Tempered Days

A Century of Newfoundland Short Fiction

Collected and Edited by

G.J. Casey
and
Elizabeth Miller

Tempered Days

A Century of Newfoundland Short Fiction

Collected and Edited by
G.J. Casey
and
Elizabeth Miller

Killick Press
St. John's, Newfoundland
1996

Appreciation is expressed to *The Canada Council* for publication assistance.

Cover: Flower's Cove, Northern Peninsula 1987
Oil on Canvas, 22.8cm x 30.4cm
Elizabeth Margot Wall
courtesy of the Ewing Gallery
collection of Yvonne Thurlow
photo by David Morrish
courtesy of Sir Wilfred Grenfell College Art Gallery

Drawings © Scott Fillier, Roddickton, Newfoundland

∝ Printed on acid-free paper

First printing, September 1996
Second Printing, September 1997

Published by
Killick Press
A CREATIVE BOOK PUBLISHING imprint
a division of 10366 Newfoundland Limited
a Robinson-Blackmore Printing & Publishing associated company
P.O. Box 8660, St. John's, Newfoundland A1B 3T7

Printed in Canada by:
ROBINSON-BLACKMORE PRINTING & PUBLISHING

Canadian Cataloguing in Publication Data

Main entry under title:

Tempered days

ISBN 1-895387-73-6

1. Short stories, Canadian (English) — Newfoundland *
2. Canadian fiction (English) — 20th century. *
I. Casey, George J. II. Miller, Elizabeth Russell.

PS8329.5.N3T46 1996 C813'.01089718 C96-950158-7
PR9198.2.N42T46 1996

Table of Contents

PREFACE

This anthology grew from the need to include a survey of short fiction for the last century (both pre-Confederation and post-Confederation) in an undergraduate English course in Newfoundland literature. We hope that the collection will not only meet that need but prove of interest to the general reader. The telling of stories is, of course, an innate feature of Newfoundland life; indeed, the people of rural Newfoundland and Labrador participated chiefly in an oral culture until the mid-twentieth century. While this volume focuses on the literary tradition, the oral influence can be seen especially in "The Legend of Ben's Rock" by Wanda Neill Tolboom and "Algebra Slippers" by Ted Russell.

Rather than provide a selection of the "best" stories, whatever that term might imply, we opted for a historical cross-section dealing with a broad range of subject matter and setting: from outport to city, from sea to parlour, from love to loss, from tragedy to joy. The other criteria applied include a representative sampling from both male and female writers, a balance between well-known and more obscure authors, and practical considerations such as availability and cost. As a result of this, some prominent writers are excluded. The number of more contemporary stories is limited, as these are readily available in individual collections as well as in the Newfoundland issue of *Canadian Fiction Magazine* (Number 72, 1990) edited by Lawrence Mathews, and *Extremities* (St. John's: Killick Press, 1994) edited by Michael Winter.

The stories presented here have been arranged chronologically according to the date of original publication. Where possible, a brief biographical sketch of each author is presented. In the case of the older stories, we have adhered as closely as possible to the stylistic features (word choice, spelling, punctuation, and use of italics) of the original. Only where such features affect clarity have changes been made.

To the students who helped in various ways through graduate assistantships and MUCEP undergraduate grants provided by Memorial University, we offer a special thank you. We are also grateful to Scott Fillier and Elizabeth Margot Wall for the use of their art. Any royalties from this book will be donated to the Michael Cook Scholarship Fund for students in Theatre and Drama at Memorial University.

G.J. Casey
Elizabeth Miller
August 1996

Rev. Geo. J. Bond

Uncle Joe Burton's Strange Xmas Box

George Bond (1850-1933) was a native of St. John's and a brother of Sir Robert Bond, Prime Minister of Newfoundland (1900-1908). He was an ordained minister of the Methodist Church and served both in Newfoundland (including Gower Street, Cochrane Street and George Street Churches) and Nova Scotia. Three times he was elected President of the Newfoundland Methodist Conference. In addition to his clerical responsibilities, Bond, a prolific writer of both fiction and non-fiction, published a novel, *Skipper George Netman* (1887), and a number of short stories.

It was Christmas Eve, and outside Uncle Joe Burton's cottage, wild and stormy enough. A strong breeze from the northwest had been blowing since noon, with frequent showers of snow, and, as the day advanced, the wind had come more from the north, and freshened to a gale. Great gusts ever and anon, sent blinding drifts of snow swirling over the roads, piling them high against the picket fences and wreathing quaint, curling masses over the firewood piles resting against the house. The windows rattled in their casements, and puffs of smoke poured frequently down the chimney, which roared and groaned like some huge animal in mortal pain.

It was a gloomy scene indeed, that Mrs. Burton looked out upon, as she went to the window to draw down the blinds. The short evening was darkening rapidly over the dreary landscape, and the houses of the little fishing village lay half-buried under a winding-sheet of snow. On the opposite side of the harbour the great cliff loomed frowningly through the flying snow-flakes, while against its base, the cold white breakers were dashing with a sullenness that was fast increasing into fury. Seaward, a hazy stretch of white capped billows chased each other tumultuously shoreward, driven hard by the fierce and still freshening wind. The good woman shuddered as she gazed. "A terrible night sure enough," she murmured. "The good Lord pity any poor fellows in craft on this shore tonight;" and then, with a sigh that might be an Amen to her kindly prayer, she drew the red curtains over the noisy windows, and set about getting her husband's supper.

It was a pleasant interior enough. In the huge chimney recess, that had been built for open fires, a well burnished cooking-stove sent out its heat, and on its top the tea-kettle sang a cheery song, in perfect harmony with the hubble-bubble of a boiler, its companion, in which a big figgy pudding, rich with galores of suet and citron, was already undergoing the beginning of its long boil for tomorrow's dinner. An appetizing odor came from the oven, where a couple of fine fat bull-birds, part proceeds of a successful day's gunning in punt a day or two before, were yielding up their juices, as they browned for the good man's supper. Mats, hooked in bright colors and quaint patterns, covered the clean floor, and a noisy American clock emphasized the flight of time on a shelf between the two small windows, flanked on the one side by a bright print cut from some illustrated periodical, and on the other by a gay pictorial advertisement of "Taylor's Soluble Cocoa." Gleams from the glowing wood inside the stove-bars lit up the rows of crockery on the tidy dresser, and glanced along the barrels of the skipper's guns, suspended on rests across the beams of the ceiling. A big black and white cat, evidently a privileged member of the household, purred contentedly on a settle on one side of the stove, while on the other, the skipper himself, with head resting on his hands and elbows on knees, stooped, sound asleep over the fire. An air of homely content and comfort pervaded the whole apartment, with which the expression of Mrs. Burton's face, as she bustled about, and the tone of her voice, as she quietly hummed a hymn-tune, were completely in unison.

In a little while the supper was ready, the tea-pot filled and set on the stove-fender to draw, and the bull-birds smoked temptingly on a big blue dish, supported on the one side by an overflowing plate of mealy potatoes, and on the other by an equally generous plate of "riz" bread and butter. As Mrs. Burton set the chairs by the table, her husband awoke with a mighty stretch and yawn, and rose to his feet.

"Why, I b'lieve I bin dozin' a bit," he said.

"Dozin'! You've been fast asleep for an hour or more, I allow," replied his wife, laughing; "an' I don't wonder, after bein' in the woods all day. Draw over now, and take hold. You must want your supper, I'm sure."

As Uncle Joe sits down at his humble board, let us have a good look at him. Short, sturdy, square-set, with a large head set firmly on his broad shoulders; the face wrinkled and weather-beaten, but fresh and ruddy, framed all round with grey whiskers; eyes that twinkled good-humoredly beneath shaggy brows; a tumbling chaos of iron-grey hair above a broad, honest forehead — a typical fisherman in build and appearance. And Aunt Betsy, as the people called her, was a fitting match for her husband. She, too, was short and square, and sturdy; but the hair beneath the trim cap was still jet black, and the placid brow unwrinkled; and, though the face had lost something of the color and contour that in youth had made her the belle of the harbour, there was a matronly sweetness about her that more than made up for any loss of youthful charms. Uncle Joe, kindly, shrewd and blunt, was, by sheer force of personal character, a "leadin' man" in the little settlement, while his wife was known for miles around as the friend and sympathizer, readiest with help of word and deed in all cases of emergency or illness; in her quiet way, a true Lady Bountiful, devoting herself in personal ministration to the sick and the poor. The worthy couple had no children; but this deprivation, while it sometimes brought secret sorrow to gentle Aunt Betsy's loving heart, made it open none the less warmly to mother the children of others, and many a little one, sick and sorrowful, had been nursed back to health and gladness in her kind embrace.

"My! 'Tis a wild night," said Uncle Joe, pausing with a cup of tea midway to his lips, as a gust of more than usual violence shook the house, "I'm afeared there's craft about, too. I seen three goin' up the Bay as I was comin' out o' the woods. People goin' up craft buildin', I s'pose, though it's very late. I hope there's no one near this shore anyway; the wind's come right in on it."

"I thought o' the same thing just now," said his wife. "I don't know how 'tis people will leave it so late. 'Tis no weather this for craft to be knockin' about in."

"But, my maid, what can 'em do, if they happens to be out and gets caught in it? You know it looked civil enough this mornin', an' I'm sure 'twas as mild as October yesterday; an' I'm afeared, as I say, that some of 'em is not far off. I do hope they got into harbour somewhere afore these snow-dwies got so bad. Wind an' sea is bad enough when you're anywhere near land, but when snow comes with 'em, 'tis awful work."

Little more was said on the subject during the meal, and the conversation branched off to other topics. Two or three hours later, as they were sitting by the fire, Aunt Betsy knitting and Uncle Joe busy putting new soles on a pair of fishing boots, a sudden hurried scuffling in the back porch, and a loud rap at the door, started them from the quiet in which they had been working. Then the door was abruptly opened and a half-dozen men appeared in the entry.

"Is Uncle Joe in?" exclaimed the first.

"Oh, yes, there he is."

"Uncle Joe, there's a craft ashore down here in the Devil's Gulch, and we want you to come and help us to get the poor creatures out of her afore she goes to pieces."

No time was lost in idle questioning, but in the few minutes it took Uncle Joe to get ready, the leader explained how he had come to know of the wreck. Living not far from the ugly chasm known as the Devil's Gulch, he had happened to be returning home a quarter of an hour before from a neighbour's house, had heard through the storm the shouts and screams which told him a craft was close to or on the rocks, and had hurried to the nearest houses for help.

In less time than it takes to write it, all was ready; and well provided with lanterns and ropes, the party started on their errand of mercy.

"Keep up a good heart, and a good fire, Betsy," was Uncle Joe's parting injunction. "I'll be back as soon as I can, an', maybe, bring some of the poor chaps home with me, please God we can save 'em. Pray for us, maid; we're in God's hands."

It was not more than a half mile to the Gulch, and amid the thick, blinding snow-storm, long before they reached it, they could hear the hoarse "rote" of the breakers and the boom of the waves, as they were hurled into the chasm.

The Devil's Gulch was appropriately named. It was a ragged rift in the steep cliffs, as if by some titanic force they had been violently torn asunder, leaving a narrow opening of perhaps a hundred feet in width, and two hundred in length, the bottom filled with huge, jagged rocks. Around it the cliffs rose sheer except where, at the extreme end, a narrow margin of shingley beach intervened at low tide between the water and the rocks. Into this narrow gulch the waves tore with relentless violence in bad weather, seething and foaming around the sharp rocks with a terrible sound; and far in through this awful chasm had a hapless craft been driven on the night in question, escaping instant destruction on the ragged teeth at the entrance, only to be hurled against the beach at the extremity. Here she lay wedged in the rocks, the waters howling like hungry wolves around her.

But not a sound came from the wreck as Uncle Joe and the rest of the men stood on the ledge immediately over her. Far down below them, a couple of hundred feet at least, they could make out a dim outline of her hull; but no shout or cry for help reached their ears. Were all dead? Were they too late? Long the men waited, peering down into the darkness and shouting. But no answering voice came back, nothing but a hollow echo from the opposite cliff, sounding as if a fiend were mocking them.

" 'Tis no use," said one of the men, at length. "They're all gone, poor fellows. We're too late."

"Aye," said another, "I'm afeared we are; and yet I could ha' sworn I heard 'em not two minutes afore we come."

"Heard 'em? To be sure we did!" exclaimed a third. "Maybe they've got ashore somehow."

"Sure you know very well they couldn't do that," answered the first speaker. " 'Tis a straight up an' down cliff, an' even if they got on that bit o' beach at the bight, they couldn't stand there a minute without being washed off. I think myself we'd best go home. They're all gone, I b'lieve, poor mortals."

All this time Uncle Joe had been creeping cautiously out to the edge of a beetling crag which projected immediately over the wreck; and stretching himself out at full length, lay with head and shoulders over the edge, peering down into the darkness and listening intently to the confused noise below. "Hark!" he cried, suddenly; and the men were silent — not a sound by the roar of the sea and the cruel hiss of the sleet laden wind. Anxiously the men listened, every ear strained, every breath hushed.

"It must ha' bin the wind," said one of them at length.

"Hush!" said Uncle Joe. "I believe I hear it again. Listen there, will you!" At that moment there was a lull in the tempest, one of those strange, short, sudden silences in which the storm-king seems to take a breath for renewed fury — and now, undoubtedly, up through the darkness there came a feeble cry — a thin, weak, pitiful wail.

"Oh, men," cried Uncle Joe, "there's a child aboard that craft — the poor little creature. There's a little child aboard that craft. We must save it — we must save it, by the help of God. Give me the end of that rope there: quick! and take a couple of turns of the other end around the tree here. I'll go down and get that child;" and he began to tie the rope securely around his body. "Let me go, Uncle Joe," said one of the others; "I'm a younger man than you, an' ought to take the risk."

"No, boy," replied Uncle Joe. "God Almighty let me hear its cry, poor little thing, an' I believe He will help me to save it. Anyhow, I'm doin' His work, an' I'm not afeared, whatever way it goes. Lower away handsomely, boys, when I give you the word, and when I pull the rope three times, you'll know I want to be hauled up. Now then, steady!"

Carefully the brave fisherman swung himself clear of the cliff, and hung suspended over the dark chasm. Down, down he went, the men above paying out the rope, inch by inch, slowly and carefully — down, down, swaying heavily in the fierce wind, half-blinded by the driving, icy snow, until at length his feet touched the deck, and he turned the light of his bull's-eye lantern around it. Alas! There was little to see; the whole fore part of the vessel had disappeared. She had parted amidships, and only the after part remained, wedged as in a vice between two huge rocks. Hurriedly, Uncle Joe hastened to the spot whence the feeble cry still proceeded. The companion way was gone, but the ladder remained in place and down it swiftly and cautiously he descended into the cabin. What a sight met his eyes as the lantern flashed upon it. The cabin was full of water, on which, as it rolled to and fro, floated the dead body of a woman; while high in an upper berth, at the side, saturated but not yet submerged by the relentless sea, was a little child of perhaps two years old, sobbing most pitifully amid its awful surroundings. There was no time to be lost, and quickly, yet very tenderly, he snatched it from the hearth, wrapped a quilt carefully around it, and regained the deck. Then, giving three tugs at the rope which still secured him, he was swung steadily off the reeling deck, the little one held safely in his strong right arm. Not a moment too soon, for scarcely had he swung clear when the pent up fury of the storm burst into the Gulch with a noise like thunder, and a huge wave, surging upon the remains of the ill-fated craft, wrenched them from their position, and dashed them to pieces against the cliff. Meantime, swaying awfully in mid-air, the two precious lives hung suspended. Up, up, up, steadily, slowly, surely they were pulled, until at length Uncle Joe heard a voice a few feet above his head, "All right, Uncle Joe?"

"Yes, boy," he said, cheerily.

"Have you got the child with you?"

"Yes boy, thank God," he answered, and a chorus of thankfulness came from the men above. As they reached the top, one of the men bending over while another held his feet, lifted the child from Uncle Joe's arms and in a moment both were safe. Untying the rope from around his body, Uncle Joe took the little one in his arms again. "It's no use waiting, boys," he said, sadly. "This is the only life that's left, and this'll be gone if we don't get shelter and warmth for it soon. I'm going to take it home. Lead the way there, boys, with the lanterns, quick." With all speed, the return journey was made, and the house was soon reached. Aunt Betsy rose from her knees as the door opened. "I've brought a Christmas Box for'ee, Bets, my maid," said her husband with a strange quiver in his voice, placing the little one in her motherly arms; and then the nerves that had been so long strung to their utmost tension suddenly gave way, and the strong man threw himself on the settle, and wept like a child.

Years have passed, many long years, since that stormy Christmas Eve. Uncle Joe and Aunt Betsy are old and feeble now, and the babe then rescued has grown into early womanhood — their more than daughter, the light of their eyes and the stay of their declining years. Yet, still, the old man's eyes will kindle, and his wife's hand stroke softly the fair hair of the girl on the low seat beside her, when at the Christmas season the friends gather round his fireside to hear anew the sad and startling story of Uncle Joe Burton's Strange Christmas Box.

[1901]

Front-Yard Figure (1980) — 32 x 29 cm., ink drawing — Filliea

Norman Duncan

The Fruits of Toil

Norman Duncan (1871-1916), a prolific writer of Newfoundland sea stories, was born at Norwich, Ontario. He first visited Newfoundland in 1900 while working as a journalist in New York. As a result of frequent visits to the Exploits area of the northeast coast, he wrote dozens of short stories and several novels about Newfoundland and Labrador, including *The Way of the Sea* (1903), *Doctor Luke of the Labrador* (1904), *Dr. Grenfell's Parish* (1905) and *The Adventures of Billy Topsail* (1906). He died at Fredonia, New York.

Now the wilderness, savage and remote, yields to the strength of men. A generation strips it of tree and rock, a generation tames it and tills it, a generation passes into the evening shadows as into rest in a garden, and thereafter the children of that place possess it in peace and plenty, through succeeding generations, without end, and shall to the end of the world. But the sea is tameless: as it was in the beginning, it is now, and shall ever be — mighty, savage, dread, infinitely treacherous and hateful, yielding only that which is wrested from it, snarling, raging, snatching lives, spoiling souls of their graces. The tiller of the soil sows in peace, and in a yellow, hazy peace he reaps; he passes his hand over a field, and, lo, in good season he gathers a harvest, for the earth rejoices to serve him. The deep is not thus subdued; the toiler of the sea — the

Newfoundlander of the upper shore — is born to conflict, ceaseless and deadly, and, in the dawn of all the days, he puts forth anew to wage it, as his father did, and his father's father, and as his children must, and his children's children, to the last of them; nor from day to day can he foresee the issue, nor from season to season foretell the worth of the spoil, which is what chance allows. Thus laboriously, precariously, he slips through life: he follows hope through the toilsome years; and past summers are a black regret and bitterness to him, but summers to come are all rosy with new promise.

Long ago, when young Luke Dart, the Boot Bay trader, was ambitious for Shore patronage, he said to Solomon Stride, of Ragged Harbour, a punt fisherman: "Solomon, b'y, an you be willin', I'll trust you with twine for a cod-trap. An you trade with me, b'y, I'll trade with you, come good times or bad." Solomon was young and lusty, a mighty youth in bone and seasoned muscle, lunged like a blast furnace, courageous and finely sanguine. Said he: "An you trust me with twine for a trap, skipper, I'll deal fair by you, come good times or bad. I'll pay for un, skipper, with the first fish I cotches." Said Luke Dart: "When I trust, b'y, I trust. You pays for un when you can." It was a compact, so, at the end of the season, Solomon builded a cottage under the Man-o'-War, Broad Cove way, and married a maid of the place. In five months of that winter he made the trap, every net of it, leader and all, with his own hands, that he might know that the work was good, to the last knot and splice. In the spring, he put up the stage and the flake, and made the skiff; which done, he waited for a sign of fish. When the tempered days came, he hung the net on the horse, where it could be seen from the threshold of the cottage. In the evenings he sat with Priscilla on the bench at the door, and dreamed great dreams, while the red sun went down in the sea, and the shadows crept out of the wilderness.

"Woman, dear," said this young Solomon Stride, with a slap of his great thigh, " 'twill be a gran' season for fish this year."

"Sure, b'y," said Priscilla, tenderly; " 'twill be a gran' season for fish."

"Ay," Solomon sighed, " 'twill that — this year."

The gloaming shadows gathered over the harbour water, and hung, sullenly, between the great rocks, rising all roundabout.

" 'Tis handy t' three hundred an' fifty dollars I owes Luke Dart for the twine," mused Solomon.

" 'Tis a hape o' money t' owe," said Priscilla.

"Hut!" growled Solomon, deep in his chest. " 'Tis like nothin'."

" 'Tis not much," said Priscilla, smiling, "when you has a trap."

Dusk and a clammy mist chased the glory from the hills; the rocks turned black, and a wind, black and cold, swept out of the wilderness and ran to sea.

"Us'll pay un all up this year," said Solomon. "Oh," he added, loftily, " 'twill be easy. 'Tis t' be a gran' season!"

"Sure!" said she, echoing his confidence.

Night filled the cloudy heavens overhead. It drove the flush of pink in upon the sun, and, following fast and overwhelmingly, thrust the flaring red and gold over the rim of the sea; and it was dark.

"Us'll pay un for a trap, dear," chuckled Solomon, "an' have enough left over t' buy a . . ."

"Oh," she cried, with an ecstatic gasp, "a sewin' machane!"

"Iss," he roared. "Sure, girl!"

But, in the beginning of that season, when the first fish ran in for the caplin and the nets were set out, the ice was still hanging offshore, drifting vagrantly with the wind; and there came a gale in the night, springing from the Northeast — a great, vicious wind, which gathered the ice in a pack and drove it swiftly in upon the land. Solomon Stride put off in a punt, in a sea tossing and white, to loose the trap from its moorings. Three times, while the pack swept nearer, crunching and horribly groaning, as though lashed to cruel speed by the gale, the wind beat him back through the tickle; and, upon the fourth essay, when his strength was breaking, the ice ran over the place where the trap was, and chased the punt into the harbour, frothing upon its flank. When, three days thereafter, a west wind carried the ice to sea, Solomon dragged the trap from the bottom. Great holes were bruised in the nets, head rope and span line were ground to pulp, the anchors were lost. Thirty-seven days and nights it took to make the nets whole again, and in that time the great spring run of cod passed by. So, in the next spring, Solomon was deeper in the debt of sympathetic Luke Dart — for the new twine and for the winter's food he had eaten; but, of an evening, when he sat on the bench with Priscilla, he looked through the gloaming shadows gathered over the harbour water and hanging between the great rocks, to the golden summer approaching, and dreamed gloriously of the fish he would catch in his trap.

"Priscilla, dear," said Solomon Stride, slapping his iron thigh, "they be a fine sign o' fish down the coast. 'Twill be a gran' season, I'm thinkin'."

"Sure, b'y," Priscilla agreed; " 'twill be a gran' cotch o' fish you'll have this year."

Dusk and the mist touched the hills, and, in the dreamful silence, their glory faded; the rocks turned black, and the wind from the wilderness ruffled the water beyond the flake.

"Us'll pay Luke Dart this year, I tells you," said Solomon, like a boastful boy. "Us'll pay un twice over."

" 'Twill be fine t' have the machane," said she, with shining eyes.

"An' the calico t' use un on," said he.

And so, while the night spread overhead, these two simple folk feasted upon all the sweets of life; and all that they desired they possessed, as fast as fancy could form wishes, just as though the bench were a bit of magic furniture, to bring dreams true — until the night, advancing, thrust the red and gold of the sunset clouds over the rim of the sea, and it was dark.

"Leave us goa in," said Priscilla.

"This year," said Solomon, rising, "I be goain' t' cotch three hundred quintals o' fish. Sure, I be — this year."

" 'Twill be fine," said she.

It chanced in that year that the fish failed utterly; hence, in the winter following, Ragged Harbour fell upon days of distress; and three old women and one old man starved to death — and five children, of whom one was the infant son of Solomon Stride. Neither in that season, nor in any one of the thirteen years coming after, did this man catch three hundred quintals of cod in his trap. In pure might of body — in plenitude and quality of strength — in the full, eager power of brawn — he was great as the men of any time, a towering glory to the whole race, here hidden; but he could not catch three hundred quintals of cod. In spirit — in patience, hope, courage, and the fine will for toil — he was great; but, good season or bad, he could not catch three hundred quintals of cod. He met night, cold, fog, wind, and the fury of waves, in their craft, in their swift assault, in their slow, crushing descent; but all the cod he could wrest from the sea, being given into the hands of Luke Dart, an honest man, yielded only sufficient provision for food and clothing for himself and Priscilla — only enough to keep their bodies warm and still the crying of their stomachs. Thus, while the nets of the trap rotted, and Solomon came near to middle age, the debt swung from seven hundred dollars to seven, and back to seventy-three, which it was on an evening in spring, when he sat with Priscilla on the sunken bench at the door, and dreamed great dreams, as he watched the shadows gather over the harbour water and sullenly hang between the great rocks, rising all roundabout.

"I wonder, b'y," said Priscilla, "if 'twill be a good season — this year."

"Oh, sure!" exclaimed Solomon. "Sure!"

"D'ye think it, b'y?" wistfully.

"Woman," said he, impressively, "us'll cotch a hape o'fish in the trap this year. They be millions o' fish t' the say," he went on excitedly; "millions o' fish t' the say. They be there, woman. 'Tis oan'y for us t' take un out. I be goain' t' wark hard this year."

"You be a great warker, Solomon," said she; "my, but you be!"

Priscilla smiled, and Solomon smiled; and it was as though all the labour and peril of the season were past, and the stage were full to the roof with salt cod. In the happiness of this dream they smiled again, and turned their eyes to the hills, from which the glory of purple and yellow was departing to make way for the misty dusk.

"Skipper Luke Dart says t'me," said Solomon, "that 'tis the luxuries that keeps folk poor."

Priscilla said nothing at all.

"They be nine dollars agin me in seven years for crame o' tartar," said Solomon. "Think o' that!"

"My," said she, "but 'tis a lot! But we be used to un now, Solomon, an' we can't get along without un."

"Sure," said he, " 'tis good we're not poor like some folk."

Night drove the flush of pink in upon the sun and followed the red and gold of the horizon over the rim of the sea.

" 'Tis growin' cold," said she.

"Leave us goa in," said he.

In thirty years after that time, Solomon Stride put to sea ten thousand times. Ten thousand times he passed through the tickle rocks to the free, heaving deep for salmon and cod, thereto compelled by the inland waste, which contributes nothing to the sustenance of the men of that coast. Hunger, lurking in the shadows of days to come, inexorably drove him into the chances of the conflict. Perforce he matched himself ten thousand times against the restless might of the sea, immeasurable and unrestrained, surviving the gamut of its moods because he was great in strength, fearlessness, and cunning. He weathered four hundred gales, from the grey gusts which come down between

Quid Nunc and the Man-o'-War, leaping upon the fleet, to the summer tempests, swift and black, and the first blizzards of winter. He was wrecked off the Mull, off the Three Poor Sisters, on the Pancake Rock, and again off the Mull. Seven times he was swept to sea by the offshore wind. Eighteen times he was frozen to the seat of his punt; and of these, eight times his feet were frozen, and thrice his festered right hand. All this he suffered, and more, of which I may set down six separate periods of starvation, in which thirty-eight men, women, and children died — all this, with all the toil, cold, despair, loneliness, hunger, peril, and disappointment therein contained. And so he came down to old age — with a bent back, shrunken arms, and filmy eyes — old Solomon Stride, now prey for the young sea. But, of an evening in spring, he sat with Priscilla on the sunken bench at the door, and talked hopefully of the fish he would catch from his punt.

"Priscilla, dear," said he, rubbing his hand over his weazened thigh, "I be thinkin' us punt fishermen'll have a . . ."

Priscilla was not attending; she was looking into the shadows above the harbour water, dreaming deeply of a mystery of the Book, which had long puzzled her; so, in silence, Solomon, too, watched the shadows rise and sullenly hang between the great rocks.

"Solomon, b'y," she whispered, "I wonder what the seven thunders uttered."

" 'Tis quare, that — what the seven thunders uttered," said Solomon. "My, woman, but 'tis!"

"An' 'He set his right foot upon the sea,' " she repeated, staring over the greying water to the clouds which flamed gloriously at the edge of the world, " 'an' his left foot on the earth . . .' "

" 'An' cried with a loud voice,' " said he, whispering in awe, " 'as when a lion roareth; an' when he had cried, *seven thunders uttered their voices.*' "

" 'Seven thunders uttered their voices,' " said she; " 'an'

when the seven thunders had uttered their voices, I was about to write, an' I heard a voice from heaven sayin' unto me, Seal up those things which the seven thunders uttered, an' write them not.' "

The wind from the wilderness, cold and black, covered the hills with mist; the dusk fell, and the glory faded from the heights.

"Oh, Solomon," she said, clasping her hands, "I wonder what the seven thunders uttered! Think you, b'y, 'twas the kind o' sins that can't be forgiven?"

" 'Tis the seven mysteries!"

"I wonder what they be," said she.

"Sh-h-h, dear," he said, patting her grey head; "thinkin' on they things'll capsize you an you don't look out."

The night had driven all the colour from the sky; it had descended upon the red and gold of the cloudy West, and covered them. It was cold and dark.

" 'An' seven thunders uttered their voices,' " she said, dreamily.

"Sh-h-h, dear!" said he. "Leave us goa in."

Twenty-one years longer old Solomon Stride fished out of Ragged Harbour. He put to sea five thousand times more, weathered two hundred more gales, survived five more famines — all in the toil for salmon and cod. He was a punt fisherman again, was old Solomon; for the nets of the trap had rotted, had been renewed six times, strand by strand, and had rotted at last beyond repair. What with the weather he dared not pit his failing strength against, the return of fish to Luke Dart fell off from year to year; but, as Solomon said to Luke, "livin' expenses kep' up wonderful," notwithstanding.

"I be so used t' luxuries," he went on, running his hand through his long grey hair, "that 'twould be hard t' come down t' common livin'. Sure, 'tis sugar I wants t' me tea — not blackstrap. 'Tis what I l'arned," he added proudly, "when I were a trap fisherman."

" 'Tis all right, Solomon," said Luke. "Many's the quintal o' fish you traded with me."

"Sure," Solomon chuckled; " 'twould take a year t' count un."

In course of time it came to the end of Solomon's last season — those days of it when, as the folk of the coast say, the sea is hungry for lives — and the man was eighty-one years old, and the debt to Luke Dart had crept up to $230.80. The offshore wind, rising suddenly, with a blizzard in its train, caught him alone on the Grappling Hook grounds. He was old, very old—old and feeble and dull: the cold numbed him; the snow blinded him; the wind made sport of the strength of his arms. He was carried out to sea, rowing doggedly, thinking all the time that he was drawing near the harbour tickle; for it did not occur to him then that the last of eight hundred gales could be too great for him. He was carried out from the sea, where the strength of his youth had been spent, to the Deep, which had been a mystery to him all his days. That night he passed on a pan of ice, where he burned his boat, splinter by splinter, to keep warm. At dawn he lay down to die. The snow ceased, the wind changed; the ice was carried to Ragged Harbour. Eleazer Manuel spied the body of Solomon from the lookout, and put out and brought him in — revived him and took him home to Priscilla. Through the winter the old man doddered about the harbour, dying of consumption. When the tempered days came — the days of balmy sunshine and cold evening winds — he came quickly to the pass of glittering visions, which, for such as die of the lung trouble, come at the end of life.

In the spring, when the *Lucky Star*, three days out from Boot Bay, put into Ragged Harbour to trade for the first catch, old Skipper Luke Dart was aboard, making his last voyage to the Shore; for he was very old, and longed once more to see the rocks of all that coast before he made ready to die. When he came ashore, Eleazar Manuel told him that Solomon Stride lay dying at home; so the skipper went to the cottage under the

Man-o'-War to say good-bye to his old customer and friend — and there found him, propped up in bed, staring at the sea.

"Skipper Luke," Solomon quavered, in deep excitement, "be you just come in, b'y?"

"Iss — but an hour gone."

"What be the big craft hangin' off shoare? Eh — what be she, b'y?"

There had been no craft in sight when the *Lucky Star* beat in. "Were she a fore-an'-after, Solomon?" said Luke, evasively.

"Sure, noa, b'y!" cried Solomon. "She were a square-rigged craft, with all sail set — a great, gran' craft — a quare craft, b'y — like she were made o' glass, canvas an' hull an' all; an' she had shinin' ropes, an' she were shinin' all over. Sure, they be a star t' the tip o' her bowsprit, b'y, an' a star t' the peak o' her mainmast — seven stars they be, in all. Oh, she were a gran' sight!"

"Hem-m!" said Luke, stroking his beard. "She've not come in yet."

"A gran' craft!" said Solomon.

" 'Tis accordin'," said Luke, "t' whether you be sot on oak bottoms or glass ones."

"She were bound down north t' the Labrador," Solomon went on quickly, "an' when she made the Grapplin' Hook grounds she come about an' headed for the tickle, with her sails squared. Sure she ran right over the Pancake, b'y, like he weren't there at all, an' — How's the wind, b'y?"

"Dead offshore from the tickle."

Solomon stared at Luke. "She were comin' straight in agin the wind," he said, hoarsely. "Maybe, skipper," he went on, with a little laugh, "she do be the ship for souls. They be many things strong men knows nothin' about. What think you?"

"Ay — maybe; maybe she be."

"Maybe — maybe — she do be invisible t' mortal eyes. Maybe, skipper, you hasn't seed her; maybe 'tis that my eyes do be opened t'such sights. Maybe she've turned in — for me."

The men turned their faces to the window again, and gazed

long and intently at the sea, which a storm cloud had turned black. Solomon dozed for a moment, and when he awoke, Luke Dart was still staring dreamily out to sea.

"Skipper Luke," said Solomon, with a smile as of one in an enviable situation, " 'tis fine t' have nothin' agin you on the books when you comes t' die."

"Sure, b'y," said Luke, hesitating not at all, though he knew to a cent what was on the books against Solomon's name, " 'tis fine t' be free o' debt."

"Ah," said Solomon, the smile broadening gloriously, " 'tis fine, I tells you! 'Twas the three hundred quintal I cotched last season that paid un all up. 'Twas a gran' cotch — last year. Ah," he sighed, " 'twas a gran' cotch o' fish."

"Iss — you be free o'debt now, b'y."

"What be the balance t' my credit, skipper? Sure I forget."

"Hem-m," the skipper coughed, pausing to form a guess which might be within Solomon's dream; then he ventured: "Fifty dollars?"

"Iss," said Solomon, "fifty an' moare, skipper. Sure, you has forgot the eighty cents."

"Fifty-eighty," said the skipper, positively. " 'Tis that. I call un t' mind now. 'Tis fifty-eighty — iss, sure. Did you get a receipt for un, Solomon?"

"I doan't mind me now."

"Um-m-m — well," said the skipper, "I'll send un t' the woman the night — an order on the *Lucky Star*."

"Fifty-eighty for the woman!" said Solomon. " 'Twill kape her off the Gov'ment for three years, an' she be savin'. 'Tis fine — that!"

When the skipper had gone, Priscilla crept in, and sat at the head of the bed, holding Solomon's hand; and they were silent for a long time, while the evening approached.

"I be goain' t' die the night, dear," said Solomon at last.

"Iss, b'y," she answered; "you be goain' t' die."

Solomon was feverish now; and, thereafter, when he talked, his utterance was thick and fast.

" 'Tis not hard," said Solomon. "Sh-h-h," he whispered, as though about to impart a secret. "The ship that's hangin' off shoare, waitin' for me soul, do be a fine craft — with shinin' canvas an' ropes. Sh-h! She do be t'other side o' Mad Mull now — waitin.' "

Priscilla trembled, for Solomon had come to the time of visions — when the words of the dying are the words of prophets, and contain revelations. What of the utterings of the seven thunders?

"Sure the Lard he've blessed us, Priscilla," said Solomon, rational again. "Goodness an' marcy has followed us all the days o' our lives. Our cup runneth over."

"Praise the Lard," said Priscilla.

"Sure," Solomon went on, smiling like a little child, "we've had but eleven famines, an' we've had the means o'grace pretty reg'lar, which is what they hasn't t' Round 'arbour. We've had one little baby for a little while. Iss — one de-ear little baby, Priscilla; an' there's them that's had none o' their own, at all. Sure we've had enough t' eat when they wasn't a famine — an' bakin' powder, an' raisins, an' all they things, an' sugar, an' rale good tea. An' you had a merino dress, an' I had a suit o' rale tweed — come straight from England. We hasn't seed a railroad train, dear, but we've seed a steamer, an' we've heard tell o' the quare things they be t' St. John's. Ah, the Lard he've favoured us above our deserts. He've been good t' us, Priscilla. But, oh, you hasn't had the sewin' machane, an' you hasn't had the peach-stone t' plant in the garden. 'Tis my fault, dear — 'tis not the Lard's. I should 'a' got you the peach-stone from St. John's, you did want un so much — oh, so much! 'Tis that I be sorry for, now, dear; but 'tis all over, an' I can't help it. It wouldn't 'a' growed anyway, I know it wouldn't; but you thought it would, an' I wisht I'd got un for you."

Landing Stage Figure with Cod's Head and Sound Bone (1980) — 29 x 29 cm., ink drawing — Filliea

" 'Tis nothin', Solomon," she sobbed. "Sure, I was joakin' all the time. 'Twouldn't 'a' growed."

"Ah," he cried, radiant, "was you joakin'?"

"Sure," she said.

"We've not been poor, Priscilla," said he, continuing, "an' they be many folk that's poor. I be past me labour now," he went on, talking with rising effort, for it was at the sinking of the sun, "an' 'tis time for me t' die. 'Tis time — for I be past me labour."

Priscilla held his hand a long time after that — a long, silent time, in which the soul of the man struggled to release itself, until it was held but by a thread.

"Solomon!"

The old man seemed not to hear.

"Solomon, b'y!" she cried.

"Iss?" faintly.

She leaned over him to whisper in his ear, "Does you see the gates o' heaven?" she said. "Oh, does you?"

"Sure, dear; heaven do be . . ."

Solomon had not strength enough to complete the sentence.

"B'y! B'y!"

He opened his eyes and turned them to her face. There was the gleam of a tender smile in them.

"The seven thunders," she said. "The utterin's of the seven thunders — what was they, b'y?"

" 'An' the seven thunders uttered their voices,' " he mumbled, " 'an'. . .' "

She waited, rigid, listening, to hear the rest; but no words came to her ears.

"Does you hear me, b'y?" she said.

" 'An' seven — thunders — uttered their voices,' " he gasped, " 'an' the seven thunders — said — said . . . ' "

The light failed; all the light and golden glory went out of the sky, for the first cloud of a tempest had curtained the sun.

" 'An' said . . . ' " she prompted.

" 'An' uttered — an' said — an' said . . .' "

"Oh, what?" she moaned.

Now, in that night, when the body of old Solomon Stride, a worn-out hulk, aged and wrecked in the toil of the deep, fell into the hands of Death, the sea, like a lusty youth, raged furiously in those parts. The ribs of many schooners, slimy and rotten, and the white bones of men in the offshore depths, know of its strength in that hour — of its black, hard wrath, in gust and wave and breaker. Eternal in might and malignance is the sea! It groweth not old with the men who toil from its coasts. Generation upon the heels of generation, infinitely arising, go forth in hope against it, continuing for a space, and returning spent to the dust. They age and crumble and vanish, each in its turn, and the wretchedness of the first is the wretchedness of the last. Ay, the sea has measured the strength of the dust in old graves, and, in this day, contends with the sons of dust, whose sons will follow to the fight for a hundred generations, and thereafter, until harvests may be gathered from rocks. As it is written, the life of a man is a shadow, swiftly passing, and the days of his strength are less; but the sea shall endure in the might of youth to the wreck of the world.

[1903]

Anastasia English

A Harmless Deception

Anastasia English (1862?-1959), born in St. John's, was Newfoundland's first notable novelist. A prolific and popular writer, she sometimes used the pen name Maria. Many of her stories and poems were published in *Yuletide Bells*, which she edited for forty years, as well as *Christmas Greeting* and *Christmas Annual*, two other local Christmas annuals. Her published works include *Only A Fisherman's Daughter* (1899), *Faithless, A Newfoundland Romance* (1901), *Alice Lester. A Newfoundland Story* (1904), *"The Queen of Fairy Dell" And Other Tales* (1912), and *When the Dumb Speak* (1938).

The Christmas snow is slowly falling, not drifting and whirling in fierce gusts, but slowly and gracefully floating down in its unsullied purity, covering road and by-way, tree and housetop, with its soft, feathery mantle, till nothing is visible outside but a white world. From the window of a wealthy suburban residence in St. John's city, a young girl of twenty gazes out upon the peaceful scene. She is slight and graceful, with a bright, beautiful face, on which is portrayed too much pride and sensitiveness for her own happiness.

Her thoughts are with the past, and she pictures a different Christmas Eve from this one, when a loving mother, a kind father were there to share with her the joy of the holy festive season. Both are dead, and she is now an inmate of her uncle's household, Richard Huntley, who, with his wife and two daughters are her only relatives. An unwelcome addition she is to the family circle, and well she knows it. Often has her heart rebelled against the taunts and unkindness she so often receives from her cousins and aunt.

Her heart is rebelling now, for, though it is nine o'clock at night, and they live in a lonely part of the city, she has been told that she must go to Water Street to purchase a particular kind of silk blouse which is needed for the morrow. That she has been there three times already the same day, does not trouble them.

As the door opens she quickly dashes away the tears from her eyes and turns round. A tall, well-dressed woman of about fifty enters.

"Here Lena," she says, "is the money. Ella says to get as delicate a shade of pink as you possibly can, and hurry because it is getting late. Your uncle may have a visitor with him when he returns, and there are still some little things to be seen to before midnight."

Without a word the girl takes the money and, turning up the collar of her coat, departs on her errand.

Meanwhile Mrs. Huntley retires to the drawing-room and throws herself into a cushioned armchair, drawn up to the fire. Her two daughters, who have just put the finishing touches to the Christmas decorations, are sitting a little distance away, fearing that the heat of the fire might spoil their complexions. Both are tall and good-looking, but of very uncertain age.

The Huntleys moved in the best St. John's society. Both girls might have married long ago, but they were not of the type who marry for love, and the eligibles were scarce. A few months before Mr. Huntley had paid a visit to an old friend of his who was living in New York, and whilst there won a promise from the son that he would spend the coming Christmas with him in Newfoundland, and he was expected to arrive tonight. Lena had been spending three months with a school friend in one of the outports, and only arrived in town a week before Christmas, so knew nothing of the expected visitor.

"What a sullen disposition Lena has," remarked Mrs. Huntley. "She did not deign to answer me one word just now when I gave the message about your blouse, Ella."

"That girl should be made to feel her dependence more than she does," answered Ella, who was the elder of the two girls.

"She shows no gratitude for what has been done for her," remarked her sister, Maude.

"It is not every girl whose father died and left her penniless, would be offered a nice home like this," said Mrs. Huntley.

"It is a great mistake, mamma, and a drawback to our prospects, to have Lena living in the same house with us. Of course she is younger, and, people seem to think, prettier, and then she has such a natural talent for claiming the attention of the male sex, that, humiliating as it is to acknowledge it, we are neglected when she is by. I do wish she had remained away till Charlie Fane's visit was over. She has heard nothing of his coming, mamma, has she?"

"I just mentioned to her now that a visitor may arrive with her uncle. I did not say from where."

"We must try and keep her in the background as much as possible," said Maude. "Papa says that Mr. Fane is worth ever so much money. Do you know at what hour the *Silvia* is due, Ella?"

"The papers say about twelve," she answered. "Of course papa will wait and bring him in."

Meanwhile Lena walked on towards town. The snow falling so softly and peacefully down had a soothing effect upon her, and, by degrees, the swelling indignation melted from her heart. It was Christmas, the time of peace and good-will, and she resolved to lay aside all unkind and bitter thoughts, and do her best to be happy and make others so.

Water Street was dazzling. The shops were ablaze with lights. Gold and silver flashed in brilliant array from jewellers' windows: everything bright and rich looking gleamed forth from those of the other stores, and all that could please the palate and sharpen the appetite was temptingly arranged in the grocery and fruit stores. Throngs of people rushed hither and thither.

Lena was young and buoyant, and soon all weariness and unpleasantness were forgotten, and her spirits rose as she mingled with the merry, moving mass of humanity. She had much difficulty in getting the blouse the exact shade which was required. She tried every shop from the West to the East End, and she began to fear she would have to return without it, when, to her relief, she found the very shade for which she was seeking.

She had also purchased a pretty Christmas card for a friend of hers, and thought that, as she was not very far from the place, she would go and leave it at the door. True, it was a lonely spot; but she decided to take Water Street until she got right opposite the house before she turned up. When she came to the unfrequented part of the street she glanced timidly around, feeling a little nervous, for it was now near ten o'clock.

She held by a chain in her hand a small purse which contained her money, and, as she quickly turned a corner leading to the next street, a man who was leaning against a door, and seemed to have imbibed too freely, rushed quickly out, and, snatching the purse from her hand, dashed past her.

Lena gave a cry of terror, and looked helplessly around.

In a moment she saw a tall, manly form stride past her in pursuit of the drunken ruffian, and in a few seconds he had him by the collar. Wrenching the purse from his hand, he then flung him to the sidewalk, saying: "Only that I cannot see a policeman about, I would give you in charge."

He then walked back to Lena, and raising his hat said: "Permit me to restore your property. I fear that scamp has given you a severe fright. It is quite fortunate that I happened to be on the spot, and saw him snatch the purse from your hand."

As he gazed upon the girl's face, he thought — even in the uncertain light — that he had never seen one to compare with her. Some dark curls had escaped from under her hat, and on them a few feathery snowflakes had found a resting place; her cheeks were deeply flushed from her walk, and a pair of large, dark eyes, eloquent with gratitude, looked up at him.

Lena knew that he was a stranger for he had the unmistakable American accent. She liked his face, not that it was handsome, but it was one that she could trust. He had a pair of honest blue eyes, was light complexioned with a golden brown moustache.

"It was indeed most fortunate for me," she answered; "not that my purse contains very much. I should not have come down here so late. Thank you a thousand times!"

"It is a great mistake to be out alone at this hour," he said, with a very grave face; "it would not do if you were living in New York."

"Oh, you are from New York, then!" she remarked.

"Yes," he replied; "I just landed from the *Silvia*, and I rejoice at the impulse which prompted me to do so, since I am so lucky as to be of service to you. The gentleman to whom I have come was to have met me, but we have arrived somewhat earlier than was expected, and I suppose he is not aware of it; so, being Christmas Eve, I thought I would take a stroll up Water Street and have a look at the stores."

"Thank you again, so much," said Lena, "but," as he seemed inclined to linger, "don't you think you ought to hurry back to the steamer, your friend may now be looking for you there?"

"I could not dream of leaving you alone and unprotected at this hour," he said. "You must allow me the privilege of accompanying you to your door."

"Oh, I could not think of troubling you so much," said Lena, "I shall be quite safe now, thank you."

"I am not so sure of that," he replied; "who knows but that scamp may be on the look out and follow you."

This was what she herself feared, but still she remonstrated: "You may miss your friend."

"That makes no difference," he answered; "I have his address, and can go there. I trust you will pardon me, young lady, if I say that I must insist on seeing you safely home, for I feel it my duty to do so."

The ring of genuineness in his voice, and the deep, respectful reverence of his demeanor, gave Lena the feeling that she was quite safe, and, with a sense of newly awakened pleasure stirring in each heart, they walked on side by side. They conversed quite pleasantly and at perfect ease during the walk. Once Lena shook out the very thin paper bag which held her cousin's silk blouse, saying, "I fear the snow will melt through this paper and spoil the silk."

"Give it to me," he said," I have a long, loose pocket in this overcoat, and can put it in without crushing it," and he took it gently from her hand. "There," he said, laughing, "you did not think when buying this that a stranger from New York would bring it home for you. Perhaps you may give me a thought sometimes when you wear it, if it is anything wearable."

Lena laughed softly as she said: "I'll never wear it; it isn't mine at all."

"And you took the trouble to go all this distance so late to buy it for someone else. You must be very obliging."

"No, I'm not one bit obliging. I stormed and raged inwardly at having to come, though outwardly I was quite calm."

"Will you think me very unkind if I say I'm glad you came?" he asked.

"I will," she answered, archly, "and I will also think you very unwise to say such a thing."

"Why?"

"Because I'm sure it's not true. I know that you are also storming and raging inwardly at being forced to perform such an onerous duty."

He looked at her a moment and then said, "I will not argue the point now."

"No," she retorted, "you have not time, for here we are at the door. Thank you so much," she said holding out her hand, "and a merry Christmas to you."

He took it, and said: "Well, I won't say I'm sorry the journey is ended, for you may tell me I'm fibbing again, but —" and he looked up at the house — "I shall see you again, unless you forbid me."

"I certainly shall not be so ungenerous," she answered, "when you have been so kind."

"My name," he said, "is Charlie Fane, at you service; would it be too presumptuous of me to ask yours?"

"I'll tell you half of it," she said, with a little touch of coquetry, "it is Eleanor," giving her full name instead of the abbreviation, Lena.

"That will do," he replied. "I'm thankful for half; it is a sweet name."

Lena laughed. "Why do you laugh?" he asked.

"Because," she answered, "if I had said it was Judy you would say the same."

He smiled in spite of himself. "Do not tell me the name of your street," he said, "or the number of your house. I'll find it out. It may prove to you, if I take a little trouble to see you, that I am possessed of more sincerity than you give me credit for."

"That's a bargain," she cried gaily, "but I'll bet you won't find me."

"We shall see," he answered.

"Shall you find your way back?" she asked, her mood changing to grave seriousness. "I almost forgot that you are in a strange city."

He laughed musically, as he said: "Oh, trust an old dog for a hard road. I'm quite used to strange cities. I daresay my friend will have found out about the arrival of the *Silvia* by the time I get there. Good-night, and a very happy Christmas to you," as he raised his hat and strode off.

As Lena entered, she was met in the hallway by Mrs. Huntley. "What a time you have been, Lena," she said, crossly; "go up to Ella's room, she is waiting to try on the blouse."

Lena had removed her hat, and was just divesting herself of her coat when, to her dismay, she remembered that the blouse was still in Charlie Fane's coat pocket; and, oh — what was she to say. Of course, when he discovered it, she felt sure that he would bring it to her immediately; but how, in the meantime, could she explain things? She would not go into all the details of what had happened. It was certainly a *harmless deception*, but could she have foreseen all the unpleasantness that would arise from it she would never have practised it. She was certainly in an awkward plight, and, acting on the impulse of the moment, said: "I have not got the blouse, Aunt Emily, but I will have it tomorrow. I left it somewhere to keep it from getting wet and forgot it."

"You have not got it!" she replied. "Did you buy it at all!"

"Yes, I bought it."

"And where did you leave it? Did you lose it?"

"No, aunt, I have not lost it. All I can say is that Ella will have her blouse tomorrow. Here is the change," she said, taking some money from her purse and handing it to her.

"Well!" exclaimed Mrs. Huntley, "If this is not cool impertinence, never mind it."

Ella and Maude, hearing voices in the hall, came downstairs. "I've had a long wait for my blouse," pointed the former.

"It seems you are to have a longer one," said her mother. "She has bought your blouse, Ella, my dear, and lost it."

"Lost it," echoed the two girls.

"I did not say I lost it," said Lena, the indignant blood mounting to her forehead.

"No, because you are not truthful enough, I suppose," said Ella Huntley.

"How dare you!" exclaimed Lena. Then, turning to Mrs. Huntley, she said: "Aunt Emily, as I find I am only subjected to insult by remaining, I will go to my room. I have told you that the blouse is safe, and you shall have it tomorrow. I can say no more." And she ran quickly upstairs, before the passionate burst of tears escaped her in their presence.

About eleven o'clock Mr. Huntley and the visitor arrived. Lena, standing at her window, was the first to see them, and knew at a glance that Mr. Huntley's companion was her champion of the night. She descended the stairs and stood at the door. The light from the hall revealed her face, and, to his astonishment, Charlie Fane recognized her.

"Well, Lena, my dear," said Mr. Huntley, "have you come down to welcome the stranger? Here he is. Mr. Charlie Fane, this," he said, turning to the young man, "is my niece, Lena Huntley."

They shook hands and exchanged glances of amusement. "So I found you," he whispered.

"Ah, but only by chance," she answered.

"Lucky chance," he said.

"Quick," she murmured, "now," glancing at her uncle, who was removing his overcoat. He understood her, and hastily drawing the parcel from his pocket slipped it into her hands.

"What a blockhead I was," he said in a low voice. She smiled, and running quickly to her room threw it on the bed and was down again by the time Charlie Fane and her uncle were entering the drawing room. All the unpleasantness was now forgotten; her hero was there in the house. If she had only told him her name, all the disagreeableness would have been avoided. Her aunt and cousins frowned upon her behind the visitor's back, but she did not mind them. When it was near midnight, and supper over, they separated for the night, Mr. Huntley saying that their young guest must feel tired after his long voyage.

Lena is standing again at her window, thinking of what a

happy Christmas it has turned out to be after all. It had stopped snowing and she wanted to hear the bells when they ushered in the Christmas morn. Suddenly she remembered the blouse, which still lay upon the bed. She took it quickly from the paper bag and shook it out fearing it might be wrinkled. As she did so a light knock came upon the door, which was immediately opened and Mrs. Huntley entered. Lena quickly dropped the blouse upon the bed and turned part of the counterpane over it, but not before the quick eye of her aunt had caught sight of it, and, hastily turning back the coverlet, she demanded, in angry tones, as she held it up: "Pray, explain what this means. Why are you hiding my daughter's property? Why did you pretend you had not got it?"

"I did not pretend anything," answered Lena. "I had not got it then. How, or where I got it makes no difference, since, as you see, it is quite safe."

"This explanation does not satisfy me, Lena Huntley," said her aunt. She left the room for a moment and summoned her two daughters, to whom she told all. Lena stood with her arm leaning on the bureau, a look of indifference upon her face.

"Did you intend appropriating it to your own use?" demanded Ella.

"Will you please explain!"

"I will explain nothing," answered Lena.

Stung to anger by the girl's seeming indifference, and heartily wishing that something would happen to take her away from the house during Charlie Fane's visit, Mrs. Huntley said: "Then nothing remains for us but to suspect you of having pretended to lose the blouse, and, when the fuss had blown over, taking it to the store again, and getting the worth of it for yourself." The girl grew pale to the lips at the insult, and her eyes blazed. "You must remember that by your silence you place yourself under suspicion," she continued, "and whilst you keep so you must find another home. We will make arrangements after tomorrow. Come girls!" and they left the room.

Lena stood like one dazed. Was it possible that she, Lena Huntley, was accused of dishonesty and called a common thief by her own relations? Her first impulse was to seek her uncle and tell him all, as he had always been kind to her; her second, was to fly from the place forever. How dared they do it? she passionately asked herself. She dressed quickly, and, unheard by anyone, descended the stairs and noiselessly opened the hall door. She stood for a moment irresolute. Where could she go at that hour? Over the snow-clad hills and through the frosty air came the musical peal of the bells, breathing their message of peace and gladness to all, speaking to each human heart of charity and forgiveness, of pity and love, of good-will towards men — but no peace found a place in her stormy, passionate, rebellious heart now. She felt bitterest anger, bitterest indignation against her kinsfolk. This was her Christmas, which, a short time ago, she thought was going to be so happy — alone on a lonely road at midnight, not knowing where to go, accused of dishonesty, and by a great condescension permitted to remain under her uncle's roof till they found a suitable place for her. Ah! Did they think for a moment that she would tamely submit; that she would accept, for one hour, the shelter of this house after such an accusation. Suddenly she thought of an old woman living some distance further on, who had but one granddaughter living with her. She was called Granny Doran, and was always fond of Lena, whom she had known in happier times. So Lena decided to seek shelter there for a few days till she could make other arrangements. She found the good woman at her door listening to the "merry bells of Yule," for, as she said, "It may be the last time I will ever hear them."

"Mercy on us!" cried Granny Doran, as Lena came up to the door. "What is the matter, child?"

"I have come to spend Christmas with you, Granny, if you

will have me," said the girl. "I have quarrelled with my aunt, and I'm never going back again."

"And right glad I am to have you, dearie," said warm-hearted Granny Doran. "Come in, you must be half frozen. I'll get you a cup of hot tea, and then the best bed in the house is yours as long as you wish to stay. I always said the Huntleys were not half kind enough to you."

Many young men and maidens, living near Granny Doran, often went to her to have their fortunes told, and when Lena had finished her tea, the old woman proceeded to "toss the cup" in the endeavour to cheer her up a bit, and predicted for her a speedy marriage with a tall, handsome man, when she should be robed in white, with veil and orange blossoms.

About nine o'clock on Christmas morning at Huntley's, all sat down to breakfast. Charlie Fane looked longingly towards the door, expecting every moment to see there the face of which he had dreamed all night. When her absence was commented upon by Mr. Huntley, his wife remarked that "she must be taking an extra long nap this morning."

"That is unlike her," he said, "she is always an early riser."

Soon after breakfast Mrs. Huntley and her daughters discovered the girl's flight and feared the consequences if Mr. Huntley found out the truth; so when seated at dinner Mrs. Huntley told him that Lena had gone to spend a few days of Christmas with a friend. "Strange that she should wish to leave us on Christmas Day," remarked Mr. Huntley, "I do not like it."

Charlie Fane sang and laughed, and talked with the Misses Huntley till they thought him charming. When nine o'clock came he could stand it no longer, and he managed to slip out unseen by anyone. The night was bright and fine; he lit a cigar and began a brisk walk on the road. He felt pained beyond measure that Lena should treat him like this. He walked on till he came to Granny Doran's house; a light gleamed from the window, and he stood watching it for some time. As he gazed, he saw a hand raise a corner of the blind, and a face looked out. His heart gave a great bound as he recognized Lena. In a moment he was at the door, and she ran out to meet him. "Answer me one question, Miss Huntley," he said. "Did you leave your uncle's house to avoid me?"

Lena answered, "No." She did not tell him everything; only that she had quarrelled, and she was not going back. So, every night for the next week he managed to go out alone, and Granny Doran's was his destination.

Soon he and Lena discovered the same thing: that one could not live without the other. One night he bade her good-bye for two or three days, as he was obliged to keep a solemn promise made to his mother before leaving New York, which was that he would visit a particular friend of hers who was living in Harbour Grace, to which place his mother belonged.

Over a week had passed and he did not return. During all this time the Huntleys endeavoured, without avail, to discover Lena's whereabouts; Charlie having, at her request, kept silent about her. Mr. Huntley was much annoyed and puzzled at her behaviour.

One night a servant of Mrs. Huntley's dropped in to Granny Doran's to have her fortune told. Granny "cut the cards" and told the girl that she was soon going to a wedding. "Oh, that's true," she answered. "We are to have one at the house tomorrow night. Miss Ella is to be married to Mr. Fane. He is in Harbour Grace, but he will be home tomorrow." Lena, who was in the next room, heard all, and her faith in mankind died. "And so," she thought, "he was but amusing himself with me after all."

"You heard, dearie, I know," said Granny Doran, coming into the room when the girl had gone, "but wait a bit. I don't care if the wedding is arranged a thousand times, there's a hitch somewhere. I have not used my eyes for nothing, and that young man is honest. I'd stake my life on it."

Next morning, as Lena was sitting near the window looking

over the want-column in the morning paper, a sleigh drove up, and Charlie Fane got out and walked slowly, and with a slight halt, up the pathway to the door. Granny was out, also her granddaughter, so Lena went to the door. She was determined not to betray herself in any way. "Good morning, Mr. Fane," she said, drawing back as Charlie opened his arms, "I hope you enjoyed your visit to Harbour Grace." He looked both hurt and puzzled.

"You are aware of how I enjoyed myself, Lena," he answered; "this does not look much like amusement," and he pointed to his foot, on which he was still limping, then showed his hand, which was bound with linen.

"Have you hurt yourself?" she asked; "I am sorry."

"Did not my letter explain all, Lena?" he said.

"I received no letter," she answered; "but of course I make all allowances. A man who is preparing for his wedding cannot have much time for letter writing, and I think it is with your intended bride you should now be instead of here."

"My intended bride!" he repeated. "What are you saying, Lena? You are my intended bride, if you will make me happy by being so. I wrote you begging that you would be prepared to marry me tonight, as a few days ago I received a cable message informing me that unforseen and important business connected with our firm required my immediate presence in New York. I cannot delay longer than to-morrow, and, Lena, darling, I wrote, explaining all this to you, for I cannot leave Newfoundland without you. I could not come sooner, for the day after I arrived in Harbour Grace I was thrown from a sleigh whilst driving. My foot caught in the runners, spraining my ankle severely. I also hurt my wrist, so that it was with much difficulty I managed to write a short letter to you. I wanted to give you a little time to be prepared for our marriage tonight."

As he spoke, all Lena's faith in him was restored, and she laughed at herself for doubting him. "Perhaps you do not know,

Charlie," she said, drawing nearer to him, "that we are out of the city limits, and our letters are not brought to us."

"Oh," he said, "that explains it."

"I am sorry you have suffered so much," said Lena, with sweet, womanly pity and love shining from her eyes, and then she told him of what she had heard on the previous night.

Charlie only laughed, saying, "Ella Huntley may be getting married tonight, but it is not to me. I have not written one of them a line since I left."

"It is strange," murmured Lena. Then a suspicion flashed across her mind, and she said, "Tell me, how did you address my letter?"

"Miss Eleanor Huntley, No.___ Road."

"Why, that is Ella's name also. We are both named `Eleanor', but our abbreviations are different."

"I did not know your cousin's name was Eleanor," he said, and they looked at each other for a moment.

"They do not know at Huntley's that I am here. They always send for their letters, and, oh, Charlie, do you know what has happened? Ella thought the number was only a mistake on your part and that the letter was for her, and she is prepared to marry you tonight."

"Good gracious, Lena, do not picture such a catastrophe. I would not wish such a mistake to happen for worlds. How could I ever face Mr. Huntley again."

"Well, you are free; go and marry her tonight, and everything will be straight: I shall not mind much," said Lena.

"I don't believe you would: but I do, and I would not marry her if you were never in the question."

"I was only trying you, Charlie," she replied, smiling fondly up at him. He smiled back and both were content.

"Our stupid mistake about the blouse on Christmas Eve, and my deception afterwards, has caused all this unpleasantness," said Lena, and she told him all about it.

"It is a terrible piece of business," he said, growing quite serious; "how am I ever to explain to them."

"You should go there right away, before things go any further," she said.

"Go there? Why I'd rather face a ravenous wolf."

"Do you know what, Charlie?" said Lena. "I am the cause of all this trouble; if I had explained all to them that night this would have been avoided, and now I will take it upon myself to smooth out things as well as can be."

"Heaven bless you, Lena, you are an angel," exclaimed the young man delightedly. "In some cases men are moral cowards, and this is one of them." So Lena wrote a note to her uncle, requesting him to come to her, which he did, and then she explained everything to him. He was pained beyond measure at the humiliation his daughter would have to endure, but, in his own mind, had to acknowledge that she deserved it.

"If there is anything which I can do to make this mistake less painful to Ella, I am willing to do it, uncle," said Lena.

The rage, mortification and indignation of Ella Huntley, when she heard her father's explanation, can be better imagined than described. "I'll sue him for breach of promise," she declared, when Mr. Huntley had left the room. "To think of that sly manoeuvring girl having the laugh on me like this. I can never live and stand it. I'll die with mortification," and she burst into a storm of tears.

A little timid knock came upon the door. It was opened gently, and Lena entered. In her great happiness, her generous heart was ready to forget and forgive everything. She felt her cousin's great humiliation, and would not be in her place for untold gold. She went to her, and threw her arms around her saying: "Oh! Ella. I would give anything to undo all this. I am to blame for it all, but I was too proud and stubborn to explain to you that night. Of course, I know none of you meant the things you said, it was only because you were vexed with me."

"It is all very well for you, Lena Huntley, to come here now when it is too late to undo what you have done," cried the miserable girl, rising to her feet. "I shall be the talk of the town."

"No, no, Ella, I can fix everything if you will only listen to me. No one but ourselves need ever know of this mistake. There have been no invitations sent?"

"No," answered Ella.

"You have had no time to get any dresses made?"

"No, only a veil and orange blossoms were ordered."

"Well," went on Lena, "the veil and orange blossoms were ordered for Miss Huntley, and I am Miss Huntley. The servants could be told that you all knew I was to be married when Mr. Fane returned, and that it was only for a joke you pretended it was yourself, and I can wear the veil and orange blossoms if you will permit me."

"And how am I to explain to Mr. Fane?" asked Ella.

"Tell him you did not intend to accept him; laugh at the fun about the mistake of the letter, and prove your indifference by acting as my bridesmaid." Lena had not the heart to tell her that he knew all.

"Are you sure you will never inform on me?" asked Ella Huntley, doubtfully.

"I pledge you, upon my word of honor, Ella," she replied, earnestly, "that he shall never hear the slightest allusion to it from me." And they knew her well enough to believe her word.

And so the wedding took place at Mr. Huntley's house, and Lena, true to Granny Doran's prediction, was robed in white, with veil and orange blossoms. Ella Huntley was bridesmaid, and all went "merry as a marriage bell."

[1904]

S.B. Harrison

Near the Walls of Fort Louis

Winter had set in early in Placentia. It was but the beginning of December, 1696, and yet the hills and beach were white with snow. The settlers were not in very good humour at this time. They had had their appetite sharpened for fighting at St. John's, and were disappointed by the disagreement between De Brouillan, the Governor, and the Canadian D'Ibberville. The Governor's naturally harsh and brutal disposition was not softened by the reports brought to him of D'Ibberville's splendid march through the country, and his success in carrying everything before him. England's power in the Island was broken, the French arms were everywhere triumphant, and the Governor of Placentia had no share in the glory. Little wonder that the settlers were gloomy and dispirited when this adventurous and hardy soldier of Frontenac was bearing off the laurels that ought to have adorned the walls of Fort Louis.

One man alone was not in any way cast down by the dispiriting influences of the Governor's frown and the settlers' gloom — it was Pierre Chavaillac, Captain of the frigate *Aurore*, waiting in the harbor to take D'Ibberville's Canadians home to Quebec. He was a blue-eyed Breton, small in stature but muscular and hardy, a thorough Croisicese, vivacious, good-tempered, and fond of the sea. He loved his friend and his wine — the latter too much so, his very few enemies said. He saw in

Placentia, with its white cottages built out in the sea and its surrounding hills, the picture of his native St. Malo — "for from St. Malo Roads to Croisic Point, what is it but a run!" Another reason there was which made Capt. Pierre fond of Placentia — he loved St. Malo and his frigate, the *Aurore*. But more than all, since his arrival in Newfoundland, he had learned to love Phemie Flechard.

Phemie was a stout, rosy-cheeked maiden, who made a pretty picture standing in the doorway of her cottage under the brow of what is now Dixon's Hill. Her picturesque Breton costume — short petticoat, blue jacket and a cotton handkerchief crossed over the bosom — her laughing eyes and white teeth had done for the gallant Captain at the first glance.

The formal rules of French courtship were not strictly adhered to in the settlement, so that often before they had been regularly betrothed in the presence of the Governor and his chaplain, Pierre and Phemie used to take many solitary rambles up the shores of the Arm, and the old tale was whispered to the listening fir-trees in Breton "patois" centuries before "the ancient capital" became the haunt of summer tourists and dark-eyed, English-speaking coquettes. Pleasant were the days they spent together; joyous were the dances they had within Pere Flechard's low-roofed cottage. Pierre cared little for the glory to be gained in fruitless assaults upon Carbonear and Bonavista, and hoped that the *Aurore* would not soon be needed to take the soldiers to stupid Quebec. He was now betrothed with all the legal formalities, and Phemie was to be entirely his after the Christmas festival.

It is Christmas Eve, and all the villagers are busy, preparing for the Midnight Mass — all work is laid aside and the houses and the church are decorated with boughs and ever-greens. Phemie Flechard is running to and fro in the little cottage, her face beaming and eyes sparkling, as here she drapes the ever-green over the chimney, and there lays out, carefully brushed, her father's goat-skin waistcoat and gaiter boots. Anon her face assumes a feminine-critical appearance, as she examines the ugly national head-dress which must be worn on Christmas Day. Captain Chavaillac, with a light step, paces the deck of the *Aurore*, giving orders and preparing to salute the arrival of the Savior King as soon as the guns of Fort Louis shall give the signal. When a man is in love he feels the influence of Christmas keenly, a soothing happiness is shed over his being, and he is willing and desirous of making those about him feel some of the joy that pervades his heart.

Now the big gun from the Fort announces midnight, the carronades of the *Aurore* are brought into play and peal forth their thunder, while the joyous sound is borne away in the distance — the North-East Arm re-echoes among its little islands and rejoices in the birth of the Son of Man. The silver tinkling of the little bell at the Church follows the booming of the guns, soft music after thunder, falling with pleasure on the ear, and proclaiming the mission of the Redeemer: "Peace on earth to men of good will."

The people throng towards the Church, lights shine from the windows and along the snow, the men and women trip forth in their finery, and merrily laugh and exchange pleasant greetings in their not unmusical dialect. Superstition marvellously affected those simple Bretons, and the strong hardy men as well as the laughing women suddenly become quiet and shiver as they pass the gloomy angles of the Fort and the frowning guns, now quiet and sullen — they fancy they see the wind-fiends of their native sea-coast rushing in fury down the Arm. The lights and the cheerful glow of the Church put them again in merry mood, dashed with a religious awe and solemnity as the priest mounts the steps of the altar. He was a tall, severe-looking, dark-faced man, a missionary of the same type as Fathers Brebeuf and Jogues, and ready too, no doubt, like them to brave all manner of tortures for the good of the faith.

The congregation is composed of the fishermen of the settlement, with their families, and the thick-set sailors of the frigate, with their light curly hair and merry blue eyes, ogling the girls on the opposite side of the Church. Near the altar rail was the Governor, stiff, sullen and severe, out of harmony with the time and place. By his side was Captain Chavaillac, restless and unstable, finding it difficult to watch the ceremony, for Phemie, with a modest blush and eyes cast down, sat close behind him.

The choir chants the "Adeste Fideles," and the people, with one accord, bow their heads, feeling that even there on the snow-covered beach of Placentia, far from their homes in Brittany, the God of all nations has come to bless and protect them, reminding them that they are as near Heaven on the Atlantic Sea as on the shores of France. "Venite adoremus" — the tough old Brouillan, a warrior careless of death and human power, bends his head; "Venite adoremus," and Pierre Chavaillac, a sturdy seaman and jovial companion, kneels and prays, with sudden fear, that his Phemie may be kept from danger. The solemn tones of the "Amen!" linger in the roof of the rough church as the congregation move towards the door and, under the stars of a Newfoundland sky, wish each other God's blessing and protection.

Captain Pierre, full of thought and more deeply in love than ever, wandered slowly towards the beach beside the great quadrangle which guarded the entrance to the town, and against which the vessels almost grazed as they passed. Here a boat was waiting to take him on board his ship.

"Give way my lads!" he said, and the boat shot quickly out into the Arm. The night was dark and heavy; threatening clouds were gradually coming up from the north-east, as the wind tore along the water, lashing it into fury.

"Steady, there!" cried Pierre calmly to the man in the bow, who in sudden nervousness had almost overturned the boat. The men were wrought up to positive fear by their superstitious fancies; the windwraith was to them an evil spirit, warring and revolting against the deliverance of mankind. The boat was filled with water, and only great coolness and steadiness would enable them to row with safety; they were not far from the *Aurore* now straining at her cable, struggling like a fiery steed to free herself. "Steady, lads, here we are!" but, ere the words left his mouth, Pierre heard a crack as if the hill were rent asunder, and saw the frigate tearing madly towards them. Too late were the orders given — the boat, struck amidships, was cut almost in two. One man alone managed to keep afloat upon a portion of the shattered boat, and was rescued in the morning. The body of the captain was found on the beach near the angle of the Fort and buried by the side of the Church on the same day.

The sun was shining brightly on the morning of the twenty-fifth of October, 1713, and there was great noise and confusion in the settlement of Placentia. The settlers were busily engaged in gathering up their effects while many a one was leaning against his door-post, gazing sadly at his cottage, the birthplace of his children and his home for many years. The Governor, no longer the rough De Brouillan, but the determined and equally reliant De Costabelle, was going about superintending the departure of the inhabitants and seeing that none remained behind. France could not afford to lose such subjects. On two frigates alone waved the lilies — the British ensign surmounted Fort Louis, and for the first time British war-ships lay quietly under its guns.

The men being arranged in order, with the Governor at their head, march gloomily and sorrowfully towards the beach; but honorable withal is their departure; they bear their arms and property with them to their new homes. The women come next, and amongst them, walking here and there, comforting and cheering her weaker sisters, a woman clothed in black, with a pale face, bearing the marks of some silent sorrow. The men remove their hats as she passes, and make room for her in the boat, while she smiles wearily and thanks them in a low, sweet voice. It is Phemie Flechard, who, for the last eighteen years, has been the good angel of the settlement, nursing the sick, feeding the poor, teaching the children, and doing many other acts which have endeared her to the people. To many of them her sorrow is but a tradition, though by all her feelings are respected and herself beloved.

All are embarked. The Governor gazes mournfully over the side of the departing ship, while the guns of Fort Louis, fired by English hands, thunder forth a last salute, the sound of the English roll-call is borne faintly to his ears, the wooded slopes of Mount Pleasant recede from his view and the French dominion in Newfoundland is at an end. A broken tombstone in the church at Placentia records the death of the Croisicese Captain Chavaillac, and they say that Phemie Flechard died in Louisberg before it passed out of the power of France.

[1908]

Addison Bown

A Picture of the Past

A Romance of Newfoundland in the Days of French Occupation

Addison Bown (1905-1988) was born in Nova Scotia and spent his early childhood on Bell Island, where his father was manager of the iron ore mine. A journalist, he was a correspondent for the *Daily News* for several years before editing his own weekly newspaper, *The Bell Island Miner*. Following a short stint in politics, he served on the Board of Public Utilities, was a member of the Canadian Authors' Association and served on the executive of the Newfoundland Historical Society. In 1957 he compiled a history of Bell Island, while his book *Newfoundland Journeys* was published in 1971.

Monsieur Le Comte D'Auxine spoke slowly, carefully, with a finger on the map of Avalon outspread before him. The young sous-lieutenant at his side had already begun to understand that this was a matter of no small importance.

"Henri," said the Count, "I have received a commission from De Frontenac, under the great seal of France, in which he bids me make ready for an attempt at the capture of St. John's. He leaves me free to make those preparations at discretion, but stresses imperatively the necessity of a successful assault. I am no less resolved that there shall be no failure. To that end, Henri,

I am of a mind to send a brave and trusty agent to St. John's to spy out the defences, and my choice has fallen on you."

Quarel, the sous-lieutenant, bowed in acknowledgment of the compliment.

"You pay me a great honour, Monsieur," he returned, "and one in the performance of which I trust I may justify your confidence."

"I have no doubt you shall," replied the Count kindly, "since I feel certain that my choice is wisely made. Come, Henri. Let us consider how best the mission may be carried out. Here is Plaisance: there, St. John's. Listen to what I propose. You are to enter St. John's: I think the best way of getting there would be to join Pierre Minot and his *coureurs-de-bois*, cross the peninsula in their company, and then allow yourself to be taken prisoner, alone you understand, in order to facilitate your movements while in your captors' hands. Hampered by the presence of others, you would be deprived of greater personal liberty, which you must endeavour to gain by complete submission to the will of your masters. I can count upon you to make use of such concessions to the best possible advantage — in the furtherance of your mission. Let me see. It is now late in the year. You must be prepared to spend part of the winter in the woods around the settlement, in order to spy out the lay of the country and to note the most convenient route for an attack by land. The rest of the winter you can spend in the town, thus permitting yourself ample opportunity for a thorough study of the fortifications. In the spring, make your escape. A corvette will be cruising near Rebou, to convey you to the harbour of Aquaforte, where I shall await your coming. What think you of the plan?"

The young sous-lieutenant made ready answer, testifying alike to his absolute comprehension and his admiring appreciation.

"Excellent, Monsieur le Comte, excellent! With skill and courage such a plan cannot but be productive of success."

"Which skill and courage, Henri," rejoined the Count, "I

know you to possess, and am fully assured of ultimate triumph." He embraced the youthful soldier. "Mon fils!" he exclaimed. "Perhaps I send you to your death, you who are so brave, but these are the fortunes of war, and France, our glorious France, must be served." There was a sparkle in his eye, a ring in his voice, which showed perceptibly how wrapped up in his duty and calling was the Governor of Placentia. "But rather let us speak of the more pleasant alternative. You are now sous-lieutenant. Come you back successful and I will make you captain. But in the meantime the sword which you have ever wielded so well must be laid aside, and from the time you leave Fort Louis until you return to open service, yours must be the garb and language of a *coureur-de-bois*."

Henri had been embarrassed by the enthusiasm of his superior, especially when its warmth had extended to himself. There was something in his nature which disapproved of this intimate congratulation so essential to the French character, and it was with feelings of relief that he welcomed the change in the conversation occasioned by mention of the sword.

"Monsieur," he answered proudly, "I shall feel no regret at laying aside my sword, since in doing so, I discard it in the service of my country. And as for the fate you hint of, I possess, as you know, neither kith-nor-kin since my foster-father, Colonel Quarel, died, and so am free to risk my life, which is dedicated to France alone!"

"Spoken like a hero!" cried M. le Comte. "And yet," he mused, "heroic though your venture be, it is but a thankless task. I and the French nation honour you, for yours is a mission reserved solely for men of proved courage, ability and skill, but the penalty of infamy alone awaits you if discovered by the English. But there is no other course. We must make certain of our work, and justify the hopes of De Frontenac, whose mind is set upon the capture of St. John's, which he means to occupy permanently and convert into the powerful naval base its strategic position warrants."

"Ah yes, Monsieur!" put in the practical sous-lieutenant. "You have not yet told me of your own share in the matter. Have you decided on the course of action?"

The Count moved once more to the map and stood gazing down on it.

"That depends largely upon your report, Henri. Still, there are certain preliminaries which I have in view, one of which entails the removal of the fleet now in harbour to the Eastern coast before the coming of the ice. I have decided that a sea and land attack must be jointly made. Of the two, the more important is the land, and I am depending principally on you to discover for me the surest route. D'Iberville captured St. John's by land. I might follow his example and use Plaisance as my base of operations, but I have no mind for that long winter march overland, especially as we are without the aid of the Canadian Indians, whose familiarity with hardship is inseparable from success in such a venture. No. A shorter march, I think, would permit a swifter attack, and with the co-operation of the fleet, I may safely say that we are safeguarded against failure. However, we are somewhat premature in discussing details. Let that be done in Aquaforte. In the meantime, you do your share and I will do mine. By the spring all will be ready for the great attempt."

Henri Quarel, perceiving that the interview was at an end, bowed his way from the presence of the Governor.

Colonel William Fetherby, Commandant of St. John's, sat with wine glass and bottle before him in his quarters at Fort William.

A hard drinker was the Colonel, and a solitary, it being his custom to pass his nights thus with those never failing companions of his in secluded peace. There was sufficient in his daily round of duties to keep him occupied, but now when the shadows had fallen and the restless roar of the Atlantic surge was echoing from the rocks, he had retired to privacy. Pleasures there were none after dark to tempt him forth. A widower, and no longer young, it would have required some powerful inducement to drag him from his cups, even had there existed any such. In this wilderness of North America the recreations of the Homeland were nowhere to be found, and when the time hung heavily upon their hands it is not a matter of great wonder that the naval and military officers of the period were compelled to seek surcease from their loneliness in sherry, port and *aguardiente*.

A most explosive temper, too, possessed Colonel Fetherby, especially when disturbed in his lonely carouse. Such an outburst was now forthcoming, for a tap on the door had given notice of the arrival of an intruder. The Colonel stood angrily to his feet as the opened door revealed the serjeant.

"What in the devil brings you here at this hour, Pyme?" he flared. "Have I not told you that I am not to be disturbed?"

The serjeant bowed his apology as he removed his hat.

"Pardin, sor," he volunteered in his broad Devon accent, "but thur be a prisner without. The scouts did capture un, and I thought as how ye'd like ter be informed."

"A prisoner? Officer — soldier?"

"Naw, sor. One of thim Frinch wood-rangers, I allow, ter take un by his dress."

"To the devil with him then! Bid them take him to the Battery and —" He was on the point of saying "Shoot him!" for the Colonel possessed an undying hatred of all things French, inanimate as well as living, but appeared suddenly to change his mind. "Nay, Pyme, bid them bring him hither, I have a fancy to see this rogue and question him."

The serjeant departed, returning shortly with a file of regulars and the prisoner. Fetherby surveyed him keenly as he stood there in his deerskin garb, face dark with beard, restless eyes roving here and there. The Colonel shot a question at him.

"Who are you?"

At first the prisoner did not comprehend, and it was only the shouted repetition of the question and the heavy accompanying step forward which brought the answer trembling from his lips. He cowered back.

"I do no harm, M'sieu," he quavered. "I — Claude Derange."

"Harm?" roared the bellicose wine-bibber. "Your very presence is an insult. What brings you here?"

"Noteeng, M'sieu. I am brought."

The Colonel's rage waxed higher still as he noted the broad smile which transfigured for a startling moment the homely features of Pyme.

"Silence, you dirty half-breed! I'll have none of your impertinence. Do you know," he thundered, thrusting his enflamed face forward until it was within an inch of the bearded *coureur-de-bois*, "that I have the power, if I will, to throw you to the fishes?" He turned away in disgust. "Ugh!" he exclaimed. "He smells of vermin! I can well believe his statement that he was brought. Take him away!" he shouted. "He has been here long enough. Perhaps even now we are afflicted with other French abominations which brought him. Take him away and lock him up!"

And laughing heartily at his own coarse wit, the Commandant went back to his wine, and so was left at peace.

The months of winter slowly passed, each with its attendant quota of storm and frost and snow, but still they passed. "Claude Derange" made himself useful to his masters. A harmless fellow, noted among the garrison for his timidity, but withal cheerful and willing, he evinced a readiness for work which found him employment at every sort of manual labour in and about the forts, and in the foraging of firewood from the woods around. He possessed a mortal dread of the fiery Commandant, which was all to the good, since it served to amuse his captors and to increase their opinion of his harmlessness. The widening scope thus afforded him by increasing personal liberty found use and benefit to the end designed, and there was prepared for the perusal of M. le Comte d'Auxine a comprehensive report on the fortifications of Fort William and the earthwork defences of the Narrows which would have greatly astonished the competent, if intemperate, Commandant, Colonel William Fetherby.

There came a day when a sudden storm raged from the North West, while Claude Derange was skating on the Harbour ice. It was a favorite occupation of his, this skating, one which attracted little attention, and no molestation, on the part of his captors. The storm was sudden, swooping down with a wild shriek to the accompaniment of driving snow which thickened quickly to a raging blizzard, and Claude Derange, upon the river, steered an uncertain way for shelter. He came upon another situated as himself, a girl as it chanced, and checked his own flying speed to aid her in her confused meanderings through the snow. They reached the shore and path in safety, but it was not until the confines of the Fort were gained that Claude Derange discovered the identity of his companion: the Colonel's ward, Nell.

At the door of her guardian's quarters, she thanked him graciously and invited him to enter to receive the Colonel's thanks.

"He will be anxious about me," she smiled, presenting a pretty picture as she stood there with her rosy cheeks and disordered hair, "and I know that he wishes to thank you for the services you have done me."

The young Frenchman bowed in silence, regretting the while that his assumed lack of English forbade his assuring in adequate terms so fair a damsel that the little he had done was a pleasure.

Colonel Fetherby had been drinking harder than his wont that evening. There was a hot flush on his face and the menace of a storm of unusual violence in his eyes as he stood to his feet at their entrance. For a moment he said nothing; then before any explanation was forthcoming from his ward, who had hastened to his side, the battery of his wrath was levelled at the Frenchman, now that he had recognized him.

"So!" he shouted. "You are here again, and this time with my ward!" He pushed her roughly to one side as he spoke and came forward. "You have insulted me before, sir, but this last is too much. Were you a gentleman I would call you out. Since you are not, I will throw you out!"

There was that in Nell Fetherby's glance which told the Frenchman more plainly than if she had spoken that she considered her guardian in these besotted moods unaccountable both for words and temper. Derange comprehended instantly, and so was able to restrain his indignation. Strangely enough, he faced the angry Colonel fearlessly now and looked him squarely in the face. He cringed no longer.

"You mistake, M'sieu," he answered boldly. "M'selle there, she tell you I am gentleman. But yes! I make no insult!"

"Mention her name again, canaille, and I will choke the life from you! 'Tis ever thus with you scum of Frenchmen. Fair words and smiling lips, but treacherous hearts as black as Erebus! Listen and I will tell you what your race has done to me. Then deny me, if you can, my just cause for hatred of your nation. Fifteen years ago I was returning to Boston from leave in England on board the *Raven* sloop. With me was my only son, a boy of ten, whose mother had died in these arms two weeks before. In the night, when nearing the American coast, we were set upon by a French Privateer of twice our strength, and boarded. My boy was torn from me and I cast into the reeking hold. They took us into Louisburgh, from which I eventually escaped and rejoined my countrymen. I have searched, do you hear: I have sought unceasingly for years for news or trace of my son, but from that day to this I have never laid eyes on him. Revenge alone remains to me, for it seems that I am doomed never to discover him, and I have sworn — aye, by the most binding of oaths — that France will yet atone to me for the wrong that she has done me! I live only to see that vow fulfilled to the very letter. And now you — one of that accursed race who have already despoiled me of one child — you come hither to lure away the only treasure left me . . . ."

His hand went out with a sudden jerk to the sword and scabbard lying on the table. With a fierce gesture he drew the blade half out; then, restraining himself by a mighty effort, he plunged it again into its sheath.

". . . You are defenceless, a hostage, and for that reason I will not soil my hands by touching you. But get you gone from this as swiftly as you may. Another time and I will not be so merciful. I warn you that, if you approach my ward again, not even the immunity of your captive state will save you. Remember that and slumber on it tonight, Frenchman. Get you hence!"

Claude Derange bowed slowly to them both, and there was something so graceful in that bow, some trace of the courtier, that the Colonel's attention was arrested.

"Who are you?" he demanded suddenly on a note of suspicion; then, as if reassured by the other's outward guise, perhaps by the thought of the craven role so cleverly enacted during the past months by Claude Derange, he turned aside contemptuously and addressed his ward. "Come, Nell," he said kindly, "you have not yet told me what delayed you."

The young Frenchman lay long that night in thought. The time had come, he decided, to leave the Fort, and although the moment of departure was earlier than he had anticipated, it were wiser to go now, when the way was open, in case the hostility of the Colonel, dangerous enough already, should be carried to such lengths as to render fruitless any effort at escape.

A favourable opportunity arrived soon afterwards. When the shade of evening fell, Claude Derange made his way unnoticed up the river from the Harbour, and was quickly lost in the Southern woods. At daybreak the waiting corvette in the harbour of Bay Bulls took him off and trimmed her sails for the open sea.

On the morning of Holy Saturday, Capitaine Henri Quarel,

with the three hundred men under his command, began his march from Bay Bulls.

M. le Comte D'Auxine, with two frigates, eight privateers, and three corvettes, had already weighed anchor and was standing out to the ice-free sea.

The object of the two parties, out of sight of one another, but nevertheless in co-operation, was the same: the strategic settlement of St. John's.

The newly-appointed Captain was in high feather that morning. Several things contributed to this elation. He was back in uniform again among his compatriots after an enforced period in unfamiliar garb; and again there was the prospect of the coming battle, which before the sun was set, would be waged for possession of the town wherein he had laboured in secret to make possible this great attempt. He could almost visualize the scene so soon to become a reality. . . . Under cover of the forest his men would creep to within musket shot of the bastions of Fort William. He could see the sentinel, blissfully unconscious of danger, pacing mechanically behind the row of cannons peeping through the embrasures. Then the sharp word of command and the flood-tide of attack across the open ground; the frenzied beat of drums within, the hasty, unsuccessful attempt to close the gate in time. A sudden boom to seaward heralding the Count's attack. . . . The plan was admirable. With Fort William in their hands, the French could turn its guns upon the defences of the Narrows, caught between Scylla and Charybdis, their surrender was a foregone conclusion, impregnable though they had ever been to attack from the sea.

But not all the Captain's thoughts were martial ones. Persistently there arose before his mental eye an entrancing picture of rosy cheeks and golden hair to urge him on towards his goal. Who knows but that his stern purpose of victory in to-day's attempt was not dictated by that lovely prize he hoped to win in the town he meant to capture?

So the leader mused pleasantly as the storming party

threaded its way across the frozen barrens, through the snow-laden thickets, and over the rocky eminences of that broken country. Anon they would dip into the shadow of the ever-greens, where the all-pervading blanket bore down the weighted branches; again they stood on higher ground, which afforded them a distant glimpse of ocean stretching away to grey infinity. Thus they marched till noon, to resume their way after a brief bivouac among the snows, onwards to the goal behind the Southside Hills.

Henri, confident of the secrecy of his movements, posted no scouts, and therein made a fatal error. He discovered it too late. A musket shot from among the rocks was his first inkling, and in a moment every boulder seemed to be raining fire. The French column stopped dead in a sudden panic. Here and there a gap showed in the ranks; those in front pressed back on those behind. A wild confusion followed, a medley of bewildered, startled men, in the mass of which the ambushed weapons of the assailants took heavy toll of life.

Unhurt, the leader shouted to his men to disperse. Those of quicker intelligence threw themselves under cover; the others turned and fled. Soon an answering rattle of musketry went rolling back in defiance, although as yet there was nothing to be seen.

The Captain, armed only with sword and pistol, both weapons of close combat, could do naught but direct the defence. A sorry task he found it. Above and all around him, shot was whistling through the air or ploughing furrows in the snow. The rocks were ringing with the sound of striking metal. Worse still, the ambush seemed to hem them in completely. The discipline of barracks and the experience of open tactics availed him nothing against the cunning of hidden foe.

The white flag of surrender fluttered unwillingly above the French position.

As the triumphant band of assailants — a motley throng of settlers, scouts and soldiery — closed about the crestfallen

Frenchman, a dull boom sounded far away in the direction of the sea. It was the opening shot of the marine attack, and the knowledge of his failure came then in the nature of a heavy blow to Henri, as he delivered up his sword.

The nearer they approached St. John's, the louder and more insistent grew the sound of firing, echoing and re-echoing among the hills. On occasions a far-off glimpse of water was revealed to them as the column stood upon the higher points of land, and once the batteries on the Northern shore were seen, wreathed in swaying smoke clouds and tinged with swiftly fading streaks of crimson. They were now descending to the lower valleys, thickly wooded, and the forward march went on with that continuous bombardment ringing in their ears. At last the stream was forded, and anon the excited English and the gloomy, depressed survivors of the French landing party stood in a position whence they could view the combat beyond range of danger.

The fight was well-nigh over. Beyond the Heads, too well received to venture farther in, the ships of the French squadron were creeping slowly through the water under furled canvas, flinging their broadsides at the land. Under the great frowning mass of Signal Hill, ably supported by its sister earthwork on the other shore, the cannon of the Battery Fort were belching forth their leaden answer, encirling the enemy craft with spurting jets of spray. Upon the Hill itself — indicative of forewarned preparation — a battery of lighter guns was raining havoc on the enemy, protected as it was by the immunity of its elevation. So near were the onlookers on that shore that, when the eddying smoke permitted, they could see the lighted matches of the gunners behind the earthworks of the Battery; could perceive too the flashes of the pieces as the burning fuses sped those liberated missles seawards. Around the French battle line that heavy, obscuring smoke wrack also hung, the taller spars and the banner of the Lilies showing clearly above it in bright sunshine. The French were drawing off. Canvas soared aloft to catch the breeze; little by little the fire slackened until it had diminished to intermittent volleys. Under a growing spread of sail the Frenchmen went about and glided out into the safety of the open sea, firing their stern-chasers as they went. A mighty shout of victory swelled up from the gallant defenders of the Forts, those hardy sons of Devon, whose deeds of heroism are written broadly across the marine history of that and many a succeeding period.

Colonel William Fetherby was in a very merry mood that afternoon. Returning from the Battery, where he had directed the efforts of his gunners, he received the uneasy leader of the French storming party in the gateway of Fort William.

"So!" The bow he swept him was ironical beyond measure. "We meet again, Monsieur. Permit me to express my deep appreciation of the high honour you have paid me by this unexpected visit!"

But the French officer held his peace.

The Colonel's play-acting dropped from him then like the mask it was. He straightened swiftly, and the humour was gone from his eye, the sneer from his lip.

"Your visit was NOT unexpected, Claude Derange. When you left this Fort, in the blissful delusion that you had cleverly fooled us, I missed you before you were very far away. My scouts pursued you through the night, but failing to overtake you, were yet in time to witness the manner of your escape. Forewarned is forearmed, 'tis said. My conjecture of what was coming closely ran the truth, for I am not the fool that you may think, and I strengthened the defences of the Forts as swiftly as I could. Yesterday a planter from Petty Harbour brought me tidings of your landing and of the presence off these shores of the hostile fleet. I think you know the rest."

This time Henri Quarel was too dumbfounded to speak.

"And so," went on the Colonel, assuming fresh his former tone of mockery, "you were naught but a slinking spy, Derange. It seems a pity does it not, that such cleverness as yours should go unrewarded? Your countrymen, I fear, will not appreciate it, but I, who perceive your true genius, will be more generous. To-morrow, at dawn, a firing party will present you with a gift in keeping with your merits, one which I beg of you to accept as a slight token of my esteem — and you will have the satisfaction of knowing that your last look on this earth is to be directed on the scene of your deservedly rewarded labours." He roared an order to his men. "Take this dog to the battery and chain him up till morning!"

Henry Quarel, with head erect, was led away.

Dawn of Easter morning!

The sun of Easter has risen on many a scene of conflict, on many a day of peace. That same sun which rose o'er Calvary's consecrated height, kissing reverently with its first beams that towering Cross whereon the Son of God had died in agony and ignominy, shone too upon the grave wherein the resurrected Victim cast aside in triumph the bond of death. Through all the years between, those same contrasts of violence and majestic calm stand revealed. Today, when the warring strife is hushed, and "Nature with her thousand voices praises God," a brave man walks forth to meet a violent end at the hands of fellow-men.

A timely interruption came even as the fatal order hovered on the lips of Colonel Fetherby. Overhead, upon the Hill, a sudden cannon-shot rolled the echoes of its discharge down to the Battery Fort. As one man, the entire garrison on the battlements, prisoner, executioners, and spectators alike, turned seawards. There, sailing majestically around the Northern Head, coursed a stately French frigate under a billowing cloud of snow-white canvas; next instant, a flash of fire leaped from her ports. Came the thunder-clap of sound, reverberating in myriad echoes in that narrow space between the mighty cliffs, and the round shot of the broadside whistled overhead. Shattered by a lucky ball, the standard which had proudly flaunted above, fluttered down, evoking a long-drawn shout of jubilation on the

French man's decks. A spark of hope glowed in the heart of Henri Quarel, to die almost instantly as he saw the *L'Aigle* yaw and go about, content with the damage she had done.

The Colonel's rage was terrible to behold. One of those ungovernable outbursts of temper had come upon him at the fall of the flag; he seemed as a man bereft of sense. Shrieking an order to his gunners, he swung to his victim, fiendishly intent on wreaking his vengeance upon an enemy who could not flee his grasp.

"By Heaven!" he roared. "Your time has come at last, you cursed spy! You die — now — now — but not in the uniform that you have lived in, Frenchman!"

He rapped out a command. The watching red-coats started forward and stripped the captive violently of his silken surcoat and his upper garments, leaving him standing there naked to the waist. The Commandant drew closer, was seen to stop, surprised, and then run forward in a state of agitation which seemed strangely out of place. To see him, one would think him anxious to delay the execution, rather than determined to enforce it. He reached the Frenchman, peered incredulously at the birthmark on the left shoulder, and then his voice went ringing through the Battery in accents that were laden with overwhelming joy and gratitude.

"Is it possible?" The watchers gaped in wonder to see the French spy whom he had so violently persecuted clasped tenderly now to the Colonel's breast. "My son!" The words trembled on the speaker's lips in the throes of his emotion.

"My long-lost Hal! My boy!"

The discovery of Hal Fetherby's true identity was as much a surprise to himself as to his father. Delivered into French hands while very young, he had come to regard himself in time as one of them, and the story told him by his dead foster-father, Colonel Quarel, of the loss of both parents at sea had been implicitly believed. A lucky circumstance removed the youthful officer from Quebec to the French capital of Terre-Neuve, a step which, though unrealized by him, was to change materially the whole current of his life. The events leading up to that change have been set forth. It remains now to tell only of Hal Fetherby's decision in the choice offered him between the rival services — a decision which may be best summed up in his own words, spoken as he stood at evening with his sweetheart on the parapet of Fort William, within sound and sight of the mighty sea:

"This day has been the most eventful of my existence, since it has brought me back from the very shadow of death to a life such as I have never known. I have no regrets, no repining, for that which is past. I have been a Frenchman, but willingly, joyfully even, I renounce my fealty. The living lilies of Easter are fairer to me than the gilded lilies of France."

[1927]

Margaret Duley

Mother Boggan

Margaret Duley (1894-1968) was Newfoundland's first major female novelist. Born in St. John's, she published extensively during the 1930s and 1940s. Her best known works include *The Eyes of the Gull* (1936), *Cold Pastoral* (1939), *Highway to Valour* (1941), *Novelty on Earth* (1942), and *The Caribou Hut* (1949). She has been critically acclaimed on both sides of the Atlantic.

Joel closed the door of his white-washed house and shambled across the meadow. As he went he plucked a taper of timothy hay, jabbing it between his teeth. It was the only way he knew of keeping his mouth shut. He was on his way to board his yellow dory and row out for a talk with Mother Boggan. The setting sun reddened her as a pillar of stone in the water with her face turned towards the horizon. More woman than rock she stood as a sentinel watching the fishermen return with the fruit of the sea. Clothed in her granite cape flowing to the water's edge, her under-skirts were of kelp, swirling like a frill. Mother Boggan's petticoats softened her Spartan figure, but Joel knew her bosom to be warm. After long sunny days he could lay his face against it and tell her about his day. The speckled hen had hatched out the gull's egg he brought from the woods, and the gull-chick was running around with the others unconscious of its difference. Annunciata Costello had sniggered at his offer of marriage, and his goat, Beaumont Hamel, bucked more every time he milked her!

Joel was the richest man in the village in actual cash, his wealth assured in the pension arriving on the second day of every month. Twelve O.H.M.S. envelopes every year, with a cheque of sixty dollars for Joel O'Toole! And he was little different at forty than he had been at nineteen when they thought he was fit to fight for his country. Except that he was lonely. Unhappiness was too definite a word for his natural state, but misery, a nag of shapeless misery oppressed him when the sun didn't shine and warm Mother Boggan's bosom. Since his mother's death in July, 1914, she was the only person with time for his conversation.

Mother Boggan belonged to Joel. To the rest of the village, "she were a nasty bit of rock to run the skiff up agin." They were mainly concerned with getting their boats past herself and Mad Moll crouching in front. Joel hated Mad Moll. Snaky and slimy with sea-weed hair she slobbered all day with the water going over her head. The sea kept Mother Boggan clean. On violent days it leaped towards her face but Joel had never seen it go over her head. In a village where dreams and omens were all of the sea, the water mustn't go over the head. When it did the people walked dumb with foreboding, waiting for the sea to take away.

Joel walked on a road separating the beach and the sea from an arm of brackish water. The beach was built up with fish-rooms, high stage-heads with boats moored at the foot of ladders. On the stage-heads the fishermen ripped out the backbones of the cod, tossing them down to rot on the beach. There was a smell of offal blended with the clean tang of the sea. The arm penetrating the spruce-clad country, with its squares of meadow-land and potato-patches, was a glazed surface of black water. In the shade it was a deep ebony, turning iridescent where it held a sunset and an upside-down world.

Walking so far Joel turned to look. Chewing his cud of hay he yearned towards the world underwater. There was the sharp line of the hills, a green keel to keel and his own house with its bright red door joining the other in the meadow. It made him feel richer to see his two homes. Some day he would enter his house through the high polish of the black water. But now Mother Boggan's bosom would be warm with sun-fire. His round eyes goggled towards the sea, seeing a bright glow on his granite-mother. Spitting out his cud his jaw sagged in welcoming delight. He sprinted awkwardly over the beach towards his yellow dory.

Joel's mother had watched over him every day of his life until she died. Then they took her to a place where tablets were white against dark trees. Aimless and reckless, Joel wandered with as much purpose as flotsam floating on the waves. He belonged to no one, and he had belonged all his life. His mother had told him when to get up, when to go to bed, when to blow his nose, when to do simple chores, and when to sit down and rest by the fire. By some dumb routine of her nineteen years' direction he went on as she had taught him. But he had no stay: nothing to rest on. His mother was dead. If he met the slightest variation from the usual he didn't know what to do.

When his solitary state had increased his weaknesses, somebody told him there was a war on. It didn't mean anything to him. He would have been happy under any flag if his mother was with him to tell him what to do, but one day a man in a neat uniform took him by the arm and told him to come along and fight for King and country. He laughed for the first time since they had taken his mother up the hill. Somebody had told him what to do! He went gladly and submitted his body to unusual examination. They found it strong, and as his mother had taught him the difference between his right and left foot, they thought he was bright enough. He was content once more under constant direction, though it was not as kindly ordered as his mother's ways. Simple and stupid, he became the tolerated butt of his platoon. His own villagers thought he was "fair daft" to go off to the war. Several told him, "he was after being a fool," and one had muttered, while heaving the fish up to the stage-head, "let de Kings and t'ings what made de wah, fight the wah." But Joel had given his guffaw of foolish laughter. He didn't know what he was going to fight for, but he was glad to do as he was told. He was sent to a barracks in the City, and across the water to another in Scotland. There he stuck closer than ever to authority, took no leave and spent no money. He was obedient to the letter, but no roystering companion could make him touch a sip of beer, or go where there were women. His mother had told him to stay clean and drink no liquor. When he got to France he was bewildered, but his first day under fire told him he would never be killed. He was doing sentry duty with his mouth sagging and his throat dry, when he heard his mother's voice, "Joel, come here; Joel, come here." Then more urgently, "Joel, come here." In responsive obedience he had stepped towards the voice and looked back to see a shell bursting where he had stood. Another time he didn't move quickly enough and a bullet went through his haversack. At Beaumont Hamel, where Newfoundlanders fell like ninepins, he couldn't be killed. His mother kept stepping between him and his falling companions. He could feel her skirts and smell the homespun of her dress. Whenever she walked through, the man next to him was always killed. The battle and carnage didn't bother him. His mother kept calling him to the places that weren't being fired over. He was the only man in France that the war didn't touch in some way, but when the Armistice was signed he went before a board of grim looking men, who found him a bad shell-shock case, and gave him a large disability. It resulted in his wealth. He went back to his house with the red door, and began to court the girls. He remembered enough from his four years' service to call his goat Beaumont Hamel.

He was twenty-four when he was demobilized, and he settled back as if he'd never been away. He ambled across the beach, went out in his yellow dory, and looked for someone to talk to. But he was lonely! Everyone was busier than he. In a village where a living was dragged from the sea, where the fish had to be split and dried, and the women worked in houses and gardens from daylight to dark, there was little time for one who didn't have to struggle for his three meals a day. Joel's wealth became well known and its details established by the post-mistress. Prematurely aged mothers with seamed faces and backs humped from toil, told their daughters "that they could do a sight worse than marry Joel." But the daughters thought differently. As they reached marriageable age he proposed to them all, but one by one they married others who went to sea for their daily bread, and planted their bit of ground for their turnips and potatoes. There was no other man in the village with ready cash like Joel, but none of the girls could marry him for it. They went the way of their mothers and became prematurely aged. His proposals were accompanied by loud guffaws of laughter, and even a marriage of expediency was repelled by his sagging mouth. Then he began to boast and accompany his proposal with a formula, "I've got a house, a goat and a dory; sixty dollars a month; a meadow and an apple-tree". He never mentioned the hens, because they varied in number, but the rest of his possessions were always static. His formula became the joke of the village on the rare occasions when there was time for joking. Girls came to nineteen and twenty, and still more girls, but none of them would ever marry Joel. After each refusal he told it all to Mother Boggan. He began to ease his dory alongside, and talk his heart out to the woman in the granite cape. Mad Moll slobbered behind him, and seemed to remind him of his own sagging mouth. His own mother never came to him unless he was in danger. Only once since his return from France had he heard her voice, and that was during a thunder-storm in the woods. The lightning was playing about the tree-tops when he heard the unmistakable command, "Joel, come here, Joel, come here!" He had run from a place to let a tree fall without crushing him. But although he was safe, he shambled in loneliness, and many times he wished for another war to get in the sanctuary of direction.

Time passed. Season succeeded season. Fugitive summer followed bleak spring. Autumn gave itself with a fierce beauty to winter. Winter took the village and cased it in snow and ice. The sharpness of living touched everyone but Joel, and over it all thundered the angry voice of the sea. It beat against caverned cliffs and ran in foaming rage up the beach. Stage-heads were sucked back, fish-rooms disappeared, to be erected again in the spring with unquestioning patience. Nature found man puny, and reminded him of his state. While the rest of the village struggled, watching the sea destroy, Joel almost hibernated. He only left his house with the red door to go and have a talk with Mother Boggan. But many times she stood remote and inaccessible, doubly petrified in a cloak of gleaming ice. Then his mouth sagged further, and he huddled back to his kitchen and piled more spruce on the fire. He found himself forty, with new generations growing up around him. He was now proposing to the daughters of the girls he had known when he came back from the war. Somewhere in the thick spiritual sense of him, he was beginning to get very tired. Misery was a dull insensate thing with thin tentacles of pain. Every now and then he had a flash of sharp unhappiness, but it fell back to formlessness before he could shape it to his mind. He came to the day when he met Annie.

Annie was twenty: a little stout, with brown eyes and creamy skin like the under-belly of a Jersey cow. She came of respectable people who had kept the breath of life in their bodies by hard work. But her father had met three bad years, and his savings were eaten up. If this summer's fishery failed, the disgrace of the dole, and the dreaded spectre of the relieving-officer lay heavily on their minds. So far the summer had been scant in returns from the sea. There was nothing in the traps, nothing on the trawls, and little to hope from the hook and the line. Starvation or the dole stared them in the face. Their few vegetables could not maintain them.

Joel met Annie on the edge of a reedy lily pond during one of his aimless wanderings inland. It was a day of sharp beauty, clear light and bold outline of distant hills. As he parted the alders and saw the pond his jaw sagged in awe of the incredible beauty. One of his few streaks of intense living pierced the dullness of his brain. The slim reeds waved on the water in long lines of purple and green shading patches of lilies. Their white petals were flung open falling away from golden hearts. Piercingly yellow and waxen white they gleamed like solidified light burning heart shaped leaves. Annie was straining towards a lily just out of reach, and Joel tried to get it for her. He fell in to the knees with loud guffaws of laughter. Clumsily he splashed out and sat down with his legs stuck out to dry in the sun. But Annie was gentle and talked to him without a snigger. Insensibly his guffaws became less frequent and more modulated. He found he could tell her about his world of little things, and she had patience to hear of the gull's egg he had brought from the woods, and put under the speckled hen. The pond, the delicate beauty of the waving reeds, Annie, and the water lilies intensified his loneliness. His eyes grew rounder and he saw Annie wistfully.

"Marry me, Annie?" he asked without a guffaw. "I got—"

"I know what you've got, Joel. Don't tell me." But she said it without a giggle, or a `get on with you' toss of the head.

He stared hopefully at her. "Marry me, A-annie?" he stuttered.

No fish! Nothing in the traps or on the trawls! Her father's face getting thinner and his stomach more shrunken. Her mother working her fingers to the bone, twisting and turning trying to make both ends meet. Already they knew the deprivation of vital necessities. It was the dole for her people with their simple pride in the independence they wrested from the sea! Joel whom no girl would marry! How impossible was it? Sixty dollars a month, and the amount he must have saved up! It was a fortune! She looked at the lily-pond and then she looked at Joel. His face was clean! His mother had taught him that, but his clothes were a mass of creases and some of his buttons were off. She raised her eyes hastily to his face seeing his sagging mouth and furry teeth! But Joel had never got so far before.

"Marry me, Annie?" he said with grinning hope.

"Joel, I, I —"

Joel felt like a man, he even snatched at her hand. His was clammy and cold with the nails almost bitten down to the moons. The clear health of her flesh recoiled. But her father and mother? If she could shut out the lily-pond with its pure white flowers.

"Marry me, Annie?" panted Joel. He was breathing down her neck, and she could see the awful wetness of his mouth.

"Joel, I-I-I —"

"Giv'us a kiss, Annie?"

She leaped to her feet and Joel stood loutishly up. He made a grab at her and held her arms. "Giv'us a kiss, Annie?"

That would tell. If she could kiss him without dying she could marry him! She closed her eyes on the lily-pond, and the kiss from the sagging mouth smacked from her chin to her nose leaving a wet horror. Her flesh crawled and she flung her people to the dole. Her eyes woke on the lily-pond and she knew the nature of defilement. She ran through the alders.

"Marry me, Annie?" shouted Joel.

"No, no, no!" A remnant of caution made her scream. "I'll tell you tomorrow night by the fish-room." The alders closed round her.

Joel sat back on the bank, and grinned at the lilies. He was going to be married, he was going to be married! Annie would have him, he knew Annie would have him. She hadn't sniggered and she talked to him like his mother. Tonight he would tell Mother Boggan, and her bosom would be warm with sun-fire. The formlessness of his mind blurred to a soft content. He was going to be married!

The setting sun poured a nasturtium red over Mother Boggan, and the grey of her cloak took on a glamorous richness. The sea was so calm that it didn't stir the frills of her petticoats. The edge of the shore held no line of white. All the men in the boats were squidding for bait, and the water was red with their teeming plenty.

Much bait and no fish, thought Annie, as she came down the hill. Some years it was all fish and no bait.

Annie lived on the other side of the arm away from Joel, and as she approached, she could see his house with the red door, and another upside down in the water. It looked a nice house under the water, a house any girl would be glad to live in. But it was like the lilies in the middle of the pond: something out of reach. It was a different house in the meadow with Joel as the reason for living there. She knew now what she was going to do to help her people. She had lain awake all night, and the pale dawn on the sea had brought her light for her darkness.

Joel was looking at Mother Boggan staring from an angle that hid Mad Moll. But even she wasn't slobbering that night, and her head rested quietly on the grey-green sea. In profile Joel's mouth was just as bad, and as he turned from his contemplation of Mother Boggan his eyes seemed so round that they couldn't close. She had the feeling that he slept with them open. He shambled towards her with a foolish grin, and they scrunched over the beach and stood in the shade of the fish-house. Annie stood looking at the back-bones of the cod-fish.

"Goin' to marry me, Annie?"

She raised her eyes. "No, Joel, I'm sorry." She was the first girl that had ever refused him gently. Joel's mind became sharper with misery.

"Not goin' to marry me, Annie?" he goggled.

"No, Joel. I'm going to the City in service. I can get a good place and I'll send money home."

"But Annie, I got—"

"I know, Joel."

"Y'couldn't do for me, Annie? No trouble t'you; shockin' lonesome; gettin' old. All the money for ye, Annie."

His eyes were a round emptiness of misery. Annie saw him pitifully.

"I'm sorry, Joel. Good-bye."

"Goin', Annie? Giv'us a kiss for good-bye now, Annie?"

"No, no," she said hastily. "Good-bye, Joel, good-bye." Her departing feet made hasty disturbance on the grey stone beach.

Joel stood leaning against the wall of the fish-room. He was still there when the red faded out of the sun leaving the world cold and grey. The sea kept spots of emerald where the water was shallow and opaque green where it deepened. The hills became hard lines against the dimming sky, and the black eyes of the caves peered out at the night. When Joel stirred towards his yellow dory the warmth had been drained from the village. When he reached Mother Boggan, she was grey stone; a hard woman with a cold bosom. He sagged in his boat and looked down at her skirts. Under the water they floated gently with tight sea-weed buds.

The sharp brilliance of summer changed to rain. The fishermen went to sea in yellow oil-skins and made no change in their work. The gardens had been parched for rain, and now they got it. In the strong excesses of nature it didn't know when to stop. For twelve days and nights it streamed down, and saturated the vegetation to damaging point. Growth came to the verge of mould, and green leaves were alive with snails. There were no intervals of sun. Perseveringly it rained in long straight lines, varying only to a slant when the wind changed. It filled the holes and hollows in the rocks and made puddles to dance on. The large surface of the sea, and the arm of brackish water rippled with the tread of rain, like a wild aquatic dance. Everybody was busy with the effort of keeping the scant catch of fish from mouldering in the fish-rooms. They were piled up head to tail, waiting for a break in the weather.

Joel's world was sodden around him. His fire-wood was always damp, his feet were wet, the goat's hair was dripping, and drops trickled on his hands when he milked her. The grass became soaked, and the tapers of timothy hay were beaten to a list. Mother Boggan had become a rain-woman, and no sun-fire warmed her bosom. All day he sat in his kitchen, in his house with the red door, and did nothing but the merest necessities of life. His formless misery changed to a wet wretchedness, but he didn't know what to do about it.

On the twelfth twilight the rain ceased, and if it had been dawning day the sun would have come through. A few gleams of hidden colour streaked in the western sky. The fishermen looked up and knew they could spread out their fish tomorrow.

Joel dragged himself through the meadow. His boots became sopping wet, but he shambled down to the beach. It was a washed world and the sun would have to be strong to drink the surplus moisture. Silently he unmoored his yellow dory and rowed out. The outline of everything was smudged, as if the rain had washed the hard edges away. He rowed between Mother Boggan and Mad Moll, and eased gently alongside of Mother Boggan. He shipped his oars, threw out his anchor and just sat. It grew dusk and he hadn't moved. A gull flew by and his round eyes followed it over Mother Boggan's head. He put out his hand and touched her grey cloak. Then he stood up and laid his face against her granite bosom. It was wet, wet, full of wet wretchedness, and all around him rolled the sea with a long oily swell. There was nothing but wetness everywhere. Miserably he put his arms around his granite Mother, and tried to press himself closer. He stood up on the seat of his dory to reach her granite neck. He put his face against it, and didn't know whether it felt cold, or wet, or both. Mad Moll slobbered a bit behind him: she seemed to be gulping down the rolling sea. He gave a loud laugh. Mad Moll must have a big stomach; his feet lost the seat of his dory and a screech came out of his mouth. Wildly he kicked with his arms round Mother Boggan's neck until the dory bobbed gently out of reach. He was panting, and his round eyes goggled and protruded. Then he heard his Mother's voice, "Joel, come here! Joel, come here!" It came from the hem of Mother Boggan's skirts. Then from further down. "Joel come here! Joel, come here!" His mouth changed to a happy grin and his round eyes smiled. The voice came again from below the sea-weed frills of Mother Boggan's skirts. "Joel, come here!"

[1940]

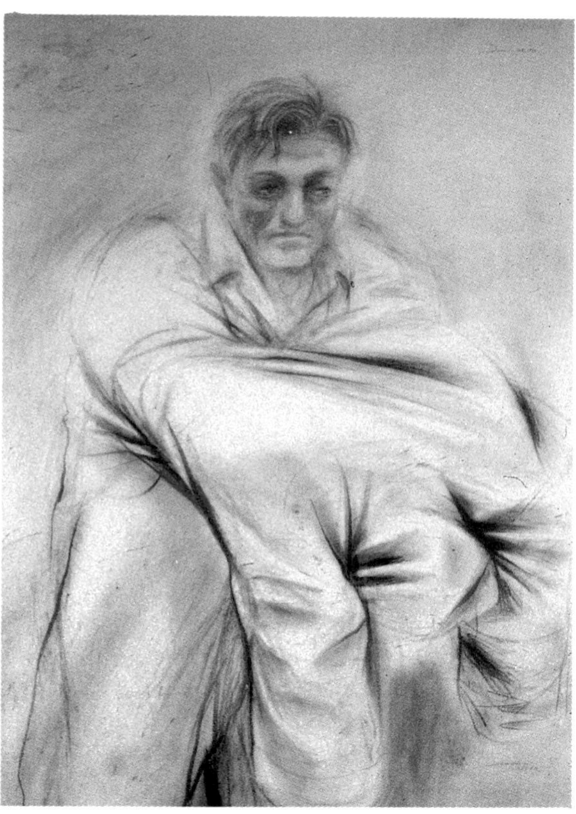

Kitchen Figure — 102 x 81 cm., oil pastel with powdered pigment — Filliea

John Avalon

Grimace of Spring

John Avalon (1901-1984), a pseudonym for **William Irving Fogwill**, was born in St. John's and was active in the Labour movement in the 1930s, having played a significant role in the founding of both the Brotherhood of Railway Clerks and the Newfoundland Trades and Labour Council. A strong supporter of Confederation, under the Smallwood administration he served as chair of the Workmen's Compensation Board. A writer of both poetry and prose, Irving Fogwill was co-editor of the literary magazine *Protocol,* where he published under the name John Avalon. His writings include two collections: *Prelude to Doom* (1931) and *A Short Distance Only* (1981).

Since leaving the movie house the erotic spell woven by the heavily romantic picture had in no way faded; if anything it had increased. The warm, humid spring night with its misty drizzle seemed to soak into his being, arousing strange feelings. The drains exuded a miasma, fetid, dank, yet darkly warm, which increased his melancholia, a pleasant, sensuous melancholia, with a feminine motif influencing its dim imagery. It had always been that way with him. Warm, wet nights filled him with an unappeasable longing, a restless madness sometimes with self-consciously heroic contemplations of suicide. When in such moods, suicide thrilled him as the final glorious gesture of defiance to the universe, and to a sentimental world, which would also thrill to the gesture in return.

He remembered, nebulously surprised at his remembering, how he had often stood on the edge of a lonely pier listening to the slap-slap of the water against the wooden piles. It affected him so that all his senses seemed to coalesce, forming one bewitched unit — a unit which absorbed, through some mystical dimension, from the music of the murmuring waters, a secret knowledge of things. He would lean over the wharf's edge, and in the waters see Marseilles and Singapore, not the cities of boulevards and great buildings but waterfronts, the brothels, and the crawling life of the nether world. He would almost groan under the weight of a nameless yearning. He wished he could be everywhere at once and for all time, to enjoy all women, to taste and to know the quintessence of things. He wanted to live a million lives and die a million deaths; his deaths were always heroic, like suicide, or being stabbed by a woman.

His train of thought engendered a feeling of irritation. Why could he not think about sensible things instead of tormenting himself with impossible dreams?

He wondered idly why his companion did not speak. A sudden incongruous idea occurred to him; perhaps she was feeling like he was. The thought clung and climbed around his brain, pleasantly worrying him, but his ego refused to accept it. It seemed to be jealous of the possibility of another, even though it be a woman, sharing his feelings.

Suddenly he became acutely conscious of the feel of her body alongside his. He had put his arm through hers when they had left the cinema, but the train of thought induced by the poisonous magic of the night had nullified the sensory consciousness of her physical nearness. Now the full tide of his sharpened sensitiveness came to bear upon her. He felt as if an intuitive sense of vision awoke inside him and went down his arm, through hers, and travelled around and about her body. He imagined he saw and knew every inch of her, nude. But there remained always an insatiableness which tortured his senses exquisitely. The intensity of his sensations made him squeeze her arm. He knew he was squeezing her arm and that he held her tightly against him because he could feel the curve of her hip and thigh against his. He purposely brushed his leg against hers as they walked, because the voluptuous feeling derived from it was a spur to his erotic imaginings.

He looked at her furtively. The beauty of her bent profile hurt as if someone was pressing him hard over the heart. She looked rather sad, he thought. He longed with an indescribable aching, to take her in his arms, to crush her, to kiss her, even to bite her lips. His sensation was like that of thirst, and that he would have to drink her to quench that thirst.

An urchin rudely broke his revery asking him for a smoke. He dropped the smoldering butt of his cigarette into his grimy outstretched hand. The interruption annoyed him exceedingly, shattering his dream. He discovered they were nearly to her home. He was absurdly surprised. Immersed, he had taken no cognition of his direction. He had an impression of intense disappointment. It would mean relinquishing his thoughts and they had been so pleasantly sensual; but the leaping thought of kisses soon to come succeeded his momentary disappointment, and his former erotic feeling returned in full flood imbued with new meanings. Dimly he felt that something momentous was going to happen.

His mind travelled back over the past few months. He had known her only several months. They had been introduced by a friend and had been keeping company ever since. She worked in an office as a stenographer and was in no way different from thousands of other girls, but she was very pretty and had a lovely figure. He supposed they would be married some day, like everybody else. He had not given it much thought.

A feeling of hopeless recklessness was gradually taking possession of him now. Things seemed to recede slowly into relative unimportance. As if he were playing a mental game, he recalled happenings that usually moved him emotionally; misery and injustice, deformity, and the death of children. He looked at them as they floated — like an irregular pictorial sequence — through his mind, grimacing and posturing, and found that he did not care. Nothing had value except things sexual.

The rain was increasing slightly and a heavy, vaporish fog obscured the street lights so that they shone with a sickly phosphoric glow in which he could discern tiny pencillings of rain which came from and disappeared into, the gloom outside the circle of phosphorescence. As he approached each light he saw the same glowing circle and the same fine pencillings.

A desultory conversation opened about the film they had just seen. It seemed, he reflected, to have gotten inside her too. He did not know whether he was glad or not. He felt that its influence on her was romantic and idealistic while its influence on him was more fleshly.

They had reached her house and she groped under the mat for the door-key. It was nearly midnight and her aunt would be in bed. She unlocked the door and they went in, as was his habit for half an hour or so before he went home. Usually she made him some tea or coffee and they enjoyed a little supper together, but tonight he pleaded a headache; so they went into the little parlor and sat together on the settee. She sighed deeply and leaned back. She seemed very pale, he noticed. It was a precursor of dark meaning to him. He sensed the completing of the metamorphosis of his mind. She slowly assumed the guise of an abstract quarry, inspiring pleasurable and sadistic waves of feeling in his thighs. He felt the necessity of stretching and yawning. All his former longings, vague and meaningless, whirled into a vortex of stark desire. He became conscious of a slowly emptying sensation which grew to a dull ache in his belly. He reached forward and pulled the light-cord of the little reading lamp which she had switched on, plunging the room into darkness which was heavy and smooth like velvet. He felt as if he were smothering, and found that he was holding his breath. He forced himself to breathe deliberately but could not inhale enough air to quiet the intensity of his feelings. He put his arm around her; it seemed without conscious motive power from his mind. The palms of his hands were sweaty and it annoyed him faintly and absently. He drew her toward him and kissed her like a man famished for water. He kissed her throat, her neck, and her lips: always he came back to her lips. It seemed to him as if his very self were turning to liquid and wanted to run out through his lips into hers. He wondered absently at her passiveness and was dimly surprised to find that he did not care much. But he noticed that her lips and cheeks were burning hot, and that her inertia had a terrible fascination.

The room was very quiet. He became aware of a dull throbbing sound. He supposed it was the heavy laboring of his heart. With a queer curiosity he put his hand over her heart and felt its quick insistent beat like his own. He felt a strange joy, and momentarily, a tender pity. The feeling of pity was soon engulfed by the feeling of joy. The feeling of joy had a tinge of predatory lust.

Indirectly, and conscious of its incongruity, he sensed an awareness of himself. It was as if he were watching a movie love drama in which he was the lover. With warm sympathy and an almost feminine love, a mystic part of him seemed to follow his every movement, even in advance of their motion; but deep down in his bowels a tiny seed of sarcastic laughter began to form, a bitter corrosive mirth at his egoism. Over and above all like a huge grey bird, hung a somber and distant melancholia that sorrowed hopelessly at the infinite and grotesque variety of his thought. The dualism of self-admiration and contempt exasperated him so that he shook his head like a dog emerging from water. He inwardly cursed the sensitivity of his mind.

With short pauses between, he was kissing her continuously. He thought he sensed a reciprocity in her lips which set leaping fires that consumed, almost, his maze of fantastic mental imagery. He caressed her deliberately, with amazing care and gentleness.

She became restless under his lips, trying weakly to avoid him, she begged him to stop, articulating her words with difficulty. Her head moved from side to side as if she were suffering pain. He knew her eyes had a peculiar cloudiness, although he could not see them. The knowledge seemed to have an evil and exquisite secretiveness about it. She appeared to be going through a terrific mental stress. She was panting heavily now and resisting him frantically. She uttered words with a sort of childish breathlessness, as if trying to hold desperately to the last vestiges of reality. He began to feel embarrassed and was glad the room was in darkness. Her breathing was like a soundless sobbing. Dismayed, he loosened his hold and let her go. His embarrassment increased and was tinged with contempt; contempt for her, for himself, and for all existence. Yet he felt that his contempt was not genuine, but was a sort of reaction to embarrassment, to save his ego from tarnish. He cursed bitterly under his breath, silly, meaningless curses. Part of himself seemed to wander off into space, searching for the silliest and most vulgar obscenities to bring back so that his mind could mouth them. There was no sound in the room save their breathing, and the grinding curses in his mind seemed to take on the properties of sound.

She had only moved once since he had let go of her, to straighten the disarray of her dress. The silence became unbearable. He felt that he must speak to relieve the unnatural tension of his mind, of its thunderous and reiterated obscenities. He essayed to speak, and his voice came huskily from a clotted throat, and was hardly above a whisper. He calmed it savagely and said that he must be going.

He arose and was surprised to find that he was deadly tired. A kind of weary *sang froid* drove his embarrassment back and he repeated with forced calmness that he must be going. She got up slowly from the settee and pulled the light string. The light, faint though it was, made him blink. His eyes felt stiff and tight, as if he had not moved his lids for hours. He noticed with a kind of evil satisfaction that she looked drawn and haggard. Catching a glimpse of himself in the mirror over the mantel he found that he too looked haggard and was immensely pleased, because he fancied that he looked striking. He was not feeling so embarrassed now. He even strutted a little as he went out into the hall for his overcoat and hat. She came to the front door with him, but did not speak, neither did he, until he was leaving, then he flung her a short good night. He heard her reply with the same words, very quietly.

He walked down the street a short distance, pausing at the corner to light a cigarette. His mind was in a turmoil. He felt savage and amused by turns. He cursed audibly now, absently and with astonishing fluency. He did not feel very good. He was too warm, and too "awake". He felt that he did not give a god damn what happened to him. A girl passed and he looked at her audaciously and lasciviously, his eyes going over the outlines of her body like a feverish hand. He was biting his lips without knowing it. Continuing, he at last came to the intersection where he had to turn up to go home. The opposite direction was down town. He stopped at this corner, inhaling deeply and rapidly from his cigarette. His mind was haunted with visions of women who walked certain streets down town. His features looked sharper than usual, and his mouth was twisted into an irresolute leer. He threw away the butt of his cigarette and mechanically extracted another from his case and lighted it. Then, slowly, as if propelled by some relentless force, he turned and went down town.

[1945]

Frederick Chafe

The Broken Mirror

Frederick Chafe (1929-   ), born in St. John's, graduated with a B.A. in English and History from McGill University in 1950. After working as a reporter and then as news editor with the St. John's *Daily News*, in 1952 he joined the Canadian Press news agency from which he retired in 1987. While attached to the agency, he lived in a number of Canadian cities and served as bureau chief in Winnipeg during the 1960s, and in Vancouver during the 1980s. His published works include hundreds of newspaper stories covering a wide range of topics, including the first session of the Newfoundland legislature after Confederation in 1949.

What, Curt wondered, stepping off his grimy ship and plodding across the old, greasy pier, does one do in a town like this on a night when it's too warm to think of doing anything?

As he scuffed up across the dusty slope, caked with a mixture of oil and horse droppings, and moved slowly down the deserted sidewalks of Water Street, his mood was one of quiet frustration — a tinge of remorse not strong enough to be oppressive, but the kind that makes you want to do something. Anything at all, as long as it is something you can really occupy yourself with so that you are not conscious of the slowness of passing time.

It comes as quite a shock, Curt reflected, when a man is jolted into a perspective of himself for the first time in his life. When you look at yourself through your own eyes, you only see what you want to and never what is really there. The picture that Curt had been seeing of himself for the twenty-five years of his life was about as perfect as he could make it, which was natural because the ego wipes the blotches from itself the way a portrait photographer removes the undesirable blemishes from a picture. The result is flattering but not very representative.

What Curt saw in himself was a powerfully built, six-foot sailor with handsome ruggedness in his face, curly black hair, and grey eyes which could radiate friendship and hate with equal facility. That was true, because his mirror confirmed it. He also saw a will that was entirely his own, a complete absence of feeling or at least the ability to control it. The master of his fate. He had read that in a poem in school once and liked it. When he put it all together he made it add up to a sense of power, of complete dominance over men and women, and that was the delusion — the delusion on which he had been living.

A delusion is abstract and empty but powerful enough to support a life if it is nourished enough. Curt's had been nourished well in the past five years. After that long at sea you are likely to become accustomed to the moving around and the impermanence of it, and Curt, up to now, thought that he had. It was a simple and undemanding life and he liked it because you didn't have to think much about it. Drop in at a port, have a good time there, maybe meet somebody and maybe not, and then leave and that's that. There was no chance to know people or to care about people and that had been fine for Curt because he wanted no responsibilities. He ruled himself and everybody else and wanted no trace of feeling to hamper his initiative. There was no caring about women because that might mean falling in love. Love was an emotion and Curt believed in squelching emotions.

But what had changed it all? It was strange the way it had

happened so suddenly, and the first he could remember was when they pulled out of Boston one day and as he stood on the deck watching the city disappear he found himself feeling lonely, when he was supposed to be feeling flippant. He tried to tell himself that it was just another port, with the same people as any other place, and why should he worry about leaving it? He'd be at another in a week or so. Nobody there knew him and he knew nobody. He'd done the same thing a thousand times before and there was nothing to it. So he shrugged his shoulders and went below.

But after two days at sea he knew that wasn't all. Standing watch at night, he saw the water boiling under the hull and listened to its seething and it no longer meant anything to him. It was not freedom nor power nor strength. It was just a senseless, aimless mass floating without direction and without purpose and taking him with it. He stood on the bridge between the water and the black sky, detached from both, feeling empty and alone, and hating the feeling because he could not understand it and it was the first emotion he could ever remember not being able to understand. He wanted to talk to someone furiously, but there was nobody to talk to because if he said anything to his shipmates he would be embarrassed and he could not quite stand embarrassment.

And then he was in St. John's and it meant nothing to him. He should have gone ashore with his friends and looked for a waterfront tavern as he had always done everywhere else. Only he didn't want to go ashore and the tavern, instead of meaning fun and freedom, meant only drabness and people talking and he could find no more pleasure in it. So he told them he had a headache and lay on his bunk, staring at the ceiling and hating the ship and the stifling heat and even hating himself.

After a while he couldn't take any more of that, so he washed and combed his hair and went ashore. All he wanted to do was get away from the ship and find something to do and try, somehow, to keep from thinking too much.

Now, where to go? He wanted to head for the bright lights section, because there seemed to be nowhere else to go. But this was a crazy town, because there didn't seem to be any sections of any kind. Business houses, stores, residences, all chopped up and thrown together like tutti-frutti. If he could find the entertainment spots he might find someone to talk to.

He began to wander uptown. A row of steps took him to Duckworth Street. Another one and he was on Gower Street, and one more brought him to Harvey Road. When he stopped climbing he was warm and sweating and his clean shirt was beginning to cling. This blasted place is worse than the tropics, he thought. It was the middle of July and the hottest night of the summer. The air was damp and full of moisture which made it seem like a Turkish bath. Why didn't the skipper find a cargo for Greenland or the South Pole?

He was a little out of breath from walking uphill and he sat on a rail for a moment. People were milling about on the sidewalks, walking slowly back and forth and talking. Teen-aged boys were sitting on the rail at the south side overlooking the harbor and shouting to passing girls in a peculiar accent with overtones of Irish. The girls had fuzzy hair and a careless way of walking, but some of them were not too bad looking and many had fair figures. After a while he got up and started to walk casually westwards, taking plenty of time. It was late dusk and the street lights had just winked on. There was no reason to hurry because he didn't know where he was going.

He passed the Paramount Theatre, its modern geometric lines looking somehow out of place in the surroundings. People were beginning to pour out of it and into the different restaurants and soda bars that lined the street. This wasn't Curt's usual sort of hangout when he went ashore. There were taverns in St. John's, all right, and the boys had told him where to find them. But tonight he didn't want any more taverns. He smiled a little. Maybe a change of atmosphere was just what he needed.

He found himself pushing open the screen door of a nice

looking little place, all shiny in chromium and fluorescent lighting. He sat at an unoccupied table in the far corner, feeling a little bewildered. He reddened a little when the waitress came over and he ordered a milkshake. Cripes, he thought, if this gets back to the boys on the ship you'll never hear the end of it. You haven't been in this kind of place in a long time. And now that you're here, what do you do? The empty feeling was there again.

After he had got accustomed to drinking through a straw, he leaned back in his chair and fished out a cigarette. He blew a cloud of smoke in the direction of the bar and looked through it at the people sitting there. The girls he saw seemed unfamiliar; they were mostly high-school kids, fresh-faced and gathered in small groups, laughing and talking loudly. If it's a change of atmosphere you want, he was thinking, you certainly have come to the right place. They were entirely unfamiliar to him, the kind of girl he had forgotten long ago, the kind of girl you don't meet in waterfront taverns, the kind who doesn't get very easily acquainted with sailors. He wanted to talk to one of them, but none of them seemed to be alone.

He caught sight of his own reflection in the corner of the mirror behind the bar. It looked all right. His blue suit fitted well and showed hardly a wrinkle, the white shirt was clean and neat at the collar, the blue tie well knotted. He reflected with satisfaction that he was about as well dressed and good looking as anyone in the place.

Then somebody moved out of a seat at the far end of the bar and he saw for the first time a girl who was sitting around the corner of it where it turned in an L-shape and met the wall. She was pretty and had long brown hair over her shoulders, with a white silk band around it. It fell down over her jacket and broke into little curls. Her left foot and a couple of inches of ankle showed around the corner of the bar, and it was smooth and clean and creamy and stockingless.

Look, he thought, why not go over and sit beside her and get acquainted? Maybe you can get her to go out somewhere with you. You don't have anything to lose. If you don't talk to somebody soon you'll go nuts.

He started to get up but restrained the impulse. Better to take it easy, to wait for a while. There might be someone else with her, and you don't want anything to happen now.

He waited five minutes, but she seemed to be alone. She wasn't looking around for anyone, just sitting there and staring at the glass in front of her with her face expressionless and her eyes averted so that he couldn't see them. He wondered what color they would be. Probably brown, considering her hair and skin. Anyway, it was about time he found out. He slowly pushed back his chair and picked his way through the tables and sat at the empty seat at the end of the bar. When he looked for a cigarette he saw that his hands were trembling slightly, and the pit of his stomach felt hollow. He bit his lip. Good Lord, he thought, is a high school kid doing this to you? Where are all your ideas now? Nothing or nobody has any effect on you, remember? Relax, you fool! He was suddenly aware of having come down a lot in the world.

He concentrated on the ash tray in front of him until his hands became steady. That made him the boss again, once more the man with the over-powering will. He felt pretty good about that. Sure, he could still do it. He could do anything.

He was deliberately casual about the whole thing, and had given no sign, as he crossed the floor and sat on the stool, that he had even noticed the girl. Probably she wouldn't like it if he immediately gave her the impression that he wanted to get acquainted. This wasn't a waterfront tavern. So he sat quietly and studied her reflection in the mirror behind the bar. Sitting diagonally opposite, he had a good view of her profile.

She was still looking at her glass, seeming almost a little sad. Yes, her eyes were brown, all right. He could barely make that out. They were brown and downcast and disinterested and not expectant. There was no doubt that she was alone. Not once did she look up at the crowd of boys and girls at the tables or glance toward the door. Maybe she was a little lonely, too. That would make it easier. But if she had even noticed him sitting there at all, she gave no indication of any kind. Curt began to feel a little puzzled, but shook off the feeling because he didn't want any doubts hampering him.

Now or never, Curt thought.

"Hello there," he said.

She looked up suddenly, surprised, almost frightened. "I beg your pardon?" she said.

"I said hello," Curt repeated.

"Oh," she said. He tried to look straight into her brown eyes, but they avoided him. They ran swiftly, hesitantly, over his neat clothes, his heavy brown wrists and powerful fingers clutching a cigarette, then back over his face and hair, but skipping over his eyes almost too quickly to follow. That's bad, he thought. How is she going to see me if she looks that way? "Do I know you?" she said. "I'm afraid I've forgotten your name."

"No," he said, "you probably don't. Ever been to New York?"

"No."

"Boston? South America?"

"I've never been outside of Newfoundland," she said.

"Then I guess maybe you don't know me. This is my first time here. But I could have sworn I saw you somewhere before." Say, he thought, that's a pretty poor approach for a guy who's supposed to know his way around. Haven't I seen you somewhere before? Why don't you tell her she looks just like Margie or something? She wouldn't laugh. She'd think you were deadly serious. She almost looks like she really thinks you did make a mistake.

She had looked away from him again, and was intently twirling the straw around in her glass. He saw that it was empty.

"Look," he said, very quietly and seriously and trying to inject a note of pleading into his voice, "I don't know a soul here and don't have a thing to do to pass the time. Mind if I talk to you for a little while?"

Her face relaxed a little and something resembling a smile flickered across her mouth. Her eyes seemed to brighten a tiny bit too, but he couldn't be sure. They were raised a little towards him, but her long lashes were downcast as if she were afraid to let him see them.

"All right," she said. Her voice was low and husky because she was trying to hide a shade of nervousness with enforced carelessness. "But I'm afraid you'll find I'm pretty dull at conversation."

Good, he thought, this isn't going to be hard at all. She really wants to talk. Just a matter of taking your time, that's all.

"Fine," he said, careful not to sound too eager. "But I'm a little hungry myself. How about a malt?"

"Thank you," she said, "but I've already had one."

"Well, have another. They're good for you. Energy food and all that."

"Thank you," she said. "I guess I'll have one if you want. Thank you very much."

He ordered two malts. While they waited he looked at her again. She wasn't saying a thing, just sitting there with her eyes averted. What's she thinking now? he wondered. She's probably wondering who I am and why I'm doing this. The more closely he looked the more he realized that she was beautiful. If only she would look at him and smile or something. He kept his eyes glued on her face until his cigarette burnt his fingers and he jumped involuntarily.

He mashed it out on the bottom of the glass ashtray, then reached into his pocket and took out a crumpled package and held it out to her. "Smoke?" he said.

"No, thank you," she said, smiling a little. "I don't smoke."

Curt lit one for himself. "I thought all girls smoked these days. I like a girl who doesn't smoke," he added.

She said nothing.

The waitress placed two frosted glasses before them. Curt sipped his a little distastefully. It was too sweet and sickly. She drank hers steadily as if she liked it.

"What's your name?" he said suddenly.

She laid the straw carefully in the glass. "Why do you want to know that?" she asked.

"I think we might as well get acquainted," he said. "My name's Curt."

"Mine's Hazel," she said.

Maybe she didn't want to talk after all. Could she be afraid of him? Obviously she was nervous. She kept putting her hands on the bar and then into her pockets or at her side or fidgeting with the little plastic ornament on her lapel. Now that he had gone this far, he was not sure what to do. Forget the whole thing and go back to the ship? That was what he had always done before. But he couldn't keep walking out forever, because he had reached the point where he could no longer walk out on himself.

"Look," he said, when she had finished her drink, "it's a nice night outside. Suppose we go for a walk?"

He thought she seemed to start a little at this, but when she spoke her voice was controlled. "No, thank you," she said. "I don't think I'd like to walk right now."

He didn't want to give up now. She was just a scared little high school kid and he couldn't expect too much at first. Somebody punched some nickels into the juke box and a bouncy tune came out over the babble. After a few seconds her shoulders started to move rhythmically with the music and it gave him an idea.

"Tell you what," he said brightly. "Let's go dancing. Know any places around here we could dance?"

She didn't answer at once. "Yes," she said, almost looking at his face. Then her eyes moved away again and her lashes dropped. "But I don't care much for dancing."

"What?" he said, disbelieving. "I thought all high school girls liked to dance."

"What makes you think I'm a high school kid?"

"I don't know," he said, puzzled. "But you are, aren't you?"

"Yes," she said, "but I don't like to dance. Some of my friends do. If you want to dance, maybe some of the other kids here would go with you."

That was the longest sentence she's spoken, he noted. The trouble was that now she sounded almost eager to get rid of him. If this keeps up, he told himself, she's going to drive you nuts. The great Curt going overboard for a school kid! He wanted to drive the toe of his shoe into the front of the bar, good and hard, and feel the plaster crumble.

He sighed, decided to try once more. "Look, Hazel," he said, sounding tired, "there's a bowling alley down the street. I saw it as I came up. Suppose we have a try at that?"

She said what he was expecting. "I'm afraid not. I've never bowled in my life."

"Well, it's about time you started. It's a good game. I bet you'd like it."

"No, thank you," she said.

He squashed out his cigarette viciously, then dropped his arms limply to his sides. "For Pete's sake," he said, irritated, "you don't dance, bowl, and you don't want to talk. What the devil *do* you want to do?"

Her eyes looked right at his for the first time. They were moist and her face was coloring and she looked very, very tired. "I didn't ask you to do anything, did I?" she said hoarsely.

"Well, no, but..."

"And I didn't ask you to sit with me or talk with me, either. I'm tired and I want to go home. My folks are calling for me here." She turned her head and seemed to shiver a little. "Why don't you go away and leave me alone?" she said finally.

Curt started to say something and decided not to. This, he thought, is what comes of your crazy ideas. Get back to the waterfront where you belong. There's only one kind of life for you and it's no good for you to try to get serious with anybody. School kids! What will you be trying next? He grabbed the check and walked over to the cashier.

As he pocketed his change, he looked through the plate glass window and noticed a car pulling up outside. A grey-haired man got out, came through the door, and walked over towards the bar. Around the end of it, the part where the girl was sitting and Curt couldn't see, he picked up a pair of crutches that were leaning against the stool. He gave them to the girl.

Curt stood still, his hands grasping the brass rail in front of him until the knuckles turned white.

The girl took the crutches, the man helped her off the stool, and she hobbled painfully across the room to the door, carefully turning her eyes away from the cashier's table. Her left ankle was smooth and clean and creamy and stockingless. Her right one wasn't there at all.

The man helped her into the car and drove away. Curt pulled the door open and walked out into the street. It was still warm and clammy. The streets were full of people, walking back and forth under the lights, and in the little park at the intersection the benches were full of people, just sitting and talking. Buses were moving in and out of the terminus and the air held the faint odor of gasoline fumes.

Curt walked slowly back Harvey Road to Cathedral Hill. The sky was hazy. It might rain. He didn't know. He didn't care.

[1948]

Janet Smith

Dark Hill

Jennifer sat alone in her favorite haunt, alone with her strange, new secret. It should have been such a wonderful secret. Her whole being should have been permeated with a yearning tenderness, a deep sense of rapture, an utter wonderment of the ineffable sublimity of the Great Master Mind which controls the Universe. For long ere the wild winds of March swept over the dusky hills of her Newfoundland home, she would have travelled that ancient and well worn roadway which lies so near the gates of Heaven and would have returned, if it pleased God, bearing in her arms the gift of the Angel of Life.

Strange, was it not, that her face wore a look of deep sadness, that those soft eyes held a look of unutterable terror, of some awful mental anguish as though the staunch, pure soul of her had been dragged through the tortures of the damned. Here in this sheltered spot which had been her retreat from childhood, where the dwarfed fir trees grew in dark, straggling masses to the beach below — here, far up the hill with its jutting crags and huge boulders, she sat and brooded, her harrying thoughts turned inward upon the shrinking misery of her mind.

How often of late as she rested here had it seemed to her that the strength of the wild, rugged scene had entered into her, that the rocky hill had given her something of itself, its calmness, its iron repose. There it remained through all the raging of the elements, wild seas that tore angrily at its base, ferocious storms, as if striving to rock its foundations.

There it remained in its immutable grandeur, a massive structure, wrapped as if with a mantle in its frowning dignity. Now, as her spirit strove for calmness, alas, there came no answer as before. It seemed to her that the very horror of the thing which ate upon her mind had wrapped itself around this retreat of hers and to her mute call for aid, there had come no answering echo, nothing but the darkness and silence.

"I will lift up mine eyes unto the Hills, from whence cometh my help." How she had loved that text in its literal sense; how often in the simple pride and joy of her life had she forgotten its deeper significance. How often had the Creator been lost sight of, in the unconscious worship of the created . . .

She raised wild eyes to the calm sky, dusky with twilight. "Oh God!" she whispered in agony. "Look upon a little child; take it back to the light of Heaven, before the light of this foul world is cast upon it . . . please God, dear God . . ."

A steamer's whistle shrilled into the stillness like the wail of a lost soul and a groan burst from the lips of the girl on the hillside. That sound would haunt her till death — for did it not seem like the harbinger of fate to her; had it not announced the approach of that which had transformed her happy life into a dark cascade of crumbling dreams. For weeks she had groped among the ruins until at last in dumb misery and fear, her proud spirit had been broken and the bright sunshine of her life had faded into the dark mists of hopelessness and utter despair.

Just a year ago tonight, she had stood, a starry-eyed bride and had spoken the sacred words of the marriage vow. She had given the pure, true love of a guileless heart into the keeping of a darkly handsome stranger. He it was who, having been rescued at sea and brought to the village by the coastal steamer, had formed a strong liking for the place and had remained; and Jennifer, wholly captivated by his compelling charm, with no one to counsel or direct her too trusting mind, entered blindly into marriage with a man of whom she knew nothing, upon whose carefully, suave features her love blinded eyes had failed to discern the mark of the beast.

A few months of happiness, a brief glimpse, as it were, into a world of bliss — then the serpent entered her Eden. The handsome lover had become a sardonic, cruel, utterly inconsiderate man, whose harshness increased even as his fondness for alcoholic liquor became more apparent, until slowly, but unmistakeably the love light and the radiance faded from her eyes.

Hoping against hope, she could not contemplate the thought of escape. To her pure, loyal mind, her marriage vows would be forever sacred. "For better, for worse till death us do part" — she had uttered these words in the sight of God and of his congregation, had heard with awe the solemn tones of the clergyman, "Those whom God hath joined together, let no man put asunder."

Ah no! The thorny road she had chosen must be travelled; she would seek further for the roses, along the way. Had she chosen another, it might, perchance, have led her soul to its eternal damnation. She had begun to attend church more frequently, but her very goodness had seemed only to infuriate the man. That Sunday morning when he had forcibly forbade her going, "To Hell with your church!" he had shouted savagely, "I would destroy them all!" He had kept her imprisoned in her room until nightfall. Then, for the first time, she had revealed the wretchedness of her life to the old clergyman. "My child," he had said, "marriage is not a garment which we may put on and off at will. We must pray for guidance and light."

He had spoken words of comfort and encouragement and had bade her come again. But he had chided himself sternly for not having given more thought, more guidance, to a young girl, bereft of her parents. Of what benefit now, he thought, to delve into the past. He had, however, written a prominent lawyer friend who had, after a series of careful investigations, succeeded in discovering certain information, which he had immediately forwarded to the clergyman. It had been that very afternoon that he had sent for Jennifer and had placed the fatal letter in her hand. He had deemed it best to do so.

With a feeling as of death itself upon her, she had read:

"Randolph Daniels is a direct member of a family whose every descendant sinks at an early age into hopeless, violent insanity. This has been established beyond any shadow of doubt. His father had died at the age of thirty in Southerly Mental Hospital at H — , where at least five other members of the family had died in previous years. There are fortunately very few descendants as it is on record that each succeeding generation is affected at a much earlier age than the preceding one."

The clergyman had been most solicitous, had told her he would think of some plan. But she had gone tremblingly from his presence, flying to her favorite retreat on the hillside. Not even to her spiritual director could she bear to unfold her secret, but in her bursting heart she was crying over and over, "My little child, doomed — doomed ere it sees the light — condemned before its birth to the awful hell of insanity."

Had Rand known, she wondered dully. Would even he have been despicable enough to have married her, knowing his ghastly heritage?

At last, the lateness of the hour disturbed her painful reverie.

"I must go," she thought hopelessly. He must have returned now from his visit up the coast. The steamer had long since gone. He would be angry at her absence, would say harsh words to her.

She had entered the house unobserved by the man who sat with bowed head in the strong glow of the lamplight. As she stood there, hesitantly, a quick rush of pity wrung her sensitive heart. She had never seen him thus, had known of late only his harshness, his drunken swagger.

"Rand," she gasped quiveringly.

He raised his head and in his naked eyes was the look of a soul lost in the depths of Hell.

"Jen-oh, Jen!" he moaned, "Forgive me!"

He opened his arms, and for a moment her sorrow gave way to a surge of joy, as she clung to him with streaming eyes and sobbing breath.

"I thought you had left me, Jen," he said, "before I could make amends. I have been a beast to you, my girl. I wanted you to leave, yet had you gone then" — there was sudden violence in his tone —"before God, I would have brought you back!"

"After I knew," he went on more quietly, "I was too cowardly to tell you the truth."

"Rand," she cried, and there was something of great gladness in her voice, "you didn't know before our marriage. Thank God — oh, thank God! Don't tell me, dear, I know all. We can face it together!" She dared not tell him then, of the new little life slowly forming beneath her heart. Not now. It might hasten that inevitable curse hovering in the background . . .

The man did not answer at once. In his new softness of heart, full contrition, although hastened by circumstances, was striving for mastery.

"One thing I did know, Jen," he said, hoarsely. "I have a living wife. She has at last discovered my whereabouts and may be here on the next steamer. Listen, Jen, I swear it to you, my girl. I have loved you best."

Was this her body, this numbed machine that turned from him without a word and moved as if propelled to the door? Where was her voice? She could not utter a sound. This last blow had paralyzed her with its crushing force. The next instant, a blinding flash and the loud report of a gun aroused her swooning senses. With a sickening lurch his falling body missed her by inches as it crashed to the floor at her feet. Through the gaping hole in his temple, the life blood welled in a tide of crimson.

A wild scream of horror broke from her lips as she fled from that house of death, out into the night. Not a light showed in the village. There was none to lend a helping hand as beside herself with terror the demented girl rushed instinctively up the hill-side. How dark the trees appeared in the pale starlight — how loud the sound of the waves rolling over the pebbled beach below . . .

The late summer night passed gently and at last a pale, cold dawn gave place to a morning golden with sunshine. But what of Jennifer in her agony? What secret do those rugged rocks guard as the soft breezes of early day blow gently on a white, upturned face? A merciful Providence had laid a healing hand on her breaking heart and had gently eased it of its cruel burden . . . They found her there in the sunshine, a lovely peace upon her features, as though the frail spirit, having passed through the dark waves, had at last found refuge.

[1950]

Michael Harrington

Lukey's Boat

Michael Harrington (1916-) was born in St. John's and has had a distinguished career as a journalist, first as "The Barrelman" on a local radio program in the 1940s and later as Editor of the St. John's *Evening Telegram*. He has chaired the Newfoundland Quarterly Foundation since 1982. A prolific writer of both poetry and prose, he has received several awards, including an honorary doctorate from Memorial University. His writings include *Newfoundland Tapestry* (1943), *Sea Stories from Newfoundland* (1958) and *Goin' to the Ice* (1986).

"O, Lukey's boat is painted green,
Aha, me b'ys,
O, Lukey's boat is painted green,
The prettiest little boat ever you seen.
Aha, me riddle I day . . ."

Everyone in Cold Harbour knew Lukey Bryan's boat. Not that it was painted green when most boats in Cold Harbour were white or black or shadings from one to the other; but because it was painted such a bright green. There was no grass, no tree near Cold Harbour as green as Lukey's boat; nor in Newfoundland neither said Tom Joseph Stone, who'd been around.

It didn't matter. Lukey Bryan was proud of his boat, and why not? He built her himself. From keel to quarter-board, from thwart to thole-pin, she was his handiwork. He had built her in the winter out of wood he had cut a year before on the back of Rainy Pond, hauling it out by horse and catamaran to Sam Raymond's sawmill. Yes, Lukey Bryan was proud of his big, green skiff; more than that — he loved her. Oldtimers thought he was too fond of his boat; they said he'd rather die than let anything happen to her.

Lukey was an odd sort. He had fished with his father for years — from the day he was twelve years old till the day he was twenty-one. Then he just quit; said he was going on his own; told his young brothers to go fish with their father. Lukey hadn't much money but he was a determined fellow — almost stubborn. So he built his boat, with his own hands in his own time and in his own way. He went in to St. John's and bought the best engine he could get, brought it home with him on the coastal steamer and installed it himself. He was proud of his boat; from enginehouse to fore-cuddy she was his masterpiece.

"O, Lukey's boat got a fine fore-cutty,
Aha, me b'ys,
O, Lukey's boat got a fine fore-cutty,
And every seam is chinked with putty.
Aha, me riddle I day . . ."

Fishing can be a very dirty business, with 'gurry' and 'slub' on the planking, and dried offal on the gunwhales, but Lukey Bryan kept his trap skiff so clean and wholesome that when the 'townies' came up from St. John's in the summer, Lukey's boat was always in demand for Sunday excursions to the Round Hill Islands. But every other day Lukey was alone. He fished cross-handed as the Newfoundlanders say. It had its advantages — a man could change his ground at will — and its disadvantages;

when there was a good 'run o' fish,' a mate could help a lot. But that was Lukey's way and it was just as well.

Perhaps some of you remember the big gale of August, just before the war, when a northeaster came out of nowhere in spite of the forecasts which do not always tell the right story on the coasts of an island stuck out like a sore thumb in the North Atlantic. Most of the Cold Harbour men were out on the grounds from before daylight. A lot of them came in about noon, well-fished, but Lukey Bryan with no one to help him stayed on. It's an extraordinary thing the way the northeaster comes in mid-summer. It can be a beautiful day, shimmering with heat, and a gentle westerly fading to a molten stillness. Vast cumulus clouds tower like mountains in the fairy blue, and the earth seems ready to go asleep.

Then suddenly — as though a blind was hauled down in a sunlit room — a darkness falls on the land and the sea. The sky turns to lead, the sea to slate, the wind comes off the water with an edge to it, and a shrillness that makes one shudder. The foam flakes blow. The rest of the Cold Harbour boats got in before the gale rose, but Lukey Bryan was far out on the Red Ledge, and he had a 'hard punch' to get in. He made it through to the harbour mouth, where now the sea was in a tumult between the cliffs and the 'sunkers.' He might have driven his skiff into the Black Gulch and got ashore, but his boat would have been demolished.

So he set her straight for the roaring channel, where already the bottom was going dry in the curl of the heavy seas, and he drove her. On came the big green boat, startling green in the waste of white foam and gray sky. Her undersides were painted red, and her bows came out of the smother like a red mouth, gasping for air. The watchers could see Lukey Bryan in his yellow oilskins in the well abaft the engine-house, holding the bucking tiller and squinting through the mist of spray above the rocks. And suddenly the boat was in the tidal race and a great sea went over her and she was lost to view for a long, unbearable moment.

But she reappeared, shooting out of the water like a bright, green arrow, into the comparatively smooth, lagoon-like harbour. But Lukey Bryan was gone, for her decks were swept as clean as ever Lukey had swabbed them when his catch had been thrown upon the stagehead. They never found him either and they towed his fine, green boat to the 'collar' near the Bryans' stagehead, and there she lies to this day; because they say no boat is worth a man's life, not when he gives his life in that fashion.

"O, Lukey's boat is painted green,
Aha, me b'ys . . ."

[1951]

Landing Stage Figure (1983) — 34 x 28 cm., ink drawing — Filliea

Ernest S. Kelly

Murder Mission

Ernest S. Kelly (1919-), born in Ireland's Eye, Trinity Bay, served in the Royal Navy during the Second World War. As an editor and writer his works have been published in *Canadian Boy, Courier, Family Herald, Golden Magazine, London Mystery, Manhunt* and *Montreal Standard* among others. His books include *How To Make Money Writing At Home* (1955), *Blue Line Lightning* (1964), *Red Line Rebel* (1965), *Duck Pond Hero* (1965) and *Murder For Fun* (1974).

Stephen Manning went down the flagstone walk and around the back of the house. His wife, Nora, was bending over a precious flower-bed, her diminutive figure looking like a large doll's, half hidden by a huge sunflower. Beyond her and past the fence, the waters of Conception Bay glistened and curled lazily in the early morning sun. Bell Island loomed large, like a sleepy whale, too lazy to swim closer to shore. A bus roared by, its straining tires swishing angrily.

Manning picked his way towards his wife, his long face settled in a grey, determined mask. He looked at her hair and his eyes filled with scorn. Once, a long time ago, he had imagined they'd looked good together. She, short, blonde and cuddlesome. He, tall, slim and darkly handsome. Now he hated the very sight of her. Hated her with all the strength in his long, powerful body. Hated her until he could think of nothing else. Hated her nagging, her penny-pinching, joy-killing ways. Hated the very sight of her!

Hate, and frustration, its evil offspring, had sunk gnarled, taunting seeds into his mind until the evil roots threatened to drive him insane. The idea of murder had lurked in the misty shadows of his subconscious until now it was full grown, a vile, soul-destroying thing that gave him no peace. There was no way out. He had to kill her.

Now that his mind was made up he felt strangely relieved. Only a few minutes and he would be free. He just had to dangle the bait in front of Nora and she'd bite. She'd never let him go into St. John's alone, not on Regatta Day — she didn't trust him that much!

It was a beautiful day for murder! He tried to keep the eager smile from showing as he walked towards her. She looked up, and seeing him, flashed a bright smile. Dropping the spade, she ran towards him, dishevelled and blushing like a young bride. That was Nora all over. Putting on an act, trying to impress the neighbours, when she knew as well as he did, that everybody knew about them, knew that they no longer lived together as man and wife; that they lived in the villa like two strangers, each behind his or her own barrier, icy and silent. All that would be finished after today. A shiver of excitement ran down his legs and he wiggled his toes in anticipation.

He flashed the expected smile, picked her up bodily and kissed her roughly on the tip of her freckled nose. Like a well trained colt, she rumpled his hair and pecked at his cheek with heavily painted lips. He looked at the lines around her eyes and laughter welled up inside, forcing him to close his mouth. A picture of married bliss. The best darn acting in the world! He clenched his teeth to keep from laughing. He thought, with contempt, she actually enjoys this, it puffs up her ego to know that I have to play ball. The bitter laughter threatened to escape.

Not after today, sister. You'll be dead soon, Nora, and I'll be free. Think of that when you're in hell and laugh if you can!

She bent over and picked up her spade.

"Where goest thou, Romeo?" she smiled but her eyes remained cold.

"Into St. John's," he said. "Coming?"

She pouted, looked longingly at her flowers and shook her head.

"I'd love to Stephen," she lied sweetly, "but I simply must weed this bed, do you mind?"

"I'd like to have you with me," he lied, "you know that."

"Of course, dear," she went on, "but I must do my chores. You go on alone. Drive carefully and watch the traffic."

He cocked his head sideways, pretending to listen. His mind was going over the murder plan, searching for the minutest flaw. He couldn't find any. He looked down at the smugness on her face, the I-own-you look in her eyes. His thoughts slapped at her face. You bitch! Lap it up, kitten, because very soon you'll be dead, see? You nagged me for the last time, Nora.

He said softly, regretfully, "Okay, sweetheart, play with your flowers but watch out for the bees and don't get stung. I won't be gone long. Bye."

She grinned up at him. "Bye, Darling." Her voice was coy, knowing.

He nodded and moved quickly towards the garage.

Suddenly he heard her running feet and turned. She came towards him, her face spread in a smile. Suddenly he hated her smugness and wanted to slap her — hard!

She grinned into his face. "I changed my mind. I'll go with you. I haven't been in St. John's for days. Besides, I want to see mother."

This was going to be easier than he'd expected. She was in a happy mood. The right mood for dying.

He forced himself to smile. "Swell, honey," he said, "let's have a drink before we start, shall we?"

"Wonderful idea," she danced towards the house, "you mix the drinks while I shed these filthy slacks. Won't be a minute."

He walked into the house and stood in the hall, listening to her moving around in the bedroom. Grinning sardonically, he walked into the living room, crossed to the liquor cabinet, took out two glasses and a bottle of Doorley's rum. The two sleeping pills were in his pocket. He palmed them and reached for her glass. He mixed the drinks slowly, watching the pills dissolve. He was surprised at his complete lack of fear. His hands had never been steadier! He had always imagined that terror and panic would seize him at such a time. All he felt was a satisfaction that left him cool and very, very sure of himself.

The bedroom door slammed and Nora came into the room. She looked cool and fresh in a cotton dress and white sandals. He watched as she drained her glass.

He grinned down at her, "Ready honey?"

She nodded, put down her empty glass and followed him out to the car.

They picked up the highway at Manuels, and turning east, followed the coast road to St. John's. Topsail, a splattering of frame houses and blue sea, swished by. The morning was still early and traffic was light. He was nearly up the top of Topsail Hill when he discovered that she was sound asleep. Grinning he pulled into the side of the road and stopped. After nudging her to make sure she was asleep he got out and lit a cigarette. The highway was empty. Suddenly the car started. Startled he turned and ran towards it. He was too late. She swung the car in a short circle and came at him, engine roaring.

He never knew that she, too, had worked out a plan for death — his death. He never knew that she had been planning for weeks. All he saw was the shiny chrome bumper coming at him. He screamed once before the car struck him.

[1951]

H.M. Heather

Troubled Waters

When the Customs cutter ran into Stag Harbor, Corporal Tobin hit the beach running and kept on going till old Jos Hiscock slammed the door in his face. Somehow or other the Corporal, who had ready ears for a rumor and a nose that could smell out a smuggled bottle from under a quintal of fish, had got an idea that the glass of toddy Jos mixed for himself at bedtime came out of a bottle without a Liquor Controller's label on it. The Corporal was only a young fellow but he made up in energy what he lacked in years. He was in his office at eight o'clock every morning, and Mrs. Harris who kept the boarding house at Westport where he had his headquarters, said that he sat in his room at nights studying lawbooks till after midnight. Certainly he knew all there was to be known about how laws are broken. Before he came to that part of the coast, folks around there had the reputation of being pretty well behaved. There was no thieving or fighting, or damaging another man's property. But after the Corporal arrived in the district, somebody always seemed to be getting into trouble for not having a gun license, or letting his dog run loose or some other thing that no one ever knew was an offence against the realm until Corporal Tobin said so. Of course, the crime he really hoped to discover was smuggling. No doubt a good many illicit bottles came ashore under jackets and inside rubber boots, but the men who knew about these transactions never talked, and those who talked knew nothing. But whatever the explanation, there Tobin was, hoping to make a really big haul which would win him another stripe for his sleeve, and transform him into a Sergeant.

When Hiscock's door slammed in his face, he hammered on it for half a minute and then shouted that he'd have the law on them anyway for obstructing an officer in his duty. So Jos came shuffling as slowly as he dared, fumbled a while with the key, and finally opened the door a couple of inches. Tobin pushed his way in.

"Bring out this liquor you've got hidden away," he said.

"What liquor?" asked Jos. "If it's a drink you're after you've come to the wrong house. There hasn't been a stain in the place since Christmas."

"None of that now," snapped the Corporal. "There's smuggled liquor in this house, and I'm going to search until I find it."

"Search away," invited Jos with a hospitable wave of his hand as he sat down in the rocker by the stove to watch. "There's only one thing," he added, taking out his knife and cutting himself a chew of tobacco, "my poor old woman's sick upstairs. I'd be obliged if you don't disturb her."

The Corporal didn't answer but started poking into cupboards, peering under the stove and rooting through a barrel of dirty linen that stood ready for the wash. He didn't miss much in the kitchen or parlor but still he didn't find what he was looking for. He was pretty red in the face by this time, and stopped to loosen the neck of his tunic, and pull out a handkerchief to wipe his forehead. Jos rocked placidly in the corner, the squeak of his chair keeping time with his jaws as he chewed. But when Tobin finished mopping the back of his neck and started for the stairs, the old man was out of the rocker and scuttling through the door as nimble as an emmet.

"Didn't you hear what I'm after telling you, Corporal?" he said, spreadeagling himself across the stairway. "There's a wonderful sick woman up there."

The Corporal's frown showed that he was in no mood for arguing and Jos reluctantly moved aside. Tobin looked under the beds, and into the cupboards of the first two rooms without reward and then hesitated for a moment outside the closed door of the old woman's bedroom. But he quickly made up his mind. With silent determination, he laid his hand on the doorknob and went in. He pulled back the curtain which shut out the morning light, letting the sun pour in across a chair hung with hastily abandoned clothes and on to the bed where the old woman huddled out of sight beneath a bright patchwork quilt. Then he stood in the middle of the room with his thumbs hooked into his belt and slowly pivoted around, running a professional eye over each individual floorboard to make sure that none of them had been pried up recently. There was no evidence there. Old Jos standing in the doorway saw the baffled look on the Corporal's face and a wicked gleam shone in his watery eye.

"Well, my son," he said sympathetically, "that's a dirty trick they played on you, sending you away out here so early in the morning. I wonder who was the scoundrel did a thing like that. Why, my dear man, there's been neither drink nor sup in this house since me birthday."

The Corporal grunted and swung towards the door but as he did so a glint from the bed caught at the corner of his eye. He ran his hand over the rumpled coverlet, threw back an edge and brought out three clear bottles of gin, three dusky bottles of rum and four of golden whiskey.

Half an hour later he came out of the back door lugging a knobbly sack. He stood on the step looking round for someone to carry it to the boat but a strange calm had come over the settlement and there wasn't a man to be seen. A few women stood in the doorways, and four or five children played in the middle of the road, but the men who usually worked about the stages or stood in groups outside the store had disappeared completely. Corporal Tobin fancied he saw a head move behind a rock on the hillside, but it might have been a goat or a grazing sheep. He shifted the bag to his other hand and set off down the hill to the harbor. When he got there and came clanking and gurgling round the end of a shed, he found that the cutter was anchored fifty yards away from the end of the wharf. A man in the stern waved and shouted, "Can't come any closer, sir. Tide's dropped." Tobin carefully set down his burden, rubbed his bloodless fingers and yelled back, "Can't you come in anywhere?"

"No, sir. We're right in the channel. Shoal all round."

"Well what the devil are you waiting for?" shouted the exasperated Corporal. "Send off a dory."

The man on board threw up his hands.

"It's gone sir. Look!" he pulled a trailing end of rope from the water and held it up. "Cut! We were all down below having a mug-up."

The Corporal gritted his teeth and turned on his heel. He would have to get hold of a dory and row it out himself. But when he looked around the harbor he realised that all the boats, like their owners, had mysteriously disappeared. The high-nosed dories which generally bobbed beside the jetties or lay drawn up on the beach were nowhere to be seen. Only their ravished floats rose and fell with the ripples, trailing their empty lines.

By this time the noon-day sun shining hot in a blue sky was making the Corporal's shoulders prickle with sweat under his neat tunic. He walked to the edge of the wharf and looked across the sparkling water to the group of men who gazed back at him from the cutter's deck. It was only a short distance to swim and the sea looked cool and inviting. He had started to undo his belt when he remembered the sack at his feet and realised that he would have to abandon the booty, which was going to mean so much to his career. Slowly he refastened his buckle and turned to look at the cluster of houses, which clung around the edge of the bay and climbed unevenly up the side of the hill. He knew that from every house a hidden face was watching, but outwardly the whole village lay asleep, drugged into unconsciousness by the warmth of the summer sun. Even the playing children had vanished from the street and only the smoke that pencilled the air above each roof showed that the settlement was not actually derelict.

Desolation descended on Harry Tobin. There was nothing for him to do but stay in that inhospitable place, with invisible eyes shooting daggers at his back, until the tide rose and the boat was able to come alongside. He hitched up an overturned bucket and sat down to consider whether he could have made a more diplomatic approach. He was on the point of deciding that an extra stripe was a poor exchange for wholesale unpopularity when a voice hailed him from the road. He raised his eyes and saw a pretty girl in an apple-green dress coming through the door of one of the fish-sheds. She looked entirely out of place in those surroundings.

"You there," she said in a crisp voice which revealed no terror at the power of the law. "Come over here."

Corporal Tobin's neck crimsoned but with a humility which surprised himself he got to his feet and walked towards her.

"I suppose you want a boat," she said.

He nodded briefly.

"There's one in here then. Help me to get it out."

He followed her into the shed where she pointed to a jumble of lobster-pots and nets which hid a small flat-bottomed dinghy. Between them they lifted it out and carried it down to one of the jetties where they pushed it off into the water. The girl climbed in and held it steady while Tobin went back for his sack of bottles and lowered it into the boat.

"I'll row," said the girl. As the Corporal hesitated, she added impatiently, "Hurry up or they'll be down to stop you."

He climbed cautiously in beside his bundle, while the light flat swayed with his weight. As soon as he was seated she pushed off and rowed strongly for the cutter.

"Thanks for helping me out," he began.

"Don't thank me," she said shortly, "I just don't believe in monkeying with the law." She looked at the sack between his feet.

"That isn't really Uncle Jos's liquor," she said. "It's my cousin Tom's. He's getting married tomorrow and of course he thought he had to have a drink in the house. I told him he would only land us all in trouble."

The Corporal decided to change the subject.

"You're not from Stag Harbor, are you?" he ventured.

"Oh yes I am," she said decidedly, "I'm Mary Hiscock. But I've been working in Halifax for the last five years. I'm only here for Tom's wedding."

She stopped abruptly as if realising that she was fraternising with the enemy. There was silence until the flat bumped gently against the cutter's bow and edged along her side.

"Haul her in, now," the girl ordered.

Tobin stood up carefully and reached for the cutter's deck. Mary lifted her oars on board but as she did so she spooned up a bladeful of sea and the stern of the flat spun round. Tobin staggered, clawed helplessly at empty air and belly-flopped into the water while Mary scrambled to her feet with a scream and a lurch, which made the small boat balance for an instant on its side, and then turn over completely.

The girl went with it and the men who were reaching out to help Tobin left him abruptly and clustered by the rail peering into the troubled water. A head broke the surface and the girl swam smoothly towards the shore.

Tobin climbed on to the deck and peered through the ripples at a scattering of bottles on the sea floor.

"Can any of you fellows dive?" he demanded.

The men shook their heads.

"We might get them at low tide," suggested one.

"Not a chance," said another. "It's still too deep. You'd want a diving suit to go after that lot."

There was a long silence. Tobin glanced across at the beach

where Mary was demurely wringing out the hem of her dress. With a resounding oath he crashed his fist against the cutter's rail and turned on the crew.

"What are we waiting for?" he barked.

The engine sputtered into life. Corporal Tobin stood on the deck in a widening pool of water and gazed darkly upon Stag Harbor.

"No witnesses; no evidence; no case," he muttered. "I've made a proper fool of myself and got nothing out of it at all."

A distant flicker of apple-green caught his eye and the gloom gradually lifted from his brow.

"I'm not so sure though," he murmured. "It's a poor wedding with nary a drink. If I chanced along with a bottle or two of Screech tonight. . . . I wonder what would happen."

[1952]

F.M. Kennedy

Smallboatmen

Fabian M. Kennedy (1922-   ), born in St. John's, was employed with the Newfoundland Railway and then the Canadian National Railways until he retired in 1986. He has lived and worked in Moncton, Montreal, Toronto, and St. John's. Two volumes of *A History of The Newfoundland Railway* (in collaboration with A.R. Penney) were published in 1988 and 1990. His writings also appeared in the *Evening Telegram* and the *Newfoundland Quarterly*. In 1952 one of his short stories won first place in the Newfoundland and Labrador Arts and Letters Competition, while in 1953 a radio script won second prize.

"Do you ever think of getting drowned?" George said.

"Yes," Peter said, "lots of times I do."

"Some mornings," said George, "do you feel that you don't want to go out? You feel like something is going to happen that day. When you touch them, the bait and the hooks feel colder, and the days feel damper and your hands feel number, and you get a feeling of dread?"

"Yes," Peter said, "lots of times."

"This time of the morning," George said, "before daylight, you can't hardly tell what kind of day it's going to be. Supposing it blows up a sou-easter. Suppose now you don't come in. Not only you; me and all hands don't come in."

Peter stopped in surprise and looked at him.

"Look, George, knock off will you. You're giving me the goosepimples. One thing, I wouldn't go out if I wasn't coming in again, and another thing, you're talking now like an old woman and that might be all right around the fire before you go to bed."

"We wouldn't be the first ones," George said darkly.

"Damn it, George," Peter said in exasperation.

"Even your father now . . ."

"That was twenty-five years ago," Peter said.

"I remember then, your mother, Lord have mercy on her, said you'd never go fishing. Why did you?"

Peter looked at him uncertainly.

"Why are you, George?"

"I never did anything else," George said. "But you did. You only came fishing this year. Why did you?"

"I don't know exactly," Peter said. "I suppose I wanted to . . ."

George

There were four men in the boat that put out in the early morning darkness on a dark, cold-looking sea. A grey chill mist hung close to the water, and the sea sounded in muffled rumbles along the rocky beach.

George huddled up back aft, trying to make a small bundle of his body. He felt cold and weary and dissatisfied, and looked over the sea with loathing. God preserve us, but this is no way for men to make a living. There's fish under this boat now. Why do we have to go so far out to catch fish when they are all around us even now? Why can't we just stop here? Fish swim around, don't they? And the fish that are out there now might be swum in here by the time we get out there. Aaaah, I spit in disgust. I spit that we can be so foolish. Nelson Hodges, our mighty skipper. Look at him there with his hand on the tiller. You wouldn't know but this twenty-eight foot tub was the *Queen Mary*. What has he got to look so God A'mighty grim about and snuff up his blue nose at us about? He needn't think because he owns the boat . . . I wish I had enough money so I could give this up. I wish I had . . . Aaaah! I spit. For you too, Cooper. You big clown. Sitting up there like that, letting the spray hit you in the big fat face. Enjoying this. Like this, don't you? Aaaah. I spit. I spit. To all of you. You make me spit. Sing, Cooper, and cheer me up.

Peter

The cold, salt spray stung Peter's face and he crouched in the lee of Cooper's big form. He couldn't see anything in front of him except the glistening back of Cooper's rubber jacket but he could imagine the dark restless sea ahead. Low, white-topped waves raced by him on the side and these he could see and almost touch.

Behind him, he could sense George's lonely antagonism towards the sea. George. No more life than a dead fish. All that gloomy talk. Well, why did I come fishing this year at all? Is this what I want to do with my life? Get up at three o'clock in the morning and live on the water? Die in it too, perhaps? George again. How old are you now? I'm thirty years old, sir. British, married and one son. What is your ambition? I want to be a fisherman, sir. I want to get up every morning before dawn and shiver in the boat. I want to bait cold hooks and catch cold fish . . . Do you want to own a boat like Hodges? Like Hodges? Behind me there is his bony hand on the tiller. Do I want to be like him? Do I want to feed two sons to this hungry ocean? Do I? No. By God I don't. I'll give this up first.

What will you do? What will I do? Lumbering? You can wake up in the camp when the gong goes for breakfast. You can hear birds sing, or hear birch trees popping with the frost and the ice on the pond cracking like a gunshot. You eat enough and you get more money. But . . . .

You miss the hiss and the rumble of the sea by your door. You want to feel the weight on your line and the strain on your shoulders hauling the heavy dead-weight of the fish into the boat. You want your body rocked emotionless in the waves and your spirit waked to the adventure and the danger.

There's the answer to George. You want the danger. You want to feel the danger. You wouldn't give it up because it was dangerous, and you might because it wasn't.

That's what's wrong with George. He fears it. I welcome it as a struggle, for I don't intend to drown. The sea will be defeated by Peter Barnes, fisherman, fighter, adventurer, bluff, liar. Bluff, Peter? Liar? Liar, Peter? Because you do fear it.

Cooper there, he doesn't fear it. Big Cooper, he fears neither God, devil or man. When it's roughest he laughs loudest and bails hardest. He's superficial, is Cooper. He wants money enough for a bottle of rum, and that's all he wants.

Ah, we're there now. I suppose now Hodges will stop sniffing through his skinny nose, and George will stop spitting, and Cooper will start to sing.

Hodges cut the engine and the boat glided up to the buoy. Cooper hefted the buoy into the boat and coiled in the buoyline from the bottom. As he lifted the end of the trawl line he could feel the weight below him.

"Glory be," said Cooper, laughing, "we're surrounded. There's thousands of fish down there."

"Now, me boys," shouted Hodges, "let's get the slippery devils aboard."

Hodges

This was the moment that was so hard to bear. Hodges almost cried when the fish were coming aboard. But he couldn't let the tears show to trickle over his cold cheeks or drip from the pointed end of his purplish nose. And it wasn't pity for the fish at all. It was a welling of gratitude and happiness. He had guided his craft across an invisible path on the ocean, into the cold wind and raining spray. Now the dawn was black masses of gold bands in the eastern sky, and the fish were at his boat.

He had prayed that morning, as every morning when he got out of bed. Prayed to Jesus on the Sea of Galilee. He remembered Fred and Arthur, dead in the sea, and recommended their eternal souls to Heaven.

While he knelt, he could hear his wife moving in the kitchen below him, preparing food for him, and in these her barren years mourning all the more the lost and only fruits of her womb.

No longer did she ask him not to go. His every return she met without emotion and he felt she would accept his loss even so.

Unto You, O Lord, who did calm the winds and the seas and did fill the nets of the Apostles, I commend my life and my boat. To Your mercy the souls of my sons Frederick and Arthur, and to Your everlasting goodness the happiness of my wife, Annie. Amen.

He had gone down to the kitchen and washed and sat in at the table.

He could easily sell his boat, and the money he had would tide them both until death. Why didn't he?

"You know what, Annie?" he said. "I've been thinking I'll sell the boat to Frank Flynn, he's after it, and stay home now. I'm getting too old for this anyhow."

She didn't seemed pleased. She didn't seem anything. Perhaps she had heard that before. Oh, how many times?

Well, I'll do it. When I come in I'll see Frank. I'll sell it. I wonder what'll she say then?

Cooper

Cooper sang; sometimes aloud, more often a hum, with words known only to himself, while he hauled fish aboard. He was a big man, about forty years old. His face was round in shape and was covered now with black stubble. He was nearly always smiling and the teeth he showed were stained brown with tobacco.

He went fishing because he had been fishing all his life and never thought of doing anything else. He enjoyed the cold tingling in his hands and arms; he enjoyed hugely the battle with the waves and the tug of the line on his shoulders.

He had no great ambition to own a boat. He liked to sit forward and feel the spray on his face; he liked to sing a little to himself while the boat cut hissing through the water, and every place on the heaving ocean looked alike to him.

He liked the thrill of falling into the trough of the waves and then bouncing up again. In the boat he felt no more sense of adventure or danger than he did at home pacing the kitchen floor. It was all life to Cooper and no dramatics.

And now his spirits were rising with the rising easterly wind and his body was braced to the easy movement of the boat.

George looked over at Cooper enviously. Cooper is a great man in a boat; look at him move. He listened to Cooper's toneless humming and laughed in friendly derision.

"That's great words to that song, Cooper," he shouted. "Learn them to me, will you?"

Cooper freed one hand from his task and wiped his nose self-consciously. He grinned.

"Sure will, Uncle George," he said.

"It's a wonder to me," said Hodges, "that a fine singer like yourself don't know them already."

Peter laughed.

"Don't do it, Cooper," he said. "It's bad enough having one hand singing like that!"

"It's sure hard to listen to," Hodges agreed, seriously. No smile betrayed his feelings. His mind dropped away from the sail of his boat and he was wrapped in warm sentiment.

"Your father, now," Hodges said to Peter, "he was a great man to sing. I mind poor Skipper Ned on the Labrador singing from one end of the voyage to the other. He was a great one to sing."

"He never left it to me then," Peter said.

Cooper's face composed itself seriously, as George began in a slow measured baritone:

" 'Twas of a young maiden this story I'll tell,
And of her young lover and what them befell.
Now her lover was a Cap'n what sailed the blue sea,
And this is the circumstances surrounding the departure of he."

Cooper's head nodded to the slow beat and he hummed in with George at the end of each line.

George was tuned to the song he sang, and he felt very close to them all. He could see in Cooper's eyes shining affection and admiration for his singing prowess.

While George sang, Peter and Hodges conversed in lowered tones.

"What's your wife say to this fishing?" Hodges asked.

Peter shrugged.

"It's a job," he said.

How could he talk now of the romance of it, to Hodges, here on the cold water. To Hodges, who had spent fifty years on the water.

"Annie don't like me at it," Hodges confided, and he managed to suggest that neither would any Annie or wife of any other man, after a time.

"But it's hard to knock off after a lifetime, and stay on the beach."

In Hodges' small face his small eyes burned.

"After a while," he said, "it's more than a job. It's a life. In bed you dream you are rocking on the water. And not till you are on the water is there any peace inside you. When you have seen two sons drown out there . . ." and he pointed his thin finger out over the sea, ". . . then it comes first, before all, before everything. It owes you something then, and you owe it something, too. Something like anger and something like revenge. And you owe yourself something too. Courage, not to fear it."

Hodges' tone was low but his voice was intense.

"Do you understand me?" he asked.

"With a boatload of salt pelt our Cap'n sailed away,
Sailed away from his true love all on a summer's day;
Now he never more was heard from nor his vessel so brave,
So 'twas figured pretty generally that he met a watery grave."

George put all the emotion he knew into his song and sent frequent glances at Cooper to note how he was receiving it.

Peter laughed softly.

"Listen to George," he said, "he's singing like a banshee."

Hodges sniffed.

"He could of sung something fast. He could have sung Bonay," he said.

They hauled the night-set trawl and the fish were there. Then they threw the bait and the trawl tubs up on the gangboards and they set another. Peter and Cooper with swift, sure vigor baited and cast the hooks behind them into the sea, like men scattering seed upon the land. Sometimes leaning back upon the line Peter could feel the tug of a fish on one of the hooks. Hodges, slowly propelling the boat, watched him thus test the line and remembered. George, the cook now, swabbed the pot out and started breakfast, still singing, looking forward now and then for Cooper's solemn nod of approval. The worm of hunger stirred in their stomachs; the flame of friendship warmed them.

The trawl was set and the breakfast fish was cooking when Cooper, going aft, with a daring laugh stepped on the bait gangboard. He stood there a moment nonchalantly while they looked at him in amusement. Then, in a sudden lurch of the boat, he toppled over the side into the water. His feet were just going over the gunwale when Hodges yelled.

"Cooper. Grab Cooper. He's going overboard!"

Hodges grabbed at the sculling oar and held the boat around. George, his mouth open in midnote, gaped incredulously, as Peter, moving quickly, threw the rope across the water.

Cooper, hitting the water, felt only surprise and anger. He took a deep gulp of water on the way down and bobbed again to the surface. What the hell had happened to him?

His feet churned but he could not stand up and his arms flailed around him at invisible enemies he could not hit. The water was gradually penetrating his clothes and his boots were filled. It was cold and a great fear took possession of him. He feared the surrounding, impenetrable, unresisting, cold and silent ocean that was gradually dragging him down; that submissively took all the blows of his great fists and kicking feet and still would smother him and defeat him while he fought. The fear lent more violence to his motions; his cape ann was gone and one of his boots had been kicked off. But for all of his being determined not to, still he was drowning, and, in sudden despair, he stopped struggling.

It was then, with the fear inside him almost deafening his ears and sea water blubbering from his lips, that he heard their voices shouting.

His body gave a jump and he fought again towards the boat and the floating end of the rope. He reached out and closed his numbed fingers around it and they tugged it eagerly out of his hands. He floundered around and grabbed it again and wrapped it under his armpits. With shouted words of encouragement they gently tugged it away from him again. Sobbing with frustration, cold and heavy and weary from fighting, big Cooper closed his eyes and started to sink.

Hodges brought the boat now almost directly above Cooper. As the side went low Peter leaned far over and sank his fingers in Cooper's hair. He lifted Cooper's shoulders over the water, and George, leaning over, caught one arm. Peter moved his hands down under Cooper's chin, and then under his arm, and with Hodges' brief help they hauled Cooper into the boat and laid him out on top of the fish.

Cooper's heavy face was grey and immobile under the dark stubble on his cheeks. From the corner of his mouth water trickled, and, as they turned him over he vomited violently, his stomach heaving in great gasps. Gradually he moaned his way back to the surface of consciousness. He opened his eyes and groaned and spat and tried to push the fish away from his face, his teeth clenched and his body shivering.

"By God, Cooper," George muttered, "you almost went under. You were almost down there with the fishes. I knew something would happen today."

Now, after the shock of the near disaster, Hodges' knees felt weak and his knuckled hand trembled as he guided the craft. Could he himself survive the loss of a man from his boat if this near loss affected him so? Would it be better now for a man to stay at home and die in bed?

Peter stripped the wet clothes from Cooper and replaced them with dry clothes from the locker.

"You had us worried, Cooper," he said.

Cooper tried to grin.

"Me too," he said. He spoke hoarsely through his clenched teeth.

But even now the fearful memory was slipping behind Cooper and the others would later remember it more vividly than he. Cooper would recover and be warm again and hungry. He'd put his face into the wind again, taste the salt spray on his lips again, and only remember with a laugh the salt water he had gulped.

Watching the color flow back into Cooper's face, and his buoyancy of spirit return, Peter laughed aloud right at him.

George's unsatisfied mind raced ahead to what might have

been. I'm going to give this up — his mind resolved — I'm going to give this up.

Hodges figured in his mind how much he could ask for his boat. I'll sell it. Sell it. Sell it.

Across their thoughts cut Peter's rising, continuous laughter. He looked at Cooper's goose-pimpled face and roared with laughter.

"By heaven, Cooper," he shouted, "they can't drown you. And if they can't drown you, then, by heaven, they won't drown me."

Cooper looked back at him wanly, puzzled, and then a small sly grin, as at some shared secret thought, spread across his face. With one large finger he wiped away the water trickling from his nose and half-lying among the fish, he laughed back.

George looked at them, and then at Hodges, and then back at them in amazement.

"They're mad," he said. "They're gone mad, they must be."

Hodges sniffed steadily. Worse things had often happened and it wasn't so bad after all.

"Sing something, George, while we're waiting for that fish," he said.

George laughed stridently and felt his agitation subside.

"Come all ye good people and listen to me,
A short, simple ditty I'll sing unto ye."

Four voices were raised in the song. "It's a bloody choir we got," George said.

"A short simple ditty that's lately in print,
Concerning one summer on Bonay I spent."

[1952]

Boat Figure — 102 x 81 cm., oil pastel with powdered pigment — Filliea

Wanda Neill Tolboom

The Legend of Ben's Rock

Wanda Neill Tolboom was born in Kelwood, Manitoba, and lived for many years in Frobisher Bay as the wife of the Hudson's Bay Company Post Manager. Living what she called her "nomadic life", she came into contact with Newfoundlanders and was sufficiently impressed to write a short story for the A.H. Murray & Co. contest for which she won second prize. "The Legend of Ben's Rock" was published in the *Atlantic Guardian* in 1952.

Almost at the extreme tip of Newfoundland's Great Northern Peninsula lies Cape Onion. On the smaller maps, one will not even so much as find her name, for what little fame and publicity she might have called her own has been snatched by her more formidable cousin, Cape Bauld, which lies only a few miles to the south-east. But, she has a secret which she quietly keeps and only the friendly fisher folk who tend their nets in the waters of Ship Cove ever speak of it. Even then it is only a passing word, a nod, a smile or an allusion, for these are busy folk who have little time to ponder over that which is past and gone.

Time has swept away almost all visible traces of the little French fishing station which once stood at Western Head. But, time has done little to Ben's Rock. The base may be a little smaller — worn by the wind and the waves — but the hollow at the top is still the same smooth recess where Ben lay sheltered as he scanned the sea each day. From this point, the broad Atlantic stretches far across to England and to France. Who was this Ben and why did he watch? Around this rock lies a legend.

Each year for three centuries the fishing boats had come from France to reap a glorious harvest of fish from Newfoundland's rocky coast and to sail for home before the coming winter. Then, in 1713, by the Treaty of Utrecht they lost complete rights to fish where and when they pleased and were forced to cast their nets only along a designated coast line which came to be known as the French Shore. Here, at intervals, they set up their crude fishing stations. They quarrelled unceasingly with the "liviers," the English settlers who were struggling to make a permanent home on the island. It was no wonder that each autumn the "liviers" were happy to see them sail for home.

Jean Paul de Benoit was no fisherman. He was of noble birth, and would never have set foot aboard a dirty, reeking derelict of a fishing schooner, had he never met Roxanne, the brazen little beauty of the blue-black hair, she with the poise of a duchess but, alas, only the daughter of a vendor of fish.

The occupation of her father was of no importance to Jean Paul for he, himself, had flouted all visible ties with his noble family. His father was well pleased when this errant second son remained away from home for long periods of time. Each occasional appearance was only a source of embarrassment to them all. His dainty mother only sighed when she looked at her tall son with his unruly shock of golden hair. He was so unlike his serious, dark-haired brothers. Not that Jean Paul was wicked, but they all agreed that he did possess an aptitude for keeping himself continually in the midst of trouble, and this was so unbefitting to his station in life. And he in turn learned to despise the bonds of tradition which had so enslaved them all.

It was in the latter part of the nineteenth century. Jean Paul had not been home for many years. One day, while loitering about the wharves, he chanced to see Roxanne. Her cheeks were pink with the sea breezes and her hair was all awry but his heart swelled with loving her. In the days which followed, they often met there among the casks and the tar. But, Roxanne only smiled and taunted him with her beauty, for had he not been so blinded by the length of her silken lashes, he would have seen that the eyes beneath were cold and cruel. She only was amusing herself with this ragged stranger, all the while nurturing a foolish dream that one day some noble man would be entranced with her beauty and beg her to be his wife. So when Jean Paul asked her to marry him, her merry laugh floated out across the harbor.

He asked her again and again, and the more often she refused him the more determined he became. How surprised she would be when he revealed his true identity. How her lovely face would light up. He smiled when he imagined how he would dress her in the finest silks and present her to his family and he laughed aloud at the thought of the expressions on their faces when he announced that she was but little Roxanne, daughter of a vendor of fish.

All this time, his beloved was scheming to send him away. A ship's captain had also begun to cast admiring glances her way. Now, Jean Paul only bored and annoyed her. She teased him about his hands which were narrow and delicate of bone and most unlike those of men she knew. They were useless for any kind of work becoming a man, she said. This angered Jean Paul, as she intended it to do, and, when he asked her what he must do to prove himself, she laughingly told him to hire aboard one of the fishing schooners which were leaving soon for the shores of the unknown land across the sea. Then she sweetly promised that when he returned in the late autumn they should be married. Light-hearted in the thought of possessing Roxanne for his own, he soon found a schooner about to sail and, although he knew little concerning the sea, and less about fishing, he was soon signed aboard.

The entire voyage was a seemingly endless nightmare of wind and waves. His body ached and his hands which Roxanne had scorned were torn by the ropes and tormented by the salt water which crept into the wounds and bit into the very bone. It seemed a miracle when, one day in June, the coast of Newfoundland sprang out of the mist and they finally dropped anchor off the Western Head of Cape Onion.

All summer he worked side by side with the other fishermen ignoring both their kindnesses and their curses. His body was only aware of the agonizing pain in his muscles, and his mind had room only for the face of Roxanne and the counting of the days until mid-September when they should sail for home with a full cargo of fish.

But Jean Paul was destined never to sail, for when it was time to leave, the captain called him aside. It had been decided, he explained, that as the return voyage would be an even more treacherous one and as his prowess as a sailor was of little note, he should remain behind. It was the custom that each year one of the men should stay to take charge of the fishing station until the following year. In vain did Jean Paul cajole and threaten but the captain was adamant. When the schooner sailed she carried not he, but only a long letter to Roxanne begging her to wait but one more year.

It was a lonely winter for Jean Paul — and most bitterly cold. A few "liviers" dwelled nearby — English folk with whom they had quarrelled over the setting of the nets, and who now passed timidly by his rough cabin as they went about laying their winter traps for foxes. They understood little of his language and he of theirs, but they talked a little now and then. They asked his name, and Jean Paul de Benoit became known to his neighbors merely as Ben.

When spring came, they used to see him in his little rowboat, going across from the fishing station to the other side of the inlet where a narrow bar of land faced the Atlantic. Then, beaching his craft he would walk down the rocky bar and climb atop a conspicuous rock which had a comfortable half-secluded recess at the summit. Here he spent long hours staring out to sea and torturing his mind with thoughts of Roxanne and what news of her the schooner might bring. As the days wore on, he found he was unable even so much as to sleep in his cabin. He then took a little food and a blanket and on clear nights slept out under the stars. The "liviers" shook their heads, and were careful they did not molest him. On sunny days, while passing his rock in their little boats, they would see the glint of his golden head and they knew Ben was still watching for the schooner. Sometimes in the evening they saw a flicker of a light and they called to him and he answered. But, mostly, they stayed away.

When Jean Paul failed to return, Roxanne was glad and did not so much as enquire what evil had befallen him, for now her ship's captain kept her thoughts well occupied. It was just by chance one day that an old newspaper with which her father had wrapped some fish, fell into her hands. Looking up at her from the printed page was a picture of Jean Paul. With trembling fingers she rubbed away the stains of fish and laboriously spelled out the words which told the story. Jean Paul was the missing son of a nobleman who had died. His elder brother had shot himself in a hunting accident and now this second son and heir was sought throughout the land. Almost hysterical with excitement and rage, Roxanne went immediately to his family with her story, but they had no reason to believe her. Many others had also gone to them with equally incredible stories and so she too was sent away.

Then Roxanne, in her simple cunning, made enquiries and soon found out what had befallen Jean Paul. She wrote him a long and loving letter with no mention of his bereavements or her knowledge of his noble birth, and she dispatched it aboard his schooner when it sailed for the fishing shores that Spring. Then, in a frenzy of delight, she awaited his return.

Now, the threads of our legend are broken a bit and have

gone astray. The schooner arrived in June as she always had. But Ben was not atop his rock. The "liviers" shook their heads when questioned as to his absence. They had seen the reflection of his hair atop the rock that same morning the schooner was sighted. They had almost surely seen the shadow of his rowboat the night before. The Frenchmen were puzzled and a little angry but did not ask again. And, that summer, the "liviers" stayed away from Western Head and set their nets elsewhere. When the schooner sailed that autumn, they watched her go and were glad.

Since that year, the summit where Ben watched has been known as Ben's Rock. The legend of Roxanne and Jean Paul has no ending. The mystery still lies at Western Head. The good people who dwell at Ship Cove today will show you the rocky bar and the vantage point which was his. On a sunny day they are not alarmed by a golden glint of something which for an instant catches the eye atop this rock. It is only a trick of the sun, perhaps. In the dusk of a summer's evening when all the little boats are beached for the night, housewives are not afraid when they see a little rowboat moving out towards Ben's Rock. Twilight plays tricks on the human eye. It is only a shadow — perhaps.

[1952]

Elizabeth Dinn

The Scarlet Jacket and the Middy Blouse

Elizabeth Dinn (1914-1972), born in Cumberland, England, was a registered nurse and midwife. Elizabeth Morrow and her future husband, John Thomas Dinn of the Goulds, met during World War II, while he was serving with the Royal Navy. "The Scarlet Jacket and the Middy Blouse" won third prize in the A.H. Murray & Co. short story contest and was published in the *Atlantic Guardian* in 1953.

The pale sunlight of a midwinter's day shone upon the little house which nestled on the hillside. With its green walls and scarlet roof, it looked as much a part of the Newfoundland landscape as the clump of spruce trees sheltering it from the stormy winds of the Atlantic Ocean which swept over the hills. Smoke puffed merrily from the chimney pot, as if defying the elements to steal away from the little house any of the warmth and happiness contained within its four stout walls.

In the kitchen a woman was busy kneading some dough, pausing now and then to gaze through the window at the snow-covered hills gleaming in the sunshine, and the homes of her neighbors. From a distance they looked like gay wooden bricks, all sizes and colors, scattered over a snowy white carpet by some mischievous child.

Smiling a little, she finished her task, feeling a sense of

contentment and peace as she covered the bread crock with a sailor's white "middy" blouse and a girl's scarlet jacket. So many times had those two discarded garments been used for that purpose — yet only at that moment did they appear to her as symbols of her present happiness — that the sailor's blouse and her old scarlet jacket, after sharing so many hazards in the past, should now find themselves a part of this cheerful kitchen.

As she went about her work, setting the bread crock on a ledge near the cooking range, upon which a pan of porridge simmered, memories took her thoughts back over the years.

The scarlet jacket had attracted her because it was such a contrast to the gloomy, "blacked-out" streets of the city in the North of England where she and her family lived during the war. After wearing the dark blue uniform of an ambulance attendant most of the week, it was a pleasant change to put on the bright little coat over a pretty dress and enjoy an evening of relaxation.

It was during one of these off-duty jaunts that she had met Jim.

A shadow crossed the woman's face as she recalled the multi-colored lights, the music and happy laughter of the dance hall, where she and a girl friend, another nurse, with two young R.A.F. men they had met at a NAAFI concert, had almost forgotten, for a time, the misery and desolation which the war had brought — until their gaiety was abruptly ended by the wail of an air raid siren. A few seconds later, with crowds of others, they were on their way to the nearest air raid shelter, the shrill whistle of a falling bomb reminding them of the dangerous reality of their situation.

In the confusion she had become separated from her companions and decided that they must be in one of the other sections; the air raid shelter had several rooms, all leading off the main tunnel.

A child, tired and fretful after being roused from sleep and hurried from his home in one of the nearby streets, began to scream indignantly.

Several other children joined him in a noisy chorus which was interrupted only by the drone of aeroplanes overhead, until the sound of a popular song filled the room. One by one, the children stopped howling, to gaze in delighted wonder at the young sailor who was playing a mouth organ, his cap perched at a precarious angle on a mop of dark hair. It was then that the girl in the scarlet coat met the young fellow wearing the navy blue uniform and white middy blouse of an able-bodied seaman.

The bare brick walls of the shelter seemed to hold a kind of magic sweeter even than the tunes which soothed the frightened children. As the dark grey eyes of the girl met the merry blue ones of the sailor, they felt themselves to be drawn together. It was as if, in some mysterious way, this meeting had been planned and all the years before they met were unimportant, except that, eventually, they had led them to each other, on this night, when the crash of bombs bringing death and destruction filled the air.

After the "all clear" had sounded its welcome message that the danger had passed, the girl made her way into the street, looking for her friends in the crowds of people thronging the pavement but not seeing any of them; they had probably left their section in time to find a seat on one of the buses which resumed its journey as soon as the raid was over. Seeing the long queue waiting for buses, she began to walk the three miles to her home in one of the suburbs.

Evidently, the shops near the shelter had been damaged by a blast — glass from the windows of one of them littered the pavement. The girl, finding her way around the broken pieces, stumbled in the darkness and might have fallen but a strong arm steadied her and she looked up to see the dim outline of the sailor's dark hair above the whiteness of his blouse. She was not at all surprised to find him at her side, the cold night air seemed full of the same strange enchantment she had felt in the air raid shelter. The girl knew, somehow, that this was but the first of many meetings with the sailor, so when he insisted upon seeing that she reached home safely, she accepted his company gladly.

His name, she learned, was Jim O'Brien; the merry blue eyes and dark hair proclaimed his Irish ancestry, though the shoulder flash showed Newfoundland to be his native land.

He had just begun fourteen days' leave and not knowing anyone in England apart from a few acquaintances and shipmates, had only the haziest idea of how those precious days of freedom would be passed, so he hoped they could spend some time together, whenever she was not on duty at the Ambulance Depot.

So Anne Brooks and Jim O'Brien met in surroundings just about as unromantic as anyone could imagine. It was a night filled, not with moonlight and star dust, or any such wonderful things with which poets and song writers for countless ages have associated with romance. If the air was filled with anything at all, it was the drone of aeroplanes, the noise of bombs, the thud of falling shrapnel, mingled with the tears of frightened children, the prayers and curses of folk driven from their warm beds by fears of death or disaster.

Yet the love which began with that meeting was to blossom into as fair a bloom as any the poets have loved to tell us about. It was to survive all the separations and anxieties of war, so that when the world was once again at peace and only rain, or snow, or the golden sunlight came from the sky, their love was stronger and more beautiful than ever, as if it was something which the forces of evil that had surrounded it for so long were unable to destroy — as indeed, it was!

Many happy hours had been spent, whenever Jim could get leave from his ship, making plans for the future, talking of the home they would build out in the quiet countryside, when Jim could return to the small Newfoundland community and his peacetime occupation of farming.

The war seemed to be going on indefinitely, so they got married and set up a temporary home in a couple of furnished rooms near the ambulance depot where Anne was stationed. The hours of duty and the work of helping those injured in the raids helped to fill in the long weeks or months, when the loneliness of their separation was bridged only by brief letters.

Anne's thoughts turned happily from the past as her son, a lively, rosy cheeked schoolboy, came into the kitchen. "G'morning Mam!" he called out cheerily, "Baby's awake, shall I bring her in here?"

"Yes, David," replied his mother, "wheel in the cot, then have your breakfast. I'll dress Margaret in a little while." The boy pushed the wicker cot into a warm corner of the kitchen, then began pouring molasses over a plate of steaming porridge.

"Dad was clever, making such a nice cot for Margaret, wasn't he, Mam? Did he make one like that for me when I was a baby?" he asked.

Anne shook her head, smiling, as she took some baby clothes from the airing rack, "No, dear, Daddy was away at sea most of the time, when you were small," she reminded the lad. A grin spread over his chubby features.

"That's right — he couldn't stay at home making cots or baskets then — but I don't mind, lots of children have a cot their father made for them — only they haven't a Daddy who sailed way across the sea and won lots of medals for being brave!" David exclaimed proudly, as he spread jam over a huge chunk of bread. "Where is Dad?" he asked, "Has he had breakfast yet?"

His mother lifted up the chuckling infant, "Yes, he had to go to town on the early bus today; he said tell you to finish your homework early tonight, if you want to hear the rest of that tale about the sailors whose ship was wrecked. Now, dear, if you've finished eating, be sure to wash that jam off your face, before you go to school." The lad gave his face a hasty rub with a damp cloth, bestowed a bear-like hug upon his mother, a light kiss on the curly head of the baby sister he adored and ran off to join a group of school children in the lane.

Anne O'Brien put the baby into her high chair, fastened the safety belt, then pushed the cot into the bedroom which was next to the kitchen. Her eyes lingered proudly on the cot and she smiled wistfully, recalling young David's pride in his Dad's war medals. It was a blessing that the child had been too young to remember much about the first few years of his life in war-time England. She would never quite forget the loneliness and anxiety of those weeks she spent in a little country town awaiting the birth of her first child, not knowing where her husband was, or how he was faring, as many weary months had gone by since the arrival of his last letter.

The town was well out of the danger zone — except for blackout regulations and ration books, it seemed little affected by the war. Yet after being there for a couple of days far away from her family and friends, Anne would have returned home if it were not for the new little life entrusted to her keeping.

On the bright spring morning when she first saw her tiny son, she had longed so much for Jim's return, to share her joy — but received, instead, an official letter, informing her that he had been wounded in action and was seriously ill.

Anne tied a bib over Margaret's dress and gave her the little spoon with which she loved to feed herself, though almost as much food fell on the bib as found its way into her rosy mouth.

Memories of the day when Jim had returned from the war, not for a brief leave but for always, rushed into Anne's mind; she remembered the flags and bunting hung across the drab street by kindly neighbors, welcoming yet another hero back home from the war. It had been wonderful to be together again at last, without having to count the days that remained before they would once again be separated.

The war had taken many years of their youth and Anne's black hair had become streaked with grey; the suffering, mental and physical, he had endured had etched grim little lines on

Jim's face. But at last it was over and the little home they had dreamed of for so long was becoming more tangible.

Jim had to attend a Rehabilitation Centre for some time before returning to his own country; his war service had rendered him unable to farm the land he loved, so before the little house over the sea could be built, he had to learn to do a different kind of work.

Fortunately, they managed to live on his disability pension without spending much of their savings, but there were times when their plans seemed almost impossible of achievement.

Anne dressed the baby for her morning crawl around the floor and began to peel some potatoes, a smile softening the thoughtful expression on her face. Jim had often been despondent in those days. It was difficult for hands unused to such work to master the weaving of intricate patterns. If David was older, he would know that the beautifully made cot represented a harder won victory than any of the shining medals.

A bus stopped by the lane leading to the O'Brien's small, one storey home and as a tall, dark haired man alighted, Anne felt the same happy enchantment she had known ever since their first meeting long ago in the air raid shelter.

His face bright with suppressed excitement, Jim entered the kitchen and produced a sheet of paper for her inspection. "I've got the contract!" he exclaimed jubilantly. "One of the best shops in town wants all the baskets and bedroom chairs we can supply. The profit from their order alone will more than pay the expenses of our workshop and showroom. See, Anne darling, what it says!"

She took the paper, seeing at a glance the typed confirmation of the news her husband had brought. "Read it out," he commanded impatiently.

Anne began to read, then hesitated. It might have been a trick of the sunshine streaming through the window, or the tears of joy which filled her eyes. But somehow, just for a moment, the paper in her hand looked like a golden scroll inscribed with the words "For Valour".

Then, once more, it became just a business agreement, as she slowly read out the facts and figures of their good fortune to the smiling man at her side who, as a result of war injuries, was totally blind.

[1953]

William E. Coady

Monday Mourning

William E. Coady (1950-), born in St. John's, is a graduate of Gonzaga High School. A self-taught accountant, Bill works with the Fisheries Association of Newfoundland and Labrador Limited. He has published poetry and short fiction. "Monday Mourning" won first prize in the 1972 short story category of the Newfoundland and Labrador Arts and Letters Competition, while his narrative poem "Fire" won second prize.

"Shudda come before. Hate workin' Mondays." Joseph slowly trod the beach, skirting a seaward stream gurgling through the smooth stones, nearing the perpendicular hillside signalling the end of the beach. The drunken sensation of openness, so alien to everyday existence, flooded his thoughts. "I 'member this . . ."

"Unless you've gone crackers." The half-forgotten voice disentangled Joseph's deliberation. Matthew suddenly appeared from the shadow afforded by a spherical boulder, the geometric exactitude made common beside the unruly beauty of nature.

"Where'dja come from? Waddaya been doin'? How's Joan?" Questions muted the ocean's roar.

"Give your mouth a rest. I've been waiting for you."

"How'dja know I was comin'?"

"The criminal always returns to the scene of the crime." Matthew smiled his knowing smile, waiting for its twin.

Images pounding for recognition — settling, sorting to explain this dawn pilgrimage. "Is this the day?" It seemed so far away.

"The day before my birthday." The smile had not been returned.

"Yea, bu' how'dja know? I didn' come las' year." Facts jumbled, fighting for importance.

"I was here. I come every morning."

"I though' ya didn' wanna see me. Every time I called ye, ye were ou'."

"Coincidence." Matthew did not smile. There was nothing to smile about.

"Two years for coincidence?" The thought was appalling.

"You didn't think we were doing it for practice."

Joseph did not respond to the preposterous statement. He had not heard it. Two long years in a short life passing by. No way to alter the past. No way to escape the present. The painful transformation from a light-hearted living entity to a nine-to-five toiler, trapped within the hours; carefree time aging.

"Don't be such a stick-in-the-mud," prodded Matthew. "Let's scale the mountain."

"Not again?" Joseph laughed. When was there laughing last? Had it been here?

"Come on." Matthew led the way to the base, idly kicking the emaciated remains of a tomcod into the waters.

The wall towered threateningly, daring them to attempt the mission. It was about forty feet high, composed of dirt-packed conglomerate freckled with weeds. Joseph went first, hugging the surface with every pore of his body, forgetting his finely pressed suit. He uttered no sound, wary that a voice might upset the delicate balance and shatter the chilling ecstasy.

"What's keeping you, sluggard?" Matthew's head jutted from the rim.

"Ya bloody bugger! Ya took the path." Wind slashing back, echoing on the stone wall and throwing dust in his face. His left foothold becoming a small mound of clay banking the stream. Mind thrilling with the dread of imminent peril. The strange silence was broken only by the voices.

"None of your low-brow garrulous diminutives. I came straight up. You've been climbing at an angle."

"Gimme a han'."

"And spoil your climb? I couldn't do that." Matthew shook his head apologetically.

"Ya won' be able ta WALK if ya don' help me!"

"Let's consider the alternatives," mused Matthew. "I think a person should stand on his own two feet, don't you?"

"I got nothin' ta stan' my friggin' feet on!"

"Well . . . " Matthew stretched the moment into infinity.

"Fer godsake, throw me a goddam rope!"

"Sorry — we're all out of ropes."

"Ya gomme up this fughin' hill!"

"Temper-temper."

"Well?" Joseph wanted a definite answer.

"You're five feet away," explained Matthew.

"Use yer friggin' coat."

"O.K." Matthew took off his jacket and threw it to Joseph, covering his head in the material.

"Ya were supposed to hang on ta the goddam sleeve," came the muffled scream.

"Sorry — I'll get you up." Matthew swung his legs over the edge for Joseph to hang on to. He inadvertently kicked Joseph in the side of the head.

"Matt! When I get up . . ." Pebbles began to trickle, then pour from the holds. Joseph followed the stones, lost in the blackness of the coat. "Wanna lan' on my back." Weighing the choices; amazed that this body falling in seconds housed a mind deliberating in minutes. Landing as planned — resting in the centre of the shallow, sand-bedded stream.

. . . Did you have to track that dirt over my floors? . . . Anne drifting about the room . . . sobbing . . . back-on . . . fluffing full cushions . . . I'm sorry, hon . . . why? . . .

"C'mon 'cross. It's not deep." Joseph motioned from behind the shrubbery for John to drive his motorcycle through the watery mud.

"Where's yer bike?" John never was one to work on blind faith. Joseph anticipated the question.

"Up ahead. Came back so ya wouldn' spen' half the day tryin' ta go aroun'."

John turned his cycle about, made a fast run at the ten foot mud-pack and promptly stopped dead in the centre. The handle bars prayed for help. "Ya said . . ." He stared in mock disbelief.

"I sunk. Why not you?" The logic was unquestionable.

John struggled to rescue the machine, only to see it more firmly set. "Well? Ain't ya gonna do somethin'?"

"Doin' it." Joseph lay in the sun smoking a cigarette; enjoying the scene he had set.

"But . . . but . . ." John was speechless, word of which he hoped would never get back to his friends. This was not part of the plot he had worked out in his mind.

"Yea? Can I help ya?"

"Sure. Gimme a han' here."

"Aren't we forgetting our manners?" Joseph raised himself on one elbow and looked at John. "Someone should be peeling me a grape," he thought.

"Lord Joe, kind master an' noble frien', would ya PLEASE help me ge' my friggin' bike outta yer yon bloody mire?" John performed an exaggerated bow and lost his helmet in the deep brown muck.

"I think I could spare ya a momen'." Joseph jumped in with gusto, feet first, showering the immediate area in dirt. "Wha's the plan?" he queried, teeth clenching a dirty, cracked cigarette.

The plan was childishly simple, becoming their genius: to lift the machine from its setting. Unfortunately, they succeeded only in pulling themselves in further. They then decided to make a human chain. John was elected anchor. He clutched the base of the nearest tree and Joseph held his ankle with one hand and used the other to tug at the motorcycle.

"Ohmagod! I'm stretchin'. Leggo my leg."

"Now ya'll be able ta play basketball," Joseph gasped sympathetically.

Joseph's decision to attempt one last titanic wrench coincided with John's discovery that he could let go of the tree. They were both hurled into the inky glue.

"Ya fughin' godforsaken excuse fer a g.d. bloody . . ." Joseph's expletives were drowned in his mud-flooded mouth.

"We gotta think o' somethin'," said John when he had regained his breath.

"YOU gotta think o' somethin'!" Joseph sat waiting for a solution, looking like a dog with discolored rabies.

"Ever read the story o' the Crow an' the Pitcher?"

"Na. I fergot ta bring the friggin' book." Joseph did not consider it the proper place to discuss literature.

"He threw stones in till the water was high enough," John continued.

"Big shit!"

"Well? Why don't we?" John finished with an air of accomplishment.

"Ya got mud in yer mind? We can't lif' the bike. How we gonna lif' the bike AND the boulders?"

"Not ON the bike; aroun' it so we can stan' on 'em."

"Believe it when I see it."

Joseph believed it.

John lay on the bank panting. Joseph had gone back into the pit. "Waddaya doin'?" John asked.

"Lookin' fer my bike."

"Ya said."

"Waddaya think? I grabbed it between my teeth an' swam

ou' with it? It's deeper than yours. It's the bottom yours landed on."

"Oh." John lit a cigarette, congratulating himself on using a plastic package.

"Well? — Are ya gonna help?"

"Waddiya say?"

"I helped you."

"Manners, please." John flicked an ash into the pool.

"Would ya help me ge' the fughin' bike outta the fughin' swamp 'fore the fughin' mud spoils all the fughin' food — PLEASE?"

"O.K. — but only 'cause ye were so polite." John repeated Joseph's dive and they quickly dislodged the machine, learning from the previous attempt. They lay exhausted in the foliage.

Joseph felt a shadow blotting the sunlight. "Get outta the goddam sun. I'm tryin' ta get a tan." The silhouette did not respond. "Well? Are ya jus' gonna stan' there like the village idiot?" Joseph insinuated. His eyes were still closed.

"Do you feel compelled to develop these ethnocentric associations?" the voice rasped.

Joseph opened his eyes, praying that this was not his tormentor. The sun was blinding. He could distinguish no features.

"Are you dependent upon your acquaintances?" the voice continued.

"Go 'way! I tol' ya notta come back again! Who are ya? Why don' ya leave me alone?" screamed Joseph.

"Do you believe in God?"

"Leave me 'lone!" sobbed Joseph, covering his ears.

"Does your mother love you?" The monotone could not be muffled.

"Waddaya wan'? I'll give ya anythin' . . . jus' leave me 'lone."

"I want to help you understand yourself." The voice was unmoved.

"I like it here. Now. I wan' it ta stay this way." Joseph could not make him understand.

"You have to know yourself," countered the shadow sternly. A dark, icy hand was laid on Joseph's head. Joseph bolted and ran straight into the mud. The slime choked and blinded him.

. . . Joe, wake up . . . Anne beside him, shaking his shoulders . . . you ripped the sheet . . . sorry, hon . . . are you alright? . . . you never said you had these dreams before . . . sorry, hon . . . you're shaking . . . Anne's eyes wet . . . worried . . . why? . . .

"Come on. Get up." Matthew's bent figure shaking Joseph's shoulders. Water splashing Joseph's face. "You'll drown in this."

Joseph arose and saw John speeding toward the beach, side-stepping potholes in the ancient lane. "How'd John get here?" he asked groggily, aching to return to the quiet of the water.

"You drove us. Don't you remember?"

"Yea. How could I ferget? Two o' ye friggin' 'roun' tryin' ta get at the bottle under the seat." Joseph did not remember. His answer accurately described any journey with Matthew and John.

John raced by onto the damp sands of the ocean's border, advancing on the receding waves, withdrawing from the attacking breakers. Matthew and Joseph watched and offered dubious strategic advice. John was unexpectedly captured by an ill-advised thigh-high wave, pausing momentarily to gather strength to suck him out. He used the seconds to escape the freezing grip and fell winded, within the range of a larger breaker. Matthew raced to save him: half lifting, half dragging him to safety. Joseph stole up behind the duo and shoved them into the harmless knee-high waters. He raced for the car, choking with laughter. They were quick on his heels promising revenge. Joseph locked the doors and displayed a triumphant grin.

"C'mon. Let us in," pleaded John.

"Yes," said Matthew, "we'll freeze out here." He pressed a decidedly frostbitten nose against the windshield.

"How do I know ya won' steal my bottle?" Joseph laughed.

"We won't." Matthew backed away from the automobile and eyed Joseph sincerely.

"If ya leave me ou' here I'll steal yer friggin' hubcaps an' slash yer tires ta light a fire in 'em." John beat his arms against his sides and jumped around the car.

"Yer threatenin' me already."

"Waddaya wan' me ta do? — thank ya?"

"No. Jus' gimme yer word."

John held one hand to his heart and raised the other. "I swear," he said, "now can I get in?" He reached for the door handle, waiting for Joseph to lift the button.

"O.K." Joseph unlocked the door. John jumped in and secured it again.

"Come on," said Matthew, "let me in. I'll freeze."

John smiled broadly but made no move to open the door.

"I got you out of the water."

"O.K. . . . I guess." John let him into the warmth.

"Gotta cigarette?"

"A' leas' they're not after my booze," thought Joseph. He produced an unopened package as retribution. They inhaled deeply and fantasized the enormity of the waves and the danger of the undertaking. Several cigarettes later they decided that they had best return to Matthew's home to dry out and have some hot tea.

The car snaked along the road. The fog had come in and Joseph strained to follow the twisting white line. Seas pounded far below the cliffs, unfettered by the flimsiest guard rail. Intimidating.

"Are you envious of your peers?" The metallic voice generated from the back of the vehicle. "Is that why you refer to yourself as the Green Ghost?" No opportunity to reply to the machine gun questions. "Do you hate your father? You can trust me. Is your sex life satisfying?" The shadow jotted notes in a tattered, wire-hinged notebook. Joseph braked the car and swung on his tormentor.

"Wadda hell are ya doin' here? I tol' ya to go 'way! Where are my friends?"

"They're gone." The tone was one of infuriating smugness. Joseph could still not picture the misty features.

"Yer lyin'! They like bein' with me. Jus' the way it was before."

"They're gone," the shadow persisted.

"Yer lyin! They were here . . . with me . . . same as before . . ." Joseph closed his eyes. Maybe the figure would fade away.

"No. They didn't come back. They've forgotten this place."

"Yer lyin'!" Joseph sobbed.

"Come with me. I'll make you happy. Everybody loves you. They miss you at work."

"Yer lyin'! Nobody knows I'm gone."

"They all miss you," droned the shadow.

"They don'!"

"Trust me."

"Get out!" Joseph raged. "Yer lyin'! Ya always spoil it." The mist vanished.

Joseph hastily returned to the beach. They were not there. There were no prints in the sand and the spherical boulder had disappeared. "Matt! John!" There was no answer. The cliffs dwarfed the solitary figure ominously and mimicked his shouts. The twisted, skeletal trees capping the cliffs circled Joseph, straining to tear at him. The stream laughed at this freakish scene.

"Stop it!" he cried, covering his ears. The screeching laughter reached an insane pitch.

"It's not the same," Joseph murmured. ". . . too long . . . can' catch the pas'." The awful screaming stopped, waiting.

Joseph scraped a hole in the wet sands the dimensions of a

shoe box. He emptied his pockets of everything: a bent comb, a wrist watch with a broken strap, a half package of cigarettes, a scratched lighter, a dog-eared, wire-hinged notebook of ideas, some loose change, a worn wallet with a card calendar in it; buried them in the hole and crossed two twigs over it. He kept the keys. He needed them. Joseph then undressed, folding all his clothes neatly and laying them on a low smooth rock. He blessed himself and left the beach. The seas rolled in.

. . . Anne, holding his coat . . . Do you have much business to clear up? . . . worried. . . smiling her mechanical smile that never broke. . . Don't wait up . . . I'll be late . . . kissing her gently and leaving . . . never really speak . . . she is so unhappy . . .

The car rocketed along the highroad.

[1972]

Jean Stacey

Just Today

Jean Edwards Stacey was born in Swansea, Wales, to Betty Kern, a Welsh war bride, and Max Edwards, a Newfoundlander from St. Lawrence, who was serving in the Royal Air Force. She grew up in Gander, and completed a B.A. in Political Science at Memorial University in 1980. The mother of three grown children, Jean is presently a Lifestyles reporter with the St. John's *Evening Telegram*.

I hate the old lady. Not for anything she does do or anything she doesn't do. But just because she is she.

Why did Frank have to bring her here? Why here? She's old, old, old. Her body is thin and wasted, her hair so thin that when I stand above her I can see her scalp glistening pink. The flesh of her neck hangs loosely to protruding sinews. Did that shrivelled belly ever swell with child? It did, I know in fact, but looking at her, seeing her, I find it impossible to believe.

Her name was — is — Gen. I've seen pictures of her with her hair long and brown and hanging to her waist and with her face round and young. But they're pictures. And pictures, old pictures, give me a choken trapped feeling, the same way I used to feel when I thought about death, about never ever being again. I don't think about death much anymore. Why should I? Living is what's important. Going on from day to day.

It's not that I'm afraid of death. Death doesn't frighten me. When my time comes I won't whimper and moan — not like her. She complains of the cold, of her bad leg, of her spells. Her spells that have me on the run all day fetching and carrying like I was some kind of maid. And sometimes she doesn't say anything — just looks at me, through me with those eyes and I can see death written in them. I can feel the ground cold and damp and deep pulling at me until the sun is swallowed up and there's nothing left but black. And why should I have to feel like that? Just because her time is come doesn't mean I have to be dragged into it.

That old lady. I never wanted her to come but Frank — ah Frank had to be big and noble. Frank had to bring her here. She's sick Velma, he'd said, I can't leave my mother when she's sick and alone. Alone, ha. What about them other fine brothers? You'd never hear from any of them if you were down. But Frank's noble. And this is what noble gets you, stuck with an old lady nobody wants.

She had to travel in the bus for two days to get here and some young fellow with a beard and long hair must have been good to her because since then it's like she's getting him and God mixed up. All her life she'd never travelled more than fifty miles from home and now here she is halfway across the country and getting ready to meet her Maker. And she is getting ready, sitting up there on that chair Frank pulled over to the window so's she could look out, sitting up there day after day fingering her beads. What do you see old lady? Do you see more than the rocks and the grass and the sky?

Frank feels that age should be bowed to. He wrote a poem once about old people. About their lives lived and packed away in tissue paper wrapping them in glory. Funny I should remember that. But Frank's got this feeling that everything that's past seems good. I certainly don't feel that way. People don't change. Most old people are no more than their greedy, grasping younger selves. They wear the mask of old age but underneath there's nothing. No mellowing, no wisdom. Nothing. I heard a fellow on TV saying that the closer you came to death the more you should realize that all things in life are trivial.

Now I don't believe that. I think you should live the best you can and when your time comes you should just slip out without any wondering and bothering other people.

I can hear her now shuffling around over my head and pulling that cursed chair back against the wall. Any minute now she'll be down to make one of her never-ending cups of tea.

She gets up early in the morning, habit Frank says, but I always feel guilty hearing her shuffle around the room, hearing her kneel heavily — at her age she still kneels to pray like a child. Through the wall which separates us I can picture her, eyes tightly closed, body rocking gently to and fro, to and fro as she does in church. She kneels out there praising God as I lie in my bed wondering what if God?

What if there's no God old woman? What then? No everlasting life. No dreams of glory.

Who made you?

God made me.

Who is God?

God is our father in Heaven.

And on the last day God will come in glory to raise both the living and the dead and of His kingdom there will be no end.

I believe in God the creator of heaven and earth and of all things visible and invisible.

Mea culpa. Mea culpa.

It's raining out now, a soft noiseless rain that touches the window panes gently. Angel's tears. God the Father weeping for His children.

Before I go I *have* to leave something of myself. Not my children or memories of me as a nice person, a good person. Christ, that phrase and the hollowness it calls up. An easter egg. No edges to disturb anyone, no edges at all. Just a round smooth harmless ball.

Why is there this feeling? Isn't just the living enough? But it's not. It never is. It's like going to the moon and leaving a flag — I Was Here. I tried to write once, a story which started

`Michael lay in the sweet long grass of summer and felt a heaviness tug at his soul.'

Old lady you don't know me at all. You think of me only as Frank's wife, Velma. You know nothing at all about the me who hides behind this body shell.

And neither does Frank. Frank doesn't want to know. He wants to keep himself tightly boxed in because then he can't get hurt. We're like strangers on a narrow path, neither daring to cross over those few steps. I watched Frank one night sitting by the fire. He'd forgotten me; he was miles and years away and watching, I caught a look on his face of such yearning, of such searching that I wanted to cry. Why can't we talk? Frank, Frank I'd like to shout — look at me, look at me. What's wrong? I know that life is not a carnival. It's not meant to be all gay and carefree, but sometimes — sometimes I look up and see this greyness stretching into infinity and it chills me. I feel inconsolable.

Frank, Frank perhaps I should have reached out to touch you but I'm like her, like my mother. She treated feelings as dirty things to be kept locked away and if you wanted to take them out and examine them you did it only when you were alone. Never in front of people. My mother was thin and hard and she didn't believe in depression.

And now every year I see the lines of disappointment etch themselves more strongly into Frank's face. Old lady what do you think now? Can you picture this young old man, my husband, as the baby you suckled? The little boy who played on your kitchen floor is now a man who looks beaten by life? How can you stand it old woman? Or do you just care about your spells and your cups of tea? Does your life just revolve around you?

Velma Hardy
her mother's nose, her father's chin, her eyes, his smile
Frank's wife
Bobby's mother
Joey's mother

this that these those

Sometimes I feel as though my mind is a filing cabinet. Under 17 there are two, at most three, memories allowed to escape. No others because then too many hurts could come. The older you get the less memories. Things blur and you can't remember just when.

Someone's spinning the world too fast.

Looking back I can see my younger days as one long summer. Day followed day with nothing harsh or jagged to break the sweet monotony. I can see now that I'd been very happy then.

She's shuffling still — shuffle shuffle over to the dresser where she keeps her photographs in the bottom drawer which sticks when you try to open it. That old lady, that Gen, she bores us silly with her memories. I feel as though she's eating away my life. The way she goes round in that old black skirt and that black cardigan and those old slippers of Frank's that must be miles too big for her. It's not that I wouldn't buy her anything; I bought her a dress first, a blue one. It's hanging in the closet now next to her old black coat. She never even bothered to take the store stickers off it.

All little things reading like a litany of complaints.

Yesterday she broke one of my good cups and when I rushed into the kitchen like a madwoman I could see myself reflected in her eyes — hair every which way, mouth tight and hard — a reflection, I realized with shock, of my own mother. If you wanted something why didn't you call, I forced out. I didn't like to trouble you, Velma, she said, with that dumb patience which reminds me of an animal. And then I hid my mother's face from her as I stooped to pick up the broken pieces of china.

If I was her own daughter perhaps it would be different. Then she could look at me and say shush girl. Lord, Lord why can't you deliver me from this old lady and the guilt she dregs up from the bottom of my soul. God grant me compassion. When I was younger I felt as though I had feelers out seeking and finding all the world's hurts. I wept for the children of Korea, for men killed and buried in unmarked graves. But now, it's as though my feelings have blunted. Lord grant me mercy and compassion.

Why hasn't she come down yet? Or did I miss her, walking slowly downstairs favoring her bad leg, holding tight to the railing and, as always, starting when she sees herself in the mirror in our front hall. I hardly recognize my legs Velma, she'd said to me, they're so skinny.

Mother, I call and yet I never call her mother — mother are you alright? Why doesn't she answer me? Old lady you'll be the death of me yet, up and down these stairs fifty times a day.

In the upstairs hall I can smell the lavender which is always with her. When I push open her door I see her chair pushed to the center of the room and beside it she's lying in a heap, like a child's broken doll. She looks up at me and tries to speak but only a sound like the mewing of a lost cat escapes. I slipped, she manages finally.

With ease — and I am not a big woman — I carry her to her bed and arrange the blankets over her. She looks at me mutely, an old woman her hair in two long spindly plaits, her hands now folded peacefully across her shrunken breasts. An old lady who waits with candles in her bedside table for the moment when she will cease to be. If I went to her now — to that old lady — to Gen and put my arms around her and said I know, I understand, would she think I'd taken leave of my senses?

If I said I'm afraid could she comfort me?

My eyes feel glued to the picture above her bed, of poppies, red as blood, stretching to the sky. I don't want to look into her eyes. But her eyes are open now; I feel them upon me and I'm forced to look. Her eyes are blue and faded and old. They dredge deep into me and see me for what I am.

I'm sorry Gen.

Old Lady I'm sorry.

[1974]

Window Figure, Listener-Watcher (1980) — 31 x 30 cm., ink drawing — Filliea

Tom Dawe

The Apple Tree

Tom Dawe (1940-   ), born in Long Pond, Manuels, is a writer of poetry, fiction and children's literature. After teaching in various Newfoundland outport schools, he joined the Department of English at Memorial University in 1969. Among his published works are four poetry collections: *Hemlock Cove and After* (1975), *In a Small Cove* (1978), *Island Spell* (1981) and *In Hardy Country* (1993).

The noise woke Sam Blane. He had been dreaming of clover and cow-bells, with a school door opening for summer holidays, and the green outport slanting towards the mirror of the sea. Now it seemed that a door slammed somewhere.

He got out of bed and crippled to the window. In the half light, the big fork of the apple tree was a horned beast and the house was right in its path. A broken limb, tossed by the wind, had hit the clapboards.

His wife had slept through the noise of the big branch clawing its way down the outside wall. Sam looked at her, slowly shaking his head before returning to the window.

The snow had stopped falling but a north-easter in from the ice-floes was tearing at the limbs, scattering twigs against the window and into the dimness beyond. He stayed at the window for several minutes, rubbing his eyes, yawning, and shivering in the draughts of March dawn whispering through the rooms of the old house. He bent to rub his legs, as if trying to awaken them, shifting from foot to foot on the frigid canvas. Though he tried to hold it back, he coughed deeply several times, cursing the dampness in whispers to himself.

His wife still slept, snoring in the clock-ticking and the complaint of old rafters high up in the roof above the bed.

He wished she would not snore so like a man. Silently he cursed her as the tree outside faded away into the greyness of drifting snow.

He moved back to the bed and laboured getting under the warm sheets. She fell against his back as the mattress depressed with his weight. Envious of her peaceful sleep, he rubbed his shoulders hard against her. She murmured softly but soon went back to snoring. He lay on his back watching the ceiling and trying to ignore her, watching the snow glow along white boards, like the sheen of ice-floes out where they always met the spring horizon.

He could not sleep, his eyes closed listening to the wind come up across the beach, the boulders, and the fields under snow. He heard it rattling the back-door latch again as north-easters always did. He imagined the ice, tons of immaculate slabs moving in from the mouth of the bay and tiny bull-birds flitting around edges of dark pools in the white dawn.

She rolled over in her sleep and moved away from him now. He reached out his hand, spreading his fingers through the warm spot she had just left. Soon he rolled to his edge of the bed and tried to read the clock on the dresser. He could not see the time though he guessed it to be somewhere near six.

It disturbed him that she always got up ahead of him in the mornings now, to do things his grandfather had always done when they were children. It was not right, he thought, that a woman should be down there in the dark morning warming the cast-iron into kettle-singing, brightening the kitchen in defiance against the wind outside and the whispering draughts through the hall and along the stairs.

Sometimes he heard her singing love songs to herself down there as the tea got darker and he waited to be called for breakfast.

The man should always be up first, he was thinking, as she snored now in clock-ticking fading into a fierce swishing of apple limbs outside the window.

Half asleep now, he was away from her, and almost dreaming. Almost. But it was more re-play than dream.

He made his first trip to the seal fishery when he was only sixteen, leaving with his father to slide away into a March daylight before the women were up. The sled ride to St. John's carried visions of giants, iron men who made the girls swoon with their stories, men who laughed at mothers and sisters who pitied baby whitecoats, men who risked their lives to lower the price of a sack of flour, . . . men . . . men . . . men? As the horse pulled away from the yard, he did not want father to see him shyly catching a glance at mother's window, dark panes with nobody watching . . .

He remembered grandfather telling him how mother planted the apple tree when she was only six. It was an afternoon in spring when grandfather returned from the seal hunt. In St. John's he bought the biggest apple he could find, a gift for her because he remembered how she had cried the year before when the men discussed the slaughter of mothers and babies. It was such a lovely apple that everyone talked of keeping the seeds. Mother did, looking after it faithfully as still seed in a can of clay, as a house plant, and later as a small tree that she planted near the house. Grandfather laughed when he told of her fight with a little boy who tried to take her shovel away from her, insisting in his tears, that digging holes was man's work, not girl's . . .

He remembered his first spring back from the ice, feeling so heroic in his wild pride, a man of sixteen. One night he and his friends had quite a time with poor, silly Marge who lived out on the Point. They used to call her "the cow." She followed them down under the long, grey poles of the fish-flakes. Later, they paid her with a guarantee coupon from a sack of flour. She thought she had a dollar. How the fellows all laughed when she tried to spend it at the store . . .

Before Sam fell asleep he was recalling his last voyage to the ice-fields. He did not notice now the tree outside flinging its limbs into the grey light, and the little fingers of broken twig tapping at the panes. He heard the whistle of the "Sealer's Pride" fading away from him just as he thought he had been rescued, fading far into white light. Now he was alone on the moving floes, separated from the boys. Except for small dark pools of ocean around him, he could not see much in this mottled-white world. Once he heard something that sounded like a crow far up somewhere above his staggering figure. His eyes pained and throbbed as if they were being sucked from their sockets. His legs were numb. He screamed in agony as the whistle sounded again, even more distant now. Then he cried and cried, like a little girl, he thought to himself then. Alone and crying. Afraid. Last night, before they had become separated, one of his companions had seen a vision, something like a great beast with horns watching them, an ominous spirit. Later, he had a vision of his own. Through the fierce pain of his eyes he saw his mother's apple tree all in pink and white blossom in front of the big house. The windows were all open and children were singing somewhere. Warm orange sun seeped into the white clapboards and all the earth smelled like a Sunday after leafy rain. He was approaching the latch of the back door . . . As he fainted and slumped to the knobby ice, he sensed something like a gull flying above his cap, and heard far-off sounds like cattle lowing on the evening hills. . . . The boat found him that afternoon. As he was lifted skyward, he heard men's voices whispering like draughts in wind-swept rooms . . . speaking of his legs gone . . . never be no more good . . . from the waist down . . . and the eyes . . . to never be the same . . . never be the same . . . never . . . same . . . A door slammed.

He sat up in bed. His wife had gone to work. She had been employed at the fish-plant for six months now. She got up at seven those mornings, prepared her own breakfast and left. The tea left in the pot was always warm, the bread was sliced. From this he prepared his own breakfast.

He feared going to the store now. The men down there who idled around the stove were no longer interested in his stories. They had grown tired of his repetitions of visions on the ice-fields. Now they were making a joke of him. Several times through the winter he had caught them winking behind his back and grinning slyly when he was talking. And one day a little girl met him down by the landwash and told him that the men up in the shop were talking about him, saying he was twenty years older than his wife, saying he was no good, saying he was soft, cracked, crippled, blind. "They says your wife goes with Fred," she said.

Sam liked Fred, a young man in his early twenties who had just come back from the seal hunt. Sam's wife had always cared for the boy ever since his mother died, giving him clothes, meals and money for cigarettes and other things. And Fred did his best to help them now that Sam was not working. Let them fools in the store talk on, thought Sam. They're jealous 'cause I'm one of the survivors, 'cause I'm one of the Iron Men from the Iron Ships, 'cause I've had visions . . . they're damn jealous.

After supper that night Sam sat by the window listening to the radio. His wife rested on the day-bed in the chimney corner. Outside, a bright moon was up but Sam did not see Fred coming across the fields. When the young man came through the door, Sam nodded silently. He continued listening to the news. Fred sat in the chair by the chimney. They were used to this; nobody needed to say much while Sam listened to his weather report, occasionally tapping the sides of the radio as it whistled and faded out for a few seconds. Fred talked to the woman and they laughed together. The night passed quietly. Sam spoke once to thank the young man for the meal of flippers he brought to the house several days ago.

Around ten o'clock there was a sharp crack just outside the house, as if somebody had snapped a big stick. Sam pressed his weak eyes to the window pane. He could not see much more than the trunk horns of the apple tree. He stayed there as if waiting for the beast to move, rubbing his knees and waiting.

"Turn off the lights and you'll see them better," whispered Fred.

"It's those youngsters from out on the Point. Playing in the tree again. They're all out tonight. They'll spoil the tree that's for sure," said the wife quietly.

"Turn them off if you want to," snapped Sam.

Fred got up and turned off the lights. He quickly returned to his place in the chimney corner.

The night slipped into silence with Sam still by the window peering out through the dark branches of the apple tree. He could see nothing over in the deep shadows by the chimney, as he looked across that way a couple of times. Now he had to make conversation:

"Thanks, Fred, for the sack of flour."

"You're welcome, boy. I won two at the card-party anyway," came Fred's voice from the day-bed.

"I'll pay you back when I'm on me feet agin," offered Sam.

"You don't need to," Fred laughed softly from the shadows.

"Thanks, boy, I won't forget it," said the old man.

"Watch out for the lads now. Could be strippin' the limbs again," warned Fred.

"I'll catch the buggers yet," Sam chuckled.

The fire had died down. There were more whisperings in the chimney corner. The old man fell asleep at the window.

Next day Sam had to go to the store for tobacco. They were all waiting for him, those men sitting on bags of oats and apple barrels, tapping their pipes on cheese boxes, spitting on the floor, winking and laughing . . . nudging each other as he came through the door.

"Tell us about the apple tree," somebody requested. Somebody else giggled.

"We'd like to hear it," said another, a fat man bending over to spit tobacco into the stove.

"But I thought you were sick of that story," replied the old man, "I've told it many times."

"No. No. Not that one," said another, "we mean the apple tree last night." There was more low laughing in the molasses background.

"Oh," said Sam, "I thought you wanted to hear again about my . . ."

"Last night's apple tree story sounds more interestin'," said another, "we heard the young fellers from the Point are tearin' her up."

"I'll catch'em," offered Sam, "I'll get 'em yet."

"Keep tryin'," snickered somebody.

"Keep trying," offered another in a serious tone.

"I'm no fool. I've survived tougher stuff than that," said Sam, "I'm not as old as they thinks. I'll still catch 'em."

"Keep the lights out," offered another. More laughing.

He tried to hurry from the store, but his legs pained.

"I'll catch 'em," he called back.

He silently cursed them as he slammed the shop door, pausing in the tinkling of a small cow-bell hanging above the entrance.

[1976]

Ted Russell

Algebra Slippers

Edward (Ted) Russell (1904-1977) was born in Coley's Point. He was a teacher, magistrate and Director of Co-operatives before joining the first Smallwood cabinet in 1949. After a short period in politics, Russell turned his attention to writing scripts for "The Chronicles of Uncle Mose", a feature of CBC Radio's "Fishermen's Broadcast". Between 1953 and 1962 he wrote several hundred scripts, some of which have been published in *The Chronicles of Uncle Mose* (1975), *Tales from Pigeon Inlet* (1977) and *A Fresh Breeze from Pigeon Inlet* (1988). He also wrote several radio plays, the best known of which are *The Holdin' Ground* and *Groundswell.*

If there's one sure proof that times are gettin' more civilized than they used to be, it's the way business is carried on nowadays. Years ago, accordin' to Grampa Walcott, 'twas something awful, and to prove his point, a thing which Grampa is always ready and willin' to do, he tells this story about how he got the pair of swileskin slippers that he's been wearin' now for nigh on thirty years (of course he's had three new pair of soles and two new pair of uppers in 'em durin' that time, but they're the same pair of slippers) and he likes to treasure'em because, he says, they remind him of the one and only time he ever got the better of old Josiah Bartle who was the merchant here thirty years ago.

And even then, he said, he'd never have got 'em only for a

thing called Algebra, and when I asked him what in the world Algebra was, he said he didn't know, but it must be a wonderful fine thing to help a poor man like him get the better of a shrewd old bird like Josiah Bartle.

'Twas along about the middle of April, 1931, says Grampa, when Liz, his missus, told him the molasses keg was empty and he'd better go down to Josiah's store and get some. Grampa wondered how he'd pay for it, because 'twas too early in the spring to get credit on next summer's account, and he certainly didn't want to disturb the bit of gold he had in the sock. 'Twas then Liz reminded him of his two swileskins. True, one of 'em had some shotholes in it, but the other was perfect and between 'em they ought to fetch enough molasses to tide 'em over till credit time. So takin' his empty molasses keg and the two swileskins, off he went.

Skipper Josiah, the merchant, was glad to see him, business bein' what it was that time of year, and told Grampa how 'lassy was current price — a dollar a gallon. Likewise swileskins was current price — a dollar a skin. Grampa asked him what about shotholes, and Josiah told him they was current price too — ten cents off for every shothole. Grampa didn't need any corner to figger he'd get one gallon for the good skin and part of a gallon for the shot-holey one. So when Josiah came back from inside where he kept his swileskins, 'lassy, and things like that, and said right friendly like, "Here you are, Ben. Here's your keg, with your half gallon of 'lassy," Grampa was took aback and said it ought to be more than that.

Josiah rubbed his hands friendlier than ever and said, "No. Half a gallon is exactly right. You see," he said, "two swileskins at a dollar each is two dollars. Then fifteen shotholes in one of 'em at ten cents a shothole, that's a dollar fifty. Take that off the two dollars and you have fifty cents left, and with 'lassy a dollar a gallon, here is your half gallon."

Grampa knowed there was something wrong. He said there was nar shot hole at all in one of 'em and he asked Josiah to give him a gallon for that one and give him back the holey one. But Josiah explained how he couldn't do that, because the two skins went together in what he called in business a package deal, where the good points in one had offset the bad points in the other. Then Grampa wanted to call the whole thing off and go home again with his two skins and his empty keg, but Josiah said no. Business was business, and what was done couldn't be undone, or the business world'd never know where it stood. Then Grampa made a remark, but Josiah threatened the law on him for it. So all was left for him to do was go home.

When Liz, his missus, (Grandma she is now), tipped up the keg that night to fill the molasses dish, she noticed there wasn't much in it, so she wormed the story out of Grampa and give him twenty-four hours to go back to Josiah and get his rights or else she'd do it. Of course, a thing like that'd disgrace Grampa completely. So he spent nearly all that night layin' awake thinkin' up a scheme. Next mornin' he had it, and went over to Uncle Phineas Prior to get his help in carryin' it out. Uncle Phin was only too glad to do it.

And so, late that evenin', Grampa visited Josiah's store and Phin Prior with two or three more had just started an argument about the big profits merchants made. They asked Grampa's opinion, and he went even further than the rest and said that merchants often sold things for ten times what they paid for 'em. Josiah got mad and poked his snout right into the trap. He told Grampa he'd be glad to sell him anything he had for ten times what he'd paid for it. "All right then," said Grampa, "sell me back that swileskin that got the 15 shot holes in it."

Well, what a hullaballoo. Everybody wanted the particulars and they all agreed Josiah hadn't paid nothin' for it. So bein' as how ten times nothin' was nothin', Josiah was bound by his word to give it back to Grampa for nothin'. If Josiah had given it right then he'd have been better off, but he couldn't bear to get the worst of it. So he said he wouldn't be guided by people with less book-learnin' than he had. Then who should come in but the school master and they put the thing square up to him. And, said Grampa, 'twas the schoolmaster brought up this business about Algebra.

Accordin' to Algebra, said the schoolmaster, Josiah hadn't just paid nothin' for the swileskin with the holes, he'd paid fifty cents less than nothin', because he'd took fifty cents off the good one on account of it. Algebra called that a minus fifty cents, and ten times that was minus five dollars, which again (accordin' to Algebra) meant that Josiah had to give Grampa back the skin and five dollars besides, and Grampa went home happy.

Liz wasn't so happy though. She said if that was Algebra 'twas no better than Bingo, and made Grampa give the five dollars to the Church Organ Fund. But she let him keep the swileskin and that's what he made the pair of slippers out of, that he wears to this very day. He calls 'em his Algebra Slippers and says that whatever Algebra is, there's no doubt 'tis a true friend to the poor man.

[1977]

Paul O'Neill

The Mulberry Bush

Paul O'Neill (1928-   ), a St. John's native, has made major contributions to the Newfoundland literary and theatrical scene, serving as founding president of both the Newfoundland Writers Guild and the Corner Brook Playmakers. He was also president of the Newfoundland Folk Arts Council and chair of the Newfoundland and Labrador Arts Council. His publications include two volumes of poetry, *Spindrift and Morning Light* (1968) and *A Sound of Seagulls* (1984), as well as a two volume history of St. John's, *The Oldest City* (1975) and *A Seaport Legacy* (1976).

Murta was fortyish and fading. It was almost as if she took pleasure in looking older than her years. Dyeing her hair to encourage the illusion of youth had become too much of a chore, so she was letting the grey grow out. She could not even be bothered any more to rub Oil of Olay into her skin at night in hopes of holding back the web of tiny wrinkles that threatened to spread over her once celebrated "peaches-and-cream" complexion. She knew that most women her age did such things in order to remain attractive as long as they could, but Murta no longer had a reason. Her husband, Stanley, spent most of his time at the hospital delivering babies, or seeing his patients, and her two children were grown up and gone from the nest.

Barbara was married across town and had an infant son, which made Murta a grandmother. Kenneth was away at university in Nova Scotia becoming an engineer, and unlikely to ever move back home again. After twenty-three years of being a wife and mother, Murta was at loose ends.

Her telephone was ringing as it did every morning after eleven o'clock. There was never any mystery about who was on the line.

"What about that Minnie Felton?"

Yes. It was Edna. It seemed every time the telephone rang it was Edna. Barbara rarely called home. Nobody got more use out of Mr. Alexander Graham Bell's invention than Edna Parsley.

"What about Minnie?" Murta asked.

"My dear . . . Didn't you hear what Annie Bradford said at bridge yesterday afternoon?"

"You mean about Minnie and Tony buying a condominium in Florida?"

"I mean precisely that. There must be a fortune to be made in wallpaper and paint. That's all Anthony Felton sells in that shop of his . . . wallpaper and paint. Imagine. There can't be much to buying a condominium in Florida these days when every Tom, Dick and Harry seems to be buying one. Of course the Felton's is in Daytona. I'd just as soon be here in Corner Brook as in Daytona. I wouldn't want to live anywhere in Florida but on the gulf coast. It's St. Pete's Beach or Clearwater for me. We go there every year."

On and on she went as she always did. Nothing malicious, just talk. When she finished with the Feltons there were half a dozen other topics that had sprung up overnight including a digest of opinions aired that morning on the open-line radio show. Murta wedged the telephone receiver between her shoulder and her jaw and buffed her nails. It was practically the last vanity she had left. Some women her age allowed their fingernails to become chipped and broken. Murta's shone and were always beautifully manicured.

Forty minutes of talking to Edna, or, more precisely, listening to Edna, brought the clock to nearly noon. She hung up and began to prepare a light lunch for herself, cottage cheese and a sectioned orange on a leaf of lettuce. It wasn't that she was watching her figure. She didn't need to as she never seemed to gain an ounce. Stanley was the one with a weight problem. She was glad she didn't have much of an appetite as there just wasn't time to prepare anything very substantial. At three the bridge crowd would be arriving and there were sandwiches to make, as well as brownies and refrigerator cookies to put on plates. Stanley always ate lunch in the hospital cafeteria. Greasy food. No wonder he had a problem. If Murta ever wondered at his spending so much time at the hospital she never thought about it for long. There was no point in cluttering the mind with foolishness.

Try as she would, she could not remember when it was that Stanley began taking her for granted. Over the years the romantic young nurse, who ran away to marry the handsome young doctor before some other girl got hold of him, had become a sort of live-in housekeeper for her husband and children. She never complained, but now that the children were gone, and Stanley seldom got home much before eight o'clock in the evening, she was beginning to fret about time on her hands.

Maybe it had been a mistake to buy the twin beds when she did. There were few demands on her ability to make love after that. But wasn't it Stanley who had suggested they should get twin beds? Yes, of course. He said something about his snoring keeping her awake. That was odd. She could hear him snore in the twin bed just as easily as she heard him snore in the double bed. Perhaps marriage was like a household plant. After a number of years it needed to be re-potted.

"But how do you re-pot a marriage?"

Murta gave voice to her discontent as she scooped the

cottage cheese from the plastic container with a spoon she had been given in exchange for gasoline coupons at a neighbourhood service station.

"Bored." She suddenly cried out. "That's what I am. Bored."

She stared out the kitchen window at the backs of the neighbour's houses. Except for the height of the trees, a different shade of paint here and there, or a small shed erected on somebody's property, nothing much had changed in the countless times she had looked out that window in more than 7000 days.

"I must do something to alter the pattern of my life," she told herself. "That's how to re-pot a marriage."

Murta realized she was not only bored with cottage cheese luncheons and the view from above her sink. She was also bored with Edna's endless telephone chatter, hours wasted listening to silly talk that could be better spent taking a course at the college, or even brushing up on her nursing. A lot of men Stanley's age were having heart attacks. She never knew when she might have to use it again to make her living. Most of all she was bored with the bridge crowd, the same old faces every afternoon, half hidden behind a mask of cards. There was social work to be done passing out cups of tea in the home for the aged, or behind-the-scenes activity with the Imperial Order of the Daughters of the Empire. She would see about making a change.

A week went by and Murta was still on the telephone every morning talking to Edna, still seated in the circle of bridge players every afternoon. A month went by, two months, three months, but nothing was any different. Perhaps if Stanley had given her some encouragement . . .

"What about the hospital auxiliary? A lot of doctors' wives are involved in that."

"A breeding ground for gossip." He dismissed the ladies' auxiliary without even looking up from his newspaper.

"I'm told there's a need at the Blind Institute for people to read books to those who can't see."

"Except for Ann Landers, or that sister of hers, whatever her name is, what have you ever read? Reading is not one of your strong points, dear. Why don't you forget this nonsense and stick to bridge?"

He still did not look up.

"Stanley, you must help me."

"I *am* helping you, Murta."

With that he put down his newspaper and went upstairs to the bathroom. She heard his cordless razor running and the sound of water splashing in the basin. A few minutes later he came back downstairs. He had changed from a white shirt and the blue striped tie Kenneth had sent him for Christmas into a tan sports shirt and brown sweater.

"Aren't you staying home this evening?" Murta asked, as he pulled the zipper of a light jacket over his paunch.

"What for?"

"We seldom ever spend an evening together anymore."

He stared at her.

"By the way, I forgot to tell my answering service where I'll be. If they call I'll be at the curling club with some of the boys."

The front door slammed. She heard the car start up and back out of the driveway. The house was silent without Barbara and Kenneth running about. Not that they ever made much noise. You couldn't allow children to run wild in a house, especially if you prided yourself on keeping the place as neat as a pin. When the kids were young, Stanley was forever asking her to go to the movies with him after dinner, but she was never able to get away. There was always so much to be done for the children, even after they were in bed. Besides, she hated having babysitters poking about the house or messing up the living room. It was funny, but now that Barbara and Kenneth weren't there any more, and she had plenty of time after dinner, Stanley never once asked her to go to the movies. It seemed like years since she was in the Majestic.

Murta picked up the *Western Star* and was turning to Ann Landers when the doorbell rang. My gracious! Who could be calling at such an hour. Nobody ever rang her doorbell in the evening except by invitation. Perhaps it was Edna stopping by with Charlie to show her the new dress she bought at Eva's boutique to wear to the retirement dinner for Charlie's boss, scheduled for eight o'clock at the Glynmill Inn.

A glance at the grandfather's clock patiently ticking in the front hall told her it couldn't be Edna. It was a few minutes before nine. She walked to the door, unbolted the lock and pulled it open. It was Jessie Barnes, still wearing the green and purple tweed suit she had worn to the bridge game at Dorothy Jesso's house that afternoon. Heather mixture, she had called it.

Jessie was pale and seemed to be quite shaken.

"My goodness, Jessie! What's wrong?"

Murta sensed it must be something terrible, from the dazed appearance of her friend. Jessie's eyes were red from weeping and still streaked from tears.

"You haven't heard the awful news?"

Her sobbing expressed genuine grief.

"What awful news?"

"Poor darling. I hate to be the one to have to tell you this. Edna Parsley is dead."

A sudden chill swept over Murta.

"Edna?"

Jessie dabbed her eyes with a yellow tissue.

"She and Charlie were backing out of their driveway to go to that dinner for Ed Tufts, when an oil truck slipped its brakes and rammed into their car on the passenger side."

"An oil truck?"

Murta was still dazed by the news.

"A truck delivering furnace oil to a house up the hill from

Edna's place. The car was nearly demolished. The miracle is that Charlie escaped with just some cuts and bruises."

Suddenly the news sank in.

Murta began to cry. Her eyes filled with tears that ran down her cheeks, as sobs shook her body. They grew louder and louder until they were a wail of agony. She and Jessie clung to each other crying in unison for a long time.

When at last she was able to speak Murta asked, "How did you find out, Jessie?"

"My boy, Norman, was on his way home from the library on his motorcycle. He just turned up the hill by Edna's as the ambulance was pulling away. I called the hospital and got hold of my Melanie. She's on duty in emergency tonight. She called back a few minutes ago to tell me Edna was dead on arrival."

Murta was badly shaken by the sudden passing of her dearest friend. Now that the telephone no longer rang every morning the house seemed empty and lonely. The perpetual silence grew to be oppressive. If Edna's chatter had been meaningless, at least she was somebody to talk to. She was sorry for the times she had been short-tempered and cut Edna off, to vacuum the carpet or dust the room, especially the Hummels which stood so precisely in their places over the years.

Not only did Murta now have her mornings to herself, but her afternoons as well. The bridge club had replaced Edna with Molly Connery, but it just wasn't the same without the presence of her best friend, so, after a couple of months, Murta dropped out of the circle.

To get away from the house, with its deep silences, and the long shadows of late autumn slowly creeping over the thick pile carpets, edged by highly polished floors, Murta decided to fly home and visit her mother in St. John's. Stanley raised no objections. In fact, he said he didn't care how long she was gone. As he was occupied at Western Memorial Hospital the morning she left, Jessie Barnes drove her to the airport in Deer Lake.

Her mother met the flight. She was still an active and

attractive widow. Murta was amazed at all the building that had gone on in St. John's since her last visit three years ago. It was no longer the cosy town of her girlhood where everyone who mattered knew everyone who mattered, and people who didn't matter knew them as well. Now that oil had been discovered a few hundred miles offshore it was bound to become a booming metropolis, like Calgary or Edmonton. Her mother predicted the boom would go to Halifax.

As they drove downtown on their way to the old home on Waterford Bridge Road, there was a new C.N. hotel going up and a couple of high-rise office buildings that were a portent of the oil boom.

Within a week Murta was having serious doubts about the wisdom of visiting with her mother for a month. The endless questions and unwanted advice were a greater strain than the silences in her own house.

"It's not for me to tell you what to do with your life, Murta, darling, but if I were your . . ."

Mrs. Bailey would then proceed to tell her exactly what to do with her life, her children, her husband and almost every hour of the day and night. If her mother's life and marriage had been a great success Murta might not have minded listening so much, but she recalled the endless years of carping, bickering and capricious behaviour when she was growing up in that house. She also remembered her father saying to her shortly before he died: "I made only one big mistake in life, Murta. I thought it was possible to make your mother happy."

She went alone to visit her father's grave in the old General Protestant Cemetery. It was only a ten minute stroll from the house. As she walked along in the bright, afternoon sunshine of an Indian summer's day she caught glimpses of the Waterford River running down the floor of the valley to the harbour. Many of the houses that now blocked her view had not existed when she was a schoolgirl walking back and forth along that road. On the slope of the Southside Hills autumn was at the peak of its gold and crimson beauty.

It took her only a few minutes to find the family plot. A brother who had died as an infant was buried there with her father. As she stood staring down at the unclipped grass, squared off by a concrete retaining wall, her mind flipped through memories of childhood like somebody thumbing the pages of a picture book. Her sisters were there, and her brothers. She saw the proud smile on her father's face as he kissed her after seeing her graduate with her class at the Grace General. Perhaps she really should take a refresher course, and go back to nursing again. It would certainly be something to occupy her time.

"Excuse me."

The voice was low and husky. She turned to see a strange man facing her over a grave.

"Yes?"

"My wrist watch has stopped. It's the old-fashioned wind-up kind. I guess I forgot to wind it this morning when I put it on. Have you the time?"

Murta glanced at the watch on her wrist. It is the human thing to form immediate opinions on meeting someone for the first time. Later they are often changed for better or worse. She felt a strong attraction to this stranger. "Four o'clock. At least it will be in two minutes. I'm right according to the CBC time signal."

"I'll take your word for it."

She watched the man take off his watch and set it. He was bareheaded and wearing a light nylon jacket. His wiry, black hair was quite thick and turning to silver at the temples. He had the wind-tanned complexion of one who spent much of his life outdoors. Although he was not handsome in the conventional sense there was something compelling about his looks.

Even from the distance at which she stood Murta noticed at once that his eyes were an unusual shade of green. His face was lean and clean shaven. A dark line of hair was visible in the V neck of his shirt. Her eyes were drawn to his hands, clasped one over the other, below his waist. They were much larger than Stanley's with exceptionally long fingers. She smiled as she remembered something Edna once told her about men who had long fingers. He smiled back.

"Your husband?"

Now she was laughing.

"No. My father."

"I'm sorry. I didn't notice the dates."

"Your wife?"

He nodded.

"I'm sorry."

"It doesn't matter. We weren't very happy. As a matter of fact, we were divorced. I've been living in Alberta for the last fifteen years working for an oil company. I'm here on business. I had the afternoon free, so I thought I should visit Diana."

Murta walked around the plot to where the man was standing. The headstone read DIANA STARR.

"We had some happy times . . . in the beginning."

"Starr. Is that your name?"

"Yes."

"It's unusual. The only Starr I ever remember here was old Mr. Starr, the watchmaker, on Adelaide Street. I think he was a Russian Jew."

"Polish. He was my father. He came here from Poland after World War One with an unpronounceable name which he shortened to Starr. My name's Mike."

"Michael Starr." She let her tongue linger sensuously over the name. "No relation to Ringo?"

He grinned. "None. Singing is not a thing I do well."

"What do you do well, Mr. Starr?" she asked coyly, amazed at her own boldness.

"Pick up strange women in cemeteries."

They both laughed aloud.

"Would you like to have dinner with me?"

"I have a husband in Corner Brook."

"I asked if you would like to have dinner with me. I hear there's a very good Italian restaurant on George Street, in what used to be an old warehouse. It's right around the corner from where my father had his jeweller's shop."

She had mentioned Stanley, so it wouldn't be false pretences.

"I'd love to have dinner with you. I'm Murta Bailey, at least I was. Murta McCabe now."

"Bailey's Five-And-Ten-Cent Store?"

"My father's. It was on New Gower Street, just west of where they built City Hall."

Leaving Mike standing over Diana's grave, she hurried to her mother's favourite beauty salon on Water Street West, and bribed Doris, a family hairdresser for many years, into giving her a quick shampoo and set.

Mike called for Murta at eight o'clock. They sat by themselves in an out-of-the-way corner of Sidestreet, the Italian restaurant. After an appetizer of Linguini, they dined on Veal Parmigiana. For some perverse reason they decided on a French wine, Chateauneuf du Pape. Framed against the ruby hue of an old brick wall, by white pots of hanging green plants, Murta seemed to glimmer with a lost enchantment. The flare of candlelight, caught by a shower of gold flecks on the black shoulders of her dress, danced in reflection.

It was after ten o'clock when they entered Mike's room at the Holiday Inn for a nightcap. As he reached down to pass her a rye and water his lips kissed her ear. She turned a willing mouth to his. The drink went untouched.

Mike tore away the years of frustration that cloaked her emotions. Murta responded with a surge of carnal anticipation. A world that had disintegrated for her long ago swirled back into being with an explosive force that shattered all caution and restraint.

It was nearly 3:00 a.m. when he let her out in front of her mother's house. Mike went around and opened the car door for her. After one more kiss in the pre-dawn stillness Murta broke away and ran up the steps. The car door slammed. She waited in the shadows of the verandah until the sound of Mike's car died away. For the first time since the early days of her marriage she felt deliciously wanton.

Mrs. Bailey was asleep so there would be no need to make up stories, or tell her mother lies in the morning. It was funny how she still treated her like a child. It was funny, and it was annoying.

Mike called again a few nights later. Soon he was at the door every other evening, then every evening. Her mother's criticism of the affair began with innuendo. Murta tried biting her tongue but that proved impossible as Mrs. Bailey's disparaging remarks grew into hostile condemnation. The inevitable scene followed with the two women shouting recriminations at each other. Her sister, Veronica, resolved the situation by inviting her to move into her big house on Winter Place. Veronica had been in school with Mike's late wife, Diana, and recalled her as "a pill."

Stanley offered no protest when Murta called home to say she was extending her visit to St. John's by a fortnight. Hadn't he told her to stay as long as she wanted? On the telephone he recalled having said just that to her when she first announced the trip to visit her mother. Stanley was also glad to hear she had moved to Veronica's as he was sure they must have lots of "girl talk" to catch up on. He hoped she was enjoying herself and having a good time.

"The time of my life," thought Murta with a grin, as she placed the white tweeter phone on the table.

Her hair was now a soft, honey gold, almost the shade it had been when she was a nursing student. Doris, the hairdresser, had done an excellent job. She was an expert at giving that distinctive personal touch in hairstyling. Years seemed to have been washed away as if by some miracle rinse. A visit to Margaret Dunn Cosmetics for a facial and some hints in make-up application seemed to dissolve the tissue of aging that had begun to cloud her once celebrated loveliness. Like a born-again Christian, Murta faced the world with the confidence of a woman reborn. Her appearance mattered because her life had a purpose again. That purpose was Mike Starr whose business in St. John's was coming to an end.

"I don't know how I'm going to be able to leave you, sweetheart, and go back to Calgary next week."

She watched as he pulled the maroon, silk dressing gown she had given him over muscular shoulders. The long, tapering fingers, one of the first things she had noticed about him, knotted the cord above his hips. Slumping in a chair, he reached for a package of cigarettes lying on the table near the window. Outside, twilight was giving way to the glare of street lamps.

The tip of Mike's cigarette glowed in the near darkness of the room. As he blew the smoke from his lungs he let his head fall back so that it rested on the chair. Murta got up slowly, crossed the room in barefeet and sank to the carpet beside his chair. She pulled up a sleeve of the dressing gown and laid a cheek against his forearm.

"Mike. . . ." The offer came in hesitating phrases. "If you want me . . . I'll come with you . . . to Calgary."

He twisted his head and stared down at her.

"You'd leave your husband?"

"What husband? Stanley? The man I share a house with? He stopped being my husband years ago. I can't remember the last time he touched me with any passion . . . any feeling . . . any desire. I haven't awakened love in him for years."

"So now you want to awaken hate?"

"At least he will respond with an emotion."

Murta was wrong about that. When she called Stanley to tell him she was leaving him for a man named Mike Starr he said remarkably little.

"Well, dear, only you know what you want to do. I think you're making a bloody fool of yourself by carrying on like a lovesick teenager. But I won't stop you. I know I couldn't. Go ahead and get it out of your system. I suppose it's a delayed seven-year-itch. Just remember, Murta, you always have a home here any time you want to come back. This is your house."

As he hung up Murta saw the real tragedy of her life. She was unable to awaken love or hate in her husband.

Mike had to stop off in Halifax for a few days on the way out to Calgary. He agreed that he would meet Murta at the Hotel Bonaventure in Montreal where he also had a business appointment. On Thursday, the day he was due to arrive, she came back to her room from the roof-top swimming pool in the hotel to find the light of the telephone flashing red. She called the message desk and within minutes a bellhop was handing her a Special Delivery letter from Halifax. Her hands trembled slightly as she tore open the flap with her fingernails. She read it in phrases.

". . . truly sorry about this . . . should have told you before that Diana was only my first wife . . . Rachel and our three kids are waiting in Calgary . . . realize now my first duty is to them . . . we had a lot of fun but . . . thinking it over away from you I have decided . . . will take this like the mature women you are . . ."

Murta read the first sentence again. The moment she unfolded the letter she had recognized it as an ominous beginning. Secretly, without even admitting it to herself, she had feared just such a letter or telephone call. It was why she had felt so on edge the last two days.

The handwriting was broad and masculine. "My meeting with the oil executive in Montreal has been cancelled as he has been called to Texas . . ."

She crumpled the two sheets of Hotel Barrington stationery and let them fall to the floor. Without moving, she stared out the window into the enclosed courtyard, feeling nothing but a kind of numbness. It was like the time she had struck her head on the floor of the gym, playing basketball in high school, and lay there dazed and disoriented for a few minutes. There had been no pain.

If she had ever imagined a moment like this in her life, Murta would have seen herself pacing the floor like a cornered animal, weeping uncontrollably, and throwing her sobbing body down on the expensive bedspread.

After several minutes of standing there doing nothing, she picked up the crumpled letter, smoothed the wrinkled pages with her hands, and this time read every word. When she finished she began to laugh. Her laughter was close to hysteria, yet it was genuine. Tears were rising behind her eyelids but they did not overflow.

Barbara met her at the airport in Stephenville.

"Daddy is sorry, but he may have to deliver Joan Anderson's baby today. He asked me to come and get you. Oh, before I forget, Mother, he wants you to pick up some pork chops on the way home and fix them for dinner the way you do, with fine herbs in mushroom sauce."

"You'll have to stop at the supermarket so I can get some fresh mushrooms."

Murta's voice was flat and expressionless. Barbara put it down to flight fatigue.

"Mrs. Barnes called this morning and told me to tell you Ethel said there's a vacancy in the bridge club if you want to rejoin. Mrs. somebody-or-other's husband has been transferred to St. John's."

"Jessie's a treasure."

"I wish you'd said you were going to Montreal, Mother, before you left. I'd have given you money to buy me some Doctor Denton's for little Alfie. The ones he has are nearly worn out and they don't have his size in Corner Brook."

Next morning Murta listened to the open-line program over the small Sony portable in the kitchen, while washing up the breakfast dishes. When it was over she switched it off. The vacuum whirred into life. As the hum died away the house seemed depressingly silent. A lot of dust had collected on the furniture in six weeks but she didn't feel like starting to dust. More than anything else she wanted to hear the sound of another voice.

She picked up the telephone and dialed.

"Jessie? . . . Yes, it's Murta . . . Yesterday. Barbara met me in Stephenville . . . Of course, dear. I'd love to rejoin the girls for bridge . . . At Mabel Cooper's place in Curling tomorrow afternoon? . . . With bells on . . . Yes. I was in Montreal a few days — to do a bit of shopping . . . Were you listening to the open-line program on your radio this morning? . . . Well, there was a woman called in from Humbermouth, and if what she said is true . . . ."

[1982]

Helen Porter

The Summer Visitors

Helen Fogwill Porter (1930-   ), born in St. John's, has been for many years an active member of the Newfoundland Status of Women Council. She has written numerous poems, short stories, articles and reviews. Her best known books are her memoir entitled *Below the Bridge* (1979) and a novel, *january, february, june or july* (1988). She also edited (with Bernice Morgan and Geraldine Rubia) *From This Place: A Selection of Writing by Women of Newfoundland and Labrador* (1977).

I had a letter from Nina this morning. She's about the only person in Newfoundland I ever hear from. Most of the people I know down there find it hard to write letters. Of course they haven't been properly educated, poor things. I thank my lucky stars I got out of there when I did. Father saw to that. He was working in Boston then. A lot of Newfoundlanders had to do that, go away to the States and work for months at a time. It was almost impossible to make a living in Newfoundland. My heavens, that must be nearly fifty years ago. Anyway, he made arrangements for me to come up and join him. I was only eighteen at the time, and green as grass. When I think about what the Americans must have thought of me I could die of embarrassment. The way I talked, for one thing. I remember a girl I worked with, Peggy, her name was. She used to make fun of me all the time. " 'allo, 'azel, 'ow are you?" she'd say to me every morning. I could have killed her then but now, when I look back, I'm grateful to her. It didn't take me long to learn to speak proper.

Of course I couldn't help talking the way I did. What chance did I have, living in a little place like Cape St. Peter? The only thing that was plentiful in Cape St. Peter was rocks. A one-room school, that's all we had to go to, and half the youngsters didn't go at all. But I went. Father made sure of that. Poor Mother, I don't think she really cared all that much whether I went or not. She was sick nearly all the time, not cut out for life in a place like that at all. But Father, he was determined. "You got the chance to get a bit of learnin', you git it," he used to roar at me. "I never had the chance meself." And then, when I got older, all he wanted to do was get me out of Newfoundland. "I don't want you marryin' no Newfoundlander," he'd tell me over and over again. "I'm gettin' you out of here if it's the last thing I ever does." Funny, though, how he went back there himself, never really left it, I suppose. He always kept his house in Cape St. Peter, even after Mother died, and he was still only middle-aged when he went back there to stay. Perhaps he didn't care about himself. He sure was determined about me, though.

He didn't take it so bad when he found out I was going to marry a Newfoundlander. He always liked Max — knew his father and uncles in Bragg's Cove. That's only about seven miles from Cape St. Peter and everyone from all those little places always knew everyone else. And then, of course, I met Max in Boston. That made a difference too. He already had a good job in the factory by that time, with no intentions of ever going back to Newfoundland. He felt something the same as Father did about it. "Who'd want to live in that God-forsaken hole, Hazel?" he used to say to me. He's not a bit ashamed of being from Newfoundland though, the way some are. I've actually met people from there who pretend to be from somewhere else. "It's what you make of yourself that counts, not what you started with." I've heard Max say that so many times. Still, he never even wanted our two boys to visit there. They used to talk about it when they were kids. "What did you play at when you were small, Daddy?" they used to ask him. You know how kids are. And he'd say, "All I ever done was work. I never knew what play was." He didn't want to talk about it at all. Max really had it hard when he was growing up, more so than I did, really. I was an only child but he was the oldest of nine. He started fishing with his father before he was ten years old. "Sending a boy to do a man's job," he called it.

Strange, though, how he wants to go back every summer. He only started that seven years ago, when he retired. Before that he'd only get two weeks vacation and that wasn't much good. But the very first spring after he retired he said to me, "Hazel, let's drive down to Newfoundland this summer." I thought he was crazy. There's nobody left there belongs to us now, only a few cousins. We sold off Father's house after he died. It didn't come into my mind that we'd ever be going back that way again. And now Max had to come up with this. I was worried about him driving all that distance. It was all right on this side, of course, but what would the roads be like down there? Probably not even paved. I was surprised to find out they even had roads. But Max had been talking to a friend of his who made the trip the year before and he said it wasn't too bad. It seems like they've made a lot of progress down there since they became part of Canada. Some people wanted to join up with the States instead. It's a pity they didn't, really.

I didn't have a clue who we'd stay with, but Max remembered his old cousin Bertha in Bragg's Cove and he got me to write her. The letter we got back was written by Bertha's daughter-in-law, Nina. I should have known Bertha wouldn't be able to read or write. Anyhow, Nina said we were welcome to come if we didn't mind putting up with what we found. Bertha was all crippled up, she said, and her house was old-fashioned, but there was a room for us if we wanted it.

The trip down wasn't all that bad. Some of the people we met on the ferry were raving about the scenery in Newfoundland; apparently they'd been there a couple of years earlier. "Ruggedly beautiful," that's what they called it. I've never been much for scenery myself. Give me comfort every time. I was surprised to find a few decent restaurants along the way. Nothing extra, you know, but passable. There was nothing like that in my day.

Well, you should have seen where we had to stay. I swear to God the house couldn't have been changed since before Max went away. Bertha still had no water or toilet in, she still used the old wood stove and the same old furniture she always had, even to the wash-stand in the bedroom with the splash towel behind it. She did have the electricity in, for a wonder. Nina lived next door, and her place was much nicer. Her husband, Gerald, is a great carpenter and he had it fixed up lovely. He put the water in himself, and they had a septic tank out back. They had nice modern furniture too, and a TV, though the reception is bad most of the time.

We took to spending most of our time at Nina's and when we were getting ready to go home she said, "Why don't you stay with us next summer? We'll have a spare bedroom by then. Gerald is goin' to build a piece on the back of the house now when the work slacks off." We jumped at the chance and we've been staying there every summer since. Max gets a charge out of going out fishing with the men, picking bakeapples and blueberries, all the stuff he hasn't done for years. He likes it a lot better now that he doesn't have to do it. I'm not so keen, but it is a change. And the air is nice and fresh, although there's getting to be a smell from the fish plant.

The first few summers Nina was wonderful to us. Funny, although she's so much younger than I am, she reminded me of my mother. Her eyes are the same colour brown as Mother's were and she's got that look about her that people have when they're not very strong. You could really talk to Nina, too. I told her things I never told anyone else. She waited on us hand and foot, although I always tried to do my share. Some of the food was strange — they call margarine butter, for instance, and they use canned milk almost all the time. I put up with that for a while, but then I found real butter and fresh milk at the new supermarket in Cape St. Peter, and after that I bought my own. Nina and Gerald used to laugh at Max and me with our own little butter dish and milk jug. They liked having us there, though. "It's so nice to have a bit of company, Hazel maid," Nina used to say. I tried to break her of that habit of saying maid but I never quite managed it. And her children, sometimes you could hardly understand what they were saying. I was always after them to come to Boston when they finished school. I know I thank God every night that I had the opportunity to go to the States when I was young.

Last summer was different. Nina seemed really altered. Gerald never did have a lot to say so we didn't see too much change in him. Of course Nina had been sick during the year, and perhaps that had something to do with it. Some days she'd hardly speak at all, and once or twice we even had to get our own meals. I believe she's having a hard time with the children. There's a bit of trouble with drugs in Newfoundland now, believe it or not. We never had any problems with our boys that way, thank heavens. There wasn't too much of it on the go when they were growing up. Anyway, I don't know if drugs had anything to do with it or not, but Nina's two children were certainly changed. They're not children anymore now. The girl, Veronica, was in university this year and the boy is planning to go to the Trade School in Clarenville. Nina is lucky she only had the two. There's still lots of big families down that way, but she always had trouble carrying children. I think she had six or seven miscarriages.

It's hard for me to get used to the idea of anyone from Newfoundland going to university. I don't suppose it's a patch on our colleges but they do get some kind of a degree. "You should come back to the States with me," I told Veronica. "You'd make something out of yourself there."

"What makes you so sure everyone wants to go to the States?" she snapped at me. She's got quite a temper, that youngster. First when we started coming back she was a sweet little thing but she changed as she got older. After that, she back-answered me a few more times and one day the young fellow, Dennis, his name is, even did it to Max when Max suggested he might be able to get him a job in the factory where he used to work. "It's just as well for me to go to work in the plant here if all I'm goin' to do up in Boston is work in a factory," Dennis said to him. "Anyhow, if I couldn't go off birdin' or snarin' rabbits every now and then I'd go foolish." I started to tell him about all the things he'd be able to do in Boston but he got up and left the room. I looked at Max. He'd never let our boys answer back like that, but I suppose he thought it wasn't his place to scold someone else's children. Nina just sat there and never said a word. She's got her hands full with those two. Herself and Gerald always did let them get away with murder.

A few weeks ago Max started talking again about going back to Newfoundland this summer. He always gets on to that right after Easter every year. So I wrote Nina, like I always do, although I hadn't heard from her since I got her card at Christmas. It was a long time before she answered but I finally got a letter this morning. It was the strangest letter I ever had from Nina. She hadn't been feeling well, she said, and she was afraid she wouldn't be able to put us up this summer. She hoped we'd understand. Poor thing. I wish I could get her up here and show her a bit of life, although I suppose it's almost too late for her to change her ways now. That's why I wanted Veronica to come, while she's young, like I was. I got Newfoundland knocked out of me years ago.

I don't know what I'm going to tell Max. He looks forward so much to going to Newfoundland every year. I'd just as soon go to Bar Harbour or Old Orchard if it was up to me. Poor Nina,

I hope there's nothing seriously wrong. I guess we'll have to stay at the tourist home in Cape St. Peter. Bertha is not around any more, she died three years ago. We thought about buying her house and doing it up for a summer place, but it would have been too expensive. The tourist home doesn't appeal to me but I guess it will be all right. Anyway, I don't see what else we can do now. I'll miss being with Nina, though. I really will.

[1982]

Kitchen Figure — 102 x 81 cm., oil pastel with powdered pigment — Filliea

Harold Horwood

Iniquities of the Fathers

Harold Horwood (1923-   ) was born in St. John's and during the 1940s he was active as a labour organizer and an editor of *Protocol*, a literary magazine. A supporter of Confederation, he sat briefly as a member of the House of Assembly. After several years as political columnist for the *Evening Telegram*, he turned his attention full-time to writing. Among his best known works are *Tomorrow Will Be Sunday* (1966), *The Foxes of Beachy Cove* (1967), *White Eskimo* (1972), *Bartlett: The Great Canadian Explorer* (1977), *Only the Gods Speak* (1979), and *A History of the Newfoundland Ranger Force* (1986).

Think not that I am come to send peace on earth: I came not to send peace, but a sword.

— attributed to Jesus

Inside the square, heavy-beamed house the kitchen fire blazed, and the flat-wicked oil lamps cast a golden glow. Beside the iron-and-nickel range, which was stuffed to the dampers with blazing logs, a huge woodbox spilled cloven lengths of spruce and fir upon the floor. The house was filled with the incense of burning spruce — the only incense its people ever knew. They did not connect this homely scent, filling and surrounding their lives, with the frankincense and myrrh of the Bible.

At a kitchen table covered with flowered oilcloth the boy Pleman worked his sums and wrote the answers to the questions in his geography book while his younger brother pestered him for help with his own lessons. Pleman, fourteen, was patient with the younger boy, with all the younger children. He helped when he was asked, returned to his work, then — the oven being recently emptied of the week's baking — got up to bring kindling from the woodshed and put it to dry in the oven, from which the scent of the hot sap arose like a forest awakening to summer. It was snowing outside, and starting to blow. In the morning there'd be shovelling to do.

Pleman's father, Lize Pike, sprawled on the wooden settle, puffing quietly at his pipe, feet propped before the fire whose front drafters cast dancing red images across his face and chest. A strong and energetic man, it never crossed his mind to fill the woodbox or bring in the kindling or do any other household chore — such tasks were for women and children. Lize (he had been christened "Eleazer" forty years before) worked his twelve-to-fourteen hours a day outdoors or in fish stores or sheds. In the house he was a pampered guest. The house really belonged to his wife Melinda. She looked after it, ran it without help from Lize, but with constant assistance from the children. This was the arrangement in the homes of most Newfoundland fishermen. They were scarcely aware that any other pattern of life existed, or could exist.

Pleman was already imitating his father's quietness, patience, stoicism. He could already endure many hours of hard labor without complaint, accept the suffering imposed by storm and frost and the inevitable injuries of the fishing trade almost cheerfully. And already he was moving away from his mother's authority. In a year or so, he would be a guest in her house, too. Lize was closer to the boy than he was to his wife — a common condition among fishermen, intensified in the Pike household by the sharp differences that had separated Lize and Melinda in recent months. These differences arose from temperament, but their proximate cause was religion, to which Melinda had a passionate, emotional attachment, while Lize looked at it coolly, on the rare occasions when he thought about it at all.

The outport in which they lived, a fifty-family village, had recently got religion in a very big way. Until then Caplin Bight had gotten along with an old United Church Minister preaching an undemanding kind of Christianity that meant little to anybody except the Women's Auxiliary and the Mission Society. Then, in a few months, everything was changed. The old minister was called elsewhere, and everybody who went to church went to the Gospel Tabernacle, where religion wasn't at all a matter of ladies' meetings and afternoon teas, but had lots of snap, crackle and pop with boisterous singing and praying, tears, prophecies and speaking in tongues.

Pleman watched his mother, Melinda, buttering the tops of the loaves she had taken from the oven, wrapping them in white cloth, and laying them to cool slowly before storing them in the pantry.

Ten years younger than Lize, she was deeply caught up in the change that had swept over Caplin Bight. She had come from a family of Bible-readers, who raised her in the belief that she was born better than others, one of the Lord's chosen. This had one good effect, at least: she could read and write passably well, whereas Lize could not. As a boy he'd been sent to school, and had gone eagerly because it was a temporary escape from the endless labors that had been imposed upon him from the age of five or six — fetching firewood, making kindling, lugging water from the well, feeding and milking the goat, weeding the cabbage patch, shovelling stinking straw from the hen-house. He had learned his letters, and how to spell a few words. He still knew figures, and could add and subtract them. But he had been taken out of school at grade three and put into a fishing boat, and he had lost, gradually, his small skill with letters. After the age of ten he had never picked up a pen or pencil, and by the age of twenty, his hands thickened with work, he had forgotten how to hold one.

Melinda was not only literate, she insisted on literacy for her children, boys as well as girls. They were not going to be lost to the world, the flesh and the devil for lack of ability to read their Bibles. She herself had been a saved Christian at the age of fifteen; she was already prodding Pleman that way, and he was digging in his toes, like his father.

Melinda had suffered lapses, but had always been received back, penitent, by the Lord, and the lapses were now long behind her. The worst lapse had been when she first met Lize and fell before the biological imperative. She wasn't a virgin, even then, but her earlier sins had been committed very young and thoroughly washed away by the blood of the Lamb. She never even thought, now, about her transgressions at the age of eleven when she had teased her older brother into a state of passionate arousal once too often, and after that had continued to enjoy secret pleasures with him until they got caught and whipped — but she'd only been found with her pants off and her brother toying with her; her parents never suspected how far they'd actually gone with their "dirty play."

Lize, who rose over her horizon when she was sixteen, was quite another matter. And Melinda, a saved Christian, knew perfectly well that she was compromising her immortal soul with him, risking the Second Death. But sex has always been stronger than the Second Death, else Christianity would have wiped itself out before the time of Mohammed. Melinda didn't rest until she'd had Lize between her strong young thighs not once, but twenty times.

Her Christian parents would never have allowed Melinda to marry a man like Lize Pike, going on twenty-seven and far gone in sin, always out to dances and times, even welcome over in the Irish end of Lattice Harbour, where sinners gathered on Friday nights to drink home brew. Except for one thing. They discovered, a few months after her sixteenth birthday, that she was incurably pregnant. There was a real knock-down-drag-out row. Her brother had to intervene to protect her from her father. They insisted that she marry the man, with just as much force as they would have used to stop her, had her womb remained unquickened.

Because Melinda was too unclean to be married at the altar, being already big with child, the pair were married on the church steps, but once delivered of Pleman (who was thus snatched as a brand from bastardy) she was reckoned purified, and even sanctified, and was received back as a communicant at the altar of her easy-going church, once more a chosen child of God.

In spite of such a beginning, the marriage succeeded. Melinda continued to read her Bible, the only printed work other than the hymn book ever to enter her house until Pleman brought home his first reader. She confined her passions to her husband's bed, quarrelled only briefly with him when he drank beer or refused to punish the children for misbehaviour, and ruled her own sphere indoors while he pursued his life with boats and horses and bucksaws.

And then the Gospel preachers arrived, saving souls from Babylon. Melinda was among the first to discover that the easy-going church in which she had been born was really an instrument of the devil, one of the daughters of the Great Whore in the Book of Revelation. She became a founding member of the new congregation of the truly saved, and received the gift of tongues almost at once. Then she set out to save others from the world. So successful was the Gospel in Caplin Bight that the old church was emptied, closed down, and the devil practically put to rout. Not quite. A few of those who showed up at the Gospel Tabernacle from time to time remained stubbornly unsaved. Among them Lize. It wasn't that he was actively opposed to religion, or what you'd call an unbeliever, like that terrible old Captain Markady who lived up The Point and scoffed openly, it was just that the seed of the Gospel had fallen on stony ground. Lize didn't have a heart receptive to grace.

Soon Melinda began to believe that it might be sinful, even a kind of fornication, for one of the children of God to allow herself to enjoy carnal pleasure with a child of the devil. She consulted Pastor Tishrite.

"Ye must bear it as best ye can, Sister," he told her. " 'Tis a cross laid upon ye by the Lord. 'Submit yerselves unto yer husbands' the Apostle Paul says, and ye must submit yerself, Sister, even if he be one of the children of darkness — but o' course ye needn't *encourage* his lust. Jest *submit*. That's all the Lord requires."

Lize accepted his wife's coldness without complaint. Sexual appetite faded with age, he supposed. His own seemed to be as strong as ever. But perhaps that was an exception. He did not force his attentions on Melinda, but began to look more attentively at the Irish girls whose fathers and brothers shared his Friday evenings in Lattice Harbour.

Pleman was aware of the tension between his parents, and aware that it was approaching a crisis. The baby was sick, and they were totally opposed about what to do. The baby — well, she was a year and a half old, actually, but they still called her "baby" — had picked up a touch of the flu. Nothing unusual in that, they all got the flu now and then and got over it, with no treatment except a day or two in bed and a liberal application of goose grease to the chest. Goose grease was most useful for chest colds, but by extension it was believed to be good for flu as well.

There was something different about the baby's illness, though. She didn't respond to goose grease and Epsom salts. Instead of getting better and wanting her Carnation milk she stopped eating, developed a dry fever, and seemed to have congestion on the chest.

"If ye had sense, woman," Lize said, not for the first time, "ye'd let me take the child to Lattice Harbour — or go with 'er yerself. Nurse there'd know what to do."

"All the youngsters been sick," Melinda pointed out, "and we ain't lost one yet. If ye'd trust in the Lord ye'd be the better for it."

"Trustin' the Lord ain't no excuse fer neglectin' yer kids," Lize said. "Thomas Gilmore's young'un died o' the croup last winter, ye mind. Mighta lived, I 'low, had she been took to the nurse."

Pleman was secretly frightened by the talk of death. Though he wouldn't have admitted it to either parent, he suspected such talk was unlucky, tempting fate. He rapped wood under the table, feeling guilty because his mother had told him that was a Romish blasphemy connected with the Lord's Cross.

"Ye want to kill 'er, is that it?" Melinda demanded sharply, turning from her work to face Lize. "Ye'd take'er in this weather, snow an' frost, three, four hours in a trap skiff, off to yer devil's friends in Lattice Harbour, and she catchin' her death an'already choked up so ye'd have 'er dead when ye got there — that what ye want?"

The wind howled outside, as if to underline her remarks. As happened from time to time, Caplin Bight was this night thrown back upon its own resources, a place no one could enter or leave. Lize backed down a little. He knew if the baby did die on the way to the nursing station he'd be blamed for killing her.

"She could be wrapped an' warm," he pointed out, "an' ye could come along and tend her."

"I'll not go. I'll take no child o' mine to heathens and Romans in that place. The Apostle James says ye shall lay hands on the sick and they shall be healed. I've already spoke to the Pastor about it."

"That fool Tishrite!"

"It ill becomes ye so to speak of the Lord's anointed!"

"Well . . . anointed 'e may be, but not fer healin', that be doctor's work, woman! Let Tishrite do e'es preachin' an' leave healin' to such as knows about it."

"I've already spoke to the Pastor," she said. "He's comin' tomorra evenin' an' the elders too, and some o' the women."

Lize got up and went to the stairs, listening. He wondered if the baby was warm enough up there. The bedrooms got their small heat, like all the rest of the house, from the kitchen stove. He climbed to his child's room and looked at her, touched her forehead. It was hot and dry, but her breath seemed less labored than it had been earlier.

"She be sleepin' a mite easier I 'low," he said, "and I s'pose prayin' over 'er can do no harm."

Pleman had been to prayer meetings with his mother, and had seen people prophesy and speak in tongues, and had even seen them fall to the floor screaming in uncontrollable laughter when moved to do so by the Holy Ghost, but he had never seen a faith healing, and all next day he looked forward with some pleasure to the magic rite that would take place that evening.

Not yet "converted," he could take no part in it himself, nor could his friend Eli Pallisher, who was brought along by his parents — Eli's father being a church elder — to see faith healing in action. The boys stood together outside the circle — for that's what there was, a circle of the faithful — with Lize and the young Pike children, watching, saying nothing, not even in a whisper.

They gathered at the home of the Pikes at eight p.m. Beside the Pastor and his wife they were mostly middle-aged, forty or more, but Jehu Gilmore who was around thirty and unmarried, and never missed any kind of religious function, was there, and so was young Sister Christina Marks, just turning seventeen, who'd been converted about three months before, and was very strong and fervent in the Lord.

They sat in the yellow light of the oil lamps in the Pike's chilly big front room, which was never used except for special events like this, and in the hush Pastor Tishrite began to pray.

He prayed eloquently, reminded God of many things that God Himself had said in His Holy Word, and he was interrupted softly by murmured "amens" and "yes, Lords" from the congregation. Only Jehu Gilmore felt the need to interject his exclamations in a loud voice.

Then the Pastor read out a hymn, and they sang "When mothers of Salem their children brought to Jesus," such unsaved, or not-yet-saved creatures as Pleman and Eli joining in on this part of the service. And then Sister Tessie Tishrite, filled with sudden illumination from the Holy Ghost, stood up and spoke of the power of faith, and how the Lord at His First Advent had healed lepers, creating a type and shadow of the Great Healing that would fall upon all nations now that His Second Coming was at hand.

The service had been very quiet, so far. Pastor Tishrite next read from the Epistle of St. James, chapter 5, verses 13 and 14, where it is explained about the elders praying over the sick. Then he began to pray again, and his voice rose, pleading, nay wrestling with the Lord, and at last he cried, "Bring in the child, Sister. The Lord will heal her." And Melinda brought the baby into the room and laid her in the circle, rigid, with blue lips, almost in a coma, but still able to cry weakly between fits of coughing for breath.

They then closed the circle, holding hands, forming an unbroken shield for faith about the child, the virtue passing from one to another so that all became exalted. And Pleman and Eli and the younger children stood outside the circle with Lize the father, feeling the vibes radiating outward from the group as the wrestling with God continued.

First one prayed in a loud voice, and then another, as the Holy Ghost moved them. And as one prayed the rest kept up an obbligato of exclamations: "Amen!"

"Yes, Lord. Yes!"

"Hear us, Lord Jesus!"

"Oh come, Lord, come!" and similar remarks.

Pleman felt the power of the prayer like a current running through his limbs and felt himself swept up, controlled, tossed along in the torrent, until he wanted to plead, himself, with God, wanted to believe in it all, wanted, this minute, to accept Jesus as his personal saviour. And then a strange thing happened. The hand of Eli Pallisher, who stood touching him, crept into Pleman's hand, and fastened tight, and held hard, like the hand of someone frightened or drowning, and Eli, he realized was whispering . . . praying? . . . no . . . faintly he could hear the whisper near his ear. Eli was reciting the multiplication table.

Pleman moved away from Eli. And the hypnosis of the prayer seized him once more, swept him up, shook him like a leaf in a storm. Each person in the circle took his turn praying, and some prayed a long time, with great power, thundering phrases from the King James Version (the true Word of God) around the painted beams of the room, until the room itself vanished and all within it stood in a haze of glory with the power of God all about them.

And then Pleman saw the miracle begin to happen. The baby was no longer crying. Her face was no longer white. Her lips were no longer blue. She was sleeping. There was a tinge of red in her cheeks, and her breath came more easily, with hardly a choke or a rattle, but a gentle flutter, as though butterflies, or perhaps an invisible angel, had settled on her bosom.

There was a quiet prayer of thanks from Pastor Tishrite, a prayer that was not interrupted by a single "amen." Pleman discovered that there were tears in his eyes. He turned away to hide them, and realized the meeting was breaking up, its mission accomplished. They went out quietly, drained of emotion, and Melinda picked up the baby and climbed the stairs with her to her bed. Then she and Lize went off to their own room, not arguing, seemingly reconciled, and Pleman said his prayers that night, something he had not done for months past.

In the morning, when Melinda went to see if the baby was well enough to want her breakfast, she found the child dead, lying in the cot stiff and cold, exactly as she had laid her there the night before. Melinda screamed, and called upon the name of the Lord Jesus, who had raised the dead, as well as healing lepers, but his time the dead was not raised.

At his mother's scream Pleman jumped from his blankets to the icy floor and ran to the room where the younger children slept, and there he saw Melinda holding the baby, shaking her, as though by violence she could shake her awake, and repeating over and over again, "Jesus! Jesus! Jesus!"

Then his father came into the room, and snatched the baby and put her back in the cot and Melinda turned on him, screaming still, "Unbeliever! Unbeliever! Ye've killed her!"

Lize grabbed her arms, when she would have struck him and thinking her hysterical, forced her to sit down.

"Go see to the fire, boy," he told Pleman. "The house mustn't be left to freeze, no matter what."

But Melinda wasn't hysterical. The look in her eyes was hate, not madness.

"It's like The Book says," she told him icily. "The Lord God is a jealous God, visiting the iniquities of the fathers upon the children. Ye've killed the baby. Ye've killed her with yer unbelief."

In an hour or two word had spread around the settlement that the Pike child was dead, and Pastor Tishrite confirmed Melinda's opinion that the faith healing had worked, but that its virtue had been undone, later, by the father's lack of faith. This explanation gained immediate currency, and Eleazer Pike, knowing what was said, refused to allow the Pastor to bury his child. Screams and tears from Melinda had no effect. Tishrite, he said flatly, would not darken his door again. Nor would any child of his be allowed to visit the Gospel Tabernacle.

After the initial tears, the savage thrusts at her husband, Melinda returned to her household work woodenly. The thought of leaving him never crossed her mind. No matter what happened between them, she would stay in this house until carried out, like her baby. And she would bear whatever the Lord sent. There was just a touch of bitter pride in her heart that He had chosen her to bear such a heavy burden.

Lize took Pleman with him to the graveyard on The Point, where all the dead of Caplin Bight lay buried, those who had died in Christ together with those who had died in sin, and the father and the brother, working together, dug the grave for the baby, chopping their way down through six inches of soil frozen almost as hard as stone into the soft earth beneath.

He put the small rag of a body into a box he made himself, and carried it on his shoulder up the hill, and there, with his children beside him, shedding tears upon the snow, he lowered the box into the grave and sprinkled clay over it, repeating in his ancient Devon accent the old formula, "Earth to earth, ashes to ashes, dust to dust."

And then, because he could not read or write, he had Pleman read from the Bible the words of the service: "I am the resurrection and the life . . . this mortal shall put on immortality . . . O death where is thy sting?" And they shovelled the clay back into the grave and trampled it down, and walked home, the younger children following.

Being too poor to buy a dress stone, Lize planed a two-inch strap of pine and had his eldest daughter, who was clever with a pencil, trace the baby's name on it, with the day and year of her birth, and the months and days of her life; then he burned the letters and figures deeply into the wood with the soldering iron that he used to mend the wiring of his engines, and set the board upright in the earth at the head of the grave. This done he turned to Pleman. "Come, boy," he said. And they went together to the net loft where Lize worked at his gear in the winter, and they sat there together, knitting a leader for a cod trap, in the firm faith that the fish would return another year.

[1986]

Percy Janes

Encounter in England

Percy Janes (1922-   ) was born in St. John's and raised in Corner Brook. He came to prominence on the Newfoundland literary scene in 1970 with the publication of his novel *House of Hate*. His writings include the novels *Eastmall* (1982), and *No Cage for Conquerors* (1984), while he has also published collections of both poetry (*Light and Dark*, 1980) and short stories (*Newfoundlanders*, 1981). In 1981 he was made an honorary member of the Newfoundland Writers Guild.

After graduating from Memorial University and, like many Newfoundland writers, making his extended pilgrimage to Toronto, Peter Baird decided to try his luck as a writer in England. In Canada he had had just one novel published along with a few stories and poems, the latter insignificant and the novel something of a critical but not a financial success.

Peter was a personable young man close to thirty, good-looking without being vain about it or crudely macho in his approach to women. He came from what used to be called in St. John's a good family; that is, they had a lot of old Water Street money behind them and had been able to send him to a private school in Ontario as well as to University afterwards.

He left Toronto because he felt frustrated there, blocked in his literary ambitions, and was in a mood to think that any change must be for the best. Also, he was at the wrong end and the goodbye end of a drawn-out love affair, needing only to get away to some place where his batteries could recharge and he would be completely free to concentrate on his own thoughts and his writing. At his age, and being now on his own in every way, he felt that he must soon make his mark or else run the risk of petering out in pipedreams and futility. By strict economical living, Peter reckoned, he might make the thousand or so dollars he had saved last long enough to put him through the crucial test of a second novel and at the same time put him on his feet.

So in the early 1980s he packed his meagre gear and hopped a plane for London, despite the fact that he knew nobody in England nor had he any kind of connection there, literary or otherwise. All he knew about the scene over there was that Newfoundland's best-selling and most popular author had been living in England for some years; she too, it seemed, having reached the top in Newfoundland and even become a national name, had decided that the Old Country would make a more suitable background for her personality and her work.

Having arrived in London, Peter had a break right away. One of the more perceptive critics there, who had written what was to Peter a heart-lifting review of his novel and whom Peter had sought out, told him that he was acquainted with Barbara Waddington MacAdoo and would be happy to bring two New*found*land-Canadian writers together, so far away from home. Peter seemed to feel the magic touch of salvation; he thought of course that this might be of use in furthering his career, but he also felt eager to meet her and find out if half the stories that circulated about her saltiness, her Newfie bluntness and rowdiness, were true. She was something of a legend at home and (about half a generation older than himself) enjoyed the added advantage of having preceded him not only in literary fame but also in the English experience.

On meeting her he was first of all amused by the Atlantic

breeziness of her quick invitation to come down and visit her — stay a while if he liked — because such spontaneity was a contrast to the tight-assed caution of many English people whom he had already met, in their social relations.

—Hell's bells, Peter, Barbara shouted from halfway across a room, come on down and spread your butt a little. I got enough room in my old tilt to play football.

Peter had thought she would have a nice cottage or at most a small house in the country, but it turned out to be something like she said: almost a 'place' in the older, English sense, and with a name to match, Laurel Manor. There were about thirteen rooms staggered along its halls and stairways and crazy corridors, and there were acres of land too with vast flowerbeds, dense gleaming-green laurel hedges, as well as a large plot of ground for vegetables which Peter felt a longing to dig into the moment he laid eyes on it.

He had no idea that Barbara Waddington MacAdoo would be so loaded, and so felt all the more eager to view her now on this home ground. At the time he arrived she was out on a patio waiting for equipment to be set up in the living-room so that she could be profiled for a major CBC (St. John's) series to be called *Newfoundland Writers Abroad*. Barbara seemed tense and preoccupied, chain-smoking, and she merely waved toward him with the large glass in her hand containing an amber liquid that did not look like ginger ale. Then she bawled out something about number five, adding:

—Just park yourself, Pete. Okay? I'm kind o'busy with the media. I got a goddam grandaddy of a summer cold too. A-a-a-a-a-w, pshitt! Hrrrn, hrrrn. Christ! I'm honkin' all the time like a Canada goose. Did I tell you five? Good. Toosh! Jesus, what a day to have to go on the tube! But time and the old CBC wait for no woman.

With his rather staid family background and boarding-school training in good manners, Peter Baird was a little put out by the style of this very casual welcome, but as he pushed his way through heavy cables past seven cats — superb animals — and blazing lighting equipment, he just thought he had arrived at an awkward moment which Barbara had not exactly forseen and would soon make up for.

On the personal side, the first thing he had noticed about his hostess was that she was a *front de boeuf*, like James Cagney, but much taller and with something of an epic touch in her whole size and presence. Her face was large and rough-hewn, dominated by that brutal brow and deep-set eyes with a perpetual light in them which might have been either the glow of genius, or of malice. Her figure was not good, not at all the kind to turn Peter on, and she had it wisely draped in a long, loose kaftan.

The only person with her in the house on a permanent basis was her daughter, Pocahontas MacAdoo, who had been born in Newfoundland during a phase of Barbara's extreme sympathy with our dwindled native people and so had to carry the burden of that name along with one or two other troubles incident to being the child of such a woman. Peter was soon to learn that in many things, Barbara was not a person to do things by half measure.

Poke herself was a dim little teenager, pale and scanty-haired, all twisted with hang-ups and what seemed to be mother resentment in various forms, so that the tension between these two females was like an activized circuit that was never turned off when they were together. Poke had just finished high school, or the English equivalent, but could not make up her mind about University or any kind of next move; she just hung around the house smoking pot, forever changing her clothes and her records, watching TV or mooning from one room to another as lost and sad as an abandoned bride. In fact, she seemed to be almost paralyzed within her mother's orbit and yet unable to break away. Peter had a clear impression too that Barbara would have loved the girl more at a greater distance.

Nobody ever mentioned Poke's father, as it seemed to be

understood among both relatives and friends that he did not match up to his wife in either achievement or reputation; it also seemed that any reference to this cast-off husband who remained back in Newfoundland was in bad taste at Laurel Manor, the divorce (or otherwise) a taboo subject.

On Peter's first evening at dinner in his new home there were several CBC or other guests whom Barbara identified for him in the most bumbling, name-slurring way, and whose chief purpose in being there was apparently to supply Barbara with an audience and adulation. All but one of them were women.

But Peter, Barbara and Poke soon settled into what might have become a pleasant enough routine. With exhilarating relief Peter found that his writing flow was coming back; that he was able to type away contentedly all morning, then spend three or four pleasant hours out in his vegetable garden before afternoon tea. Such a regular and quiet schedule was exactly what he needed after all the frustration and the amorous agitation in Toronto, so that he felt no desire to do anything else but live like this until his new book was finished, at least in the first version.

It was the custom at Laurel Manor for everyone to get their own breakfast and lunch, which left Barbara free all day to get on with her own writing; then around five o'clock she would quit work, bathe and start dinner, and finally summon all those in the house to her vaulted living-room with its huge stone fireplace, for a drink and a pre-dinner chat. That was okay. Peter would fiddle with his white wine or cider, not being a drinker or overly robust, while the others, Poke excepted, bit into the hard liquor and got a glow on even before the meal. He was happy to have landed on such pleasant ground, and for a while relations between him and Barbara were quite amiable. He started kidding her about being a Chatelaine and she in turn took a gruff, slightly patronizing tone toward his serious nature and his published work. Once in a relaxed moment he called her Barb, at which she reared up like a duchess who had been goosed, giving him a stony look.

—I have never permitted anybody to call me that.

And she went on calling him Pete. Barbara was a mite drunk when she came out with her little speech, and yet after it had been uttered, Peter could never feel the same about her. Not quite. Pomposity was one of his loathings. At first such failings in her were partly cancelled out in his view by the fact that her writing, the best of her early novels and short stories, was really good and, if she had maintained her quality, would have approached the magic status of art. About her poetry he had more doubts, which were confirmed one day when he heard her call out to her daughter:

—Poke, this morning I'm going to write a poem. Bring me my Roget.

Before he came to Laurel Manor Peter had had a vision of long, deep literary talks with her, i.e. bull sessions about their craft; yet this dream did not materialize, possibly because her fictional territory was much the same as his own, and where Newfoundland life was concerned she might have feared some copy-catting, even plagiarism. Barbara refused point-blank his suggestion that they exchange manuscripts just for reading and criticism, and the odd look she gave him when he made the suggestion made Peter wonder what kind of remarks and material she put in that journal she was rumoured to be keeping so assiduously.

Therefore they avoided the topic of literature during the week, and on weekends the house was always crawling with guests.

Unlike Peter, Barbara revelled in all the fuss and commotion of having company. After her writing was done she never seemed to tire of entertaining or helping people, being in material things one of the most generous women he had ever met. Her grand climactic social hour came after dinner on Saturday evening when all the inmates and guests were assembled in her living-room, provided with booze and, once Barbara had made her entrance, just expected to listen. That entrance was often startling in itself, if she were (not wisely) wearing her toreador pants and a coruscating yellow poncho, with a thirteen-inch cheroot sticking up and out from her teeth at a decidedly phallic angle. She always set her own stage by having several bottles of Scotch and a gallon jug of red wine on the table near her carved antique chair beside the fireplace. And when she came into the room she always paused in expectation — the most obvious display of the queen bee complex that Peter had ever seen.

It was unfortunate that her talk did not match her best writing, being mostly a New Left condemnation of the Establishment to which she belonged. It was all more radical chic than political conviction. And she went on for hours. Poke would groan almost audibly as it went on and *on*, and sometimes would look over to Peter for sympathy or perhaps in the hope that he might inject a change of subject. Once or twice when he had tried this while Barbara was at full steam, she just brushed him aside with a casual put-down.

—Oh, bullshit, Pete. Grow up.

As her growling, gravelly voice kept echoing through the large room Peter sometimes had the fancy that she was miscast as a woman, and should have been a sea captain in the rowdy old days of sail, or perhaps a great general or explorer. She certainly *was* tough. Her performance carried on well into Sunday morning, Barbara eating and drinking copiously, but she never showed any signs of malaise or nausea. She had a stomach like a cement mixer. The only sign she ever gave of Monday morning hangover and blues was that before having her coffee on Monday she would generally open the kitchen door and one by one hurl all seven of her cats out into the back garden because they were getting under her feet and making her stumble. Then by Wednesday she would have recovered to the point where she was filled with remorse and so began spoiling the cats by getting them fresh fish to eat and expensive preparations from the chemist to make their fur thicker and even more beautiful.

If her boozing and garrulous mania had been confined to

the weekends Peter might have been able to hack it, but when she started going for the sauce all week, he began to feel distinctly uncomfortable and apprehensive about the future. Of course he was at liberty to leave, and yet Laurel Manor was not costing anything, and he had a strong prejudice against leaving this comfortable berth until his literary purpose had been achieved.

Once or twice he tried to reason with her in a friendly way by reminding her that she had a lot of blessings to count — health, a host of friends, a child, and no money worries — and that it seemed a shame to . . . well, to downgrade it all in the way she was doing. Peter tried to be tactful, but Barbara just gave him a bitter look, waved an arm as though to take in her mansion and her entire life, and spat out one violent word:

—Shit!

All the same, she continued in her former style, so that eventually Peter took to joining Poke in the TV room on Saturday evenings, hoping that in her preoccupation with other guests Barbara might not notice his absence. This was naive. Barbara was hardly the woman to overlook a defection on the part of a houseguest, even though for a while she said nothing about it. The first ominous reverberation came one Monday evening when he again sat watching TV with Poke. Barbara suddenly barged into the room and sat down near him on the small sofa that had come to be his place during these companionable sessions of viewing with Poke. For a few seconds Barbara even managed to keep quiet and watch; then there came an abrupt movement which took Peter by surprise, as she had shoved her ass up against him in a very suggestive way. Another moment, and at a funny part of the program, she cackled with laughter, raised one hand and brought it down on his thigh with a resounding smack. She left it there too. And squeezed.

Poke snuffled an incredulous laugh into both her hands and rushed out of the room to let herself go. Peter himself suddenly had the thought that he would have, after all, to provide some quid for all Barbara's quo in having him there, but right now he was jammed up against the arm of the sofa and somewhat in a panic about what to do next. He had never had the slightest sexual feeling about Barbara at all and had no intention of becoming a Lover in Residence.

He escaped from the sofa by saying he had to go to the bathroom; and the next time Barbara came into the TV room under the same circumstances she found him seated in a small armchair at some distance from the sofa. At this point there was a moment of palpable tension, but no word was spoken; she merely lowered her massive head like an angry bull, and charged out of the room again.

In a vague way Peter hoped that as a mature, intelligent woman, Barbara might understand his feelings without his having to wound her by expressing them; moreover, that once this crisis had been surmounted, she would come to accept him as a friend and they would be at ease with each other. No chance! There was a brief lull, a silent truce, but no feeling of peace achieved. Perversely she gave no more sign of turfing him out than he did of wanting to leave, and this Peter believed he understood. She was not the kind of woman to accept an unresolved situation like the present one, nor to accept defeat from any bloody male. So this interim period was really a silent preparation for battle.

She astonished Peter at first by using tactics that might have come from a more conventional and submissive type of woman. She started to dress in what she apparently thought was a more feminine way; she took more trouble with his dinner; and once or twice, in the early days of this campaign, even served him with a tankard of chilled cider as he sat by the fire after his day's work. All this Peter accepted with his usual polite thanks, and did not change his mind or his feeling about anything.

In so far as she was capable of subordinating herself, Barbara's effort to do so lasted about two weeks, after which there came another lull, no more cider, and mounting tension while she was obviously considering her next move. In her whole manner and aura at this time (what Poke called 'her vibes') there was sultry thunder. Imminent explosion. So Poke tried to warn Peter what it would be like.

Then Poke left. It was unexpected, fantastic; but, unable to bear the added tension, she ran off to London with a yippee musician she had met on a weekend in Brighton, and swore she was *never* coming back. Her departure took place on a weekday, at which moment the two older people realized, with an almost furtive crossing of glances, that for the first time they would be alone in the house overnight.

Nothing was said after Poke left, but Peter tried to indicate his feelings again by swinging his hoe out in the garden for an extra hour. He did not go into the house for tea. Barbara showed her irritation at this change in routine by coming out twice and telling him it was time to quit if he were going to shave and shower as usual before dinner. In her state of tension she bungled the meal, except for the oysters, and while they were eating hardly made any conversation at all.

When he had finished helping her with the dishes she invited (urged) him into her living-room for another drink, but the devil of quiet obstinacy that was one of his ruling spirits now linked up with his passion for self-determination in all things, to make Peter say no. With an ominous growl Barbara followed him into the TV room, carrying her bottle, and sat down on the little sofa. He took his armchair after switching on the set.

Now she began to infuriate him by talking all through the programs. Peter stood it until about ten o'clock, when he made the true excuse of being tired after a hard day's work and started upstairs for bed. Barbara swore obscenely under her breath, and there was no answer to his civil 'Good night' and 'See you tomorrow'.

Fearing rape, he locked his door, then hoped for restful silence.

No actual violence took place that night. Barbara did not

even try his door; she limited herself to prowling and later staggering around the landing outside his room, until about midnight, while her language passed from the obscene to the blasphemous as it became more and more incoherent. At long last Peter heard her stomp off to her own room and he was able to fall into a much-needed sleep.

The war that followed was a cold and in its early stages a silent one, as Barbara Waddington MacAdoo, without grace and with visible relish, let her wrath be felt. All through the war, of course, she had the advantage of being on home ground, while Peter felt that he was the one with greater provocation, at least in the psychological sense. It seemed to him that in her crude, hippopotamic amorous advances Barbara had never stopped to reflect that he was neither an idiot nor a cripple, and would have been quite capable of approaching her in a personal way if he had been so inclined. Why the hell couldn't the woman see that he had never even *thought* of her in relation to sex? Peter did not like the feeling of having been staked out and pre-empted in this arbitrary way. And an added grievance was that Barbara, for all her reputed skill at portraying character in her fiction, still took his mild manner for *his* character, quietness for weakness, never coming close to his real nature. It seemed that her vision was blinkered along the path of her own desires.

Barbara started real hostilities by firing ricochet shots at Peter off one or another of her guests. Was she, like a Nazi, bent on humiliating him before finishing him off? There was certainly no subtle touch in her attacks, which took the form of cheap shots about one-book authors, gutless masturbators and/or queers: zombies living emotionally in a concrete shell. If any guest should ask him how his new book was going Barbara would quash the question with a remark totally off the subject and with never a shadow of apology. Clearly she had taken him up unceremoniously, and now was just as unceremoniously letting him down. If Peter himself said anything that was not kosher in her eyes, she would emit a massive sigh of boredom, stare at him with a mixture of patronizing pity and disgust, then bawl out raucously:

—Horse piss! Goddam male chauvinist guck.

Before leaving Newfoundland Peter had heard that Barbara was a keen feminist. Now he saw that she was rabid.

At another of those weird dinner parties it was a casual guest who drew her main fire, although Peter was indirectly and innocently the cause of it. This woman just happened to pay him a compliment on his ruddy, garden-fresh appearance, right in the midst of one of Barbara's strident monologues, and this made the hostess cut in harshly:

—Oh, for Christ's sake, shut up.

For a moment the embarrassed guest thought this might be one of Barbara's unpredictable jokes and tried to pass it off with a nervous laugh. No go. Barbara added with a blank stare:

—And fuck off.

That sent the victim off to her room in mortification, vowing instant flight. Barbara just sat at the table as before, glowering at everybody in turn as if demanding to be told that she was totally right in dismissing such a bore. Later that evening when Peter tried to protest about the incident, in what he felt were mild terms, she publicly ordered him to bed, and in the tone of a master addressing a wayward dog. One that would not run with the pack.

At this particular time Peter was on a nostalgia kick, watching old Hollywood movies five or six nights a week, and his obvious enjoyment of these seemed to irk Barbara beyond all reason. She would make a show of joining him now and then, but her ribald comments soon became for him little less than persecutions. She was really obstreperous if the film were one of those Errol Flynn-Olivia de Havilland cloak and daggers with plenty of mush and passion thrown into the blood, and she kept grunting at it as 'corny crap'; if she stayed she would frequently struggle up from the sofa, blocking the screen with her bulky form, and brand anyone who could watch that kind of ancient chauvinism as a hopeless nitwit bordering on the moronic. When really soused, Barbara had a regular series of epithets, or condemnations. First:

—Yuck!

Then came her favourite admonition:

—*Vom-it* now.

And finally, when the hero was overbearing the heroine with his macho embrace at the end of the film, now addressing Olivia directly:

—Aw, go on, kiddo. Let him have it. Get him! Knee him in the balls, baby.

Sometimes Peter wondered if she were starting to flip. Certainly she seemed erratic in other ways too, as household plans were made for days ahead, obliging him to change his cherished routine, and then abruptly the whole thing would be reversed without any warning. Impulse and caprice came to rule the house. It often happened that Peter came down to breakfast by himself and found at the table three or four people he had never even seen before. At such times he had the feeling that Barbara, knowing how such things upset him and threw him off his writing, was doing it on purpose.

Bad manners and devious ways were one thing: radical personal hostility another. The day that Barbara, in another of her wild moods, got on Poke's old bicycle and wobbled all over Peter's garden, eventually toppling into the brussels sprouts, he was truly disturbed by the symbolic quality of her vandalism.

If her own writing was going badly he could sympathize, of course, but when she started interrupting his morning's stint to change his towel or check the meter on his gas fire, he felt his irritation mounting to anger. One writer doing this to another was against all the rules — unless, of course, she now thought his work so unimportant that those rules did not apply. She continued to butt in on him, and he was left to draw his own conclusions.

Flipping? Or lonely and hypersensitive like himself? Again Peter wondered about this when Poke came back for a brief visit and caught pneumonia, her temperature shooting up to 104 within a few hours. Eventually she had to be rushed off to hospital, in real danger. After Peter and Barbara got back to the Manor, exhausted, he heard her in the den sobbing and weeping like a frightened child; and on going in found her all huddled up in a chair beating her head against the hard wooden back while muttering savage imprecations on herself as a mother.

Peter's sympathy was genuine, yet as soon as Poke was getting well Barbara's persecution of him started all over again, this time with what seemed to be a touch of hysteria. In a way, the worst and most revealing thing happened one day when Peter said to her, again attempting some kind of reconciliation so that he would be able to finish his book in peace, that after all she had a fine literary reputation as one of the blessings she should count, as well as the high opinion of the critics to comfort her.

But with these remarks he had only stirred up the fire once more. She gripped his arm and dragged him into the study; then began plucking down from the shelves the rows of her own books (sparing her deluxe and first editions) and hurling them into a pile near the fireplace. All this time she was letting out a gush of oaths and obscenities expressing an attitude of total, rancid disillusion. After a pause for breath Barbara stood back from the pile, rushed forward and gave the books a solid punt that sent most of them into the flames. With a vicious frown on her face she then turned toward Peter.

—There! That's what I think of my *literary* reputation. Comfort — my goddam grandmother's fucking asshole.

As a young and ambitious writer, Peter was really shocked by this performance. It was not her language that was shocking, but his realization that with all her success, money and prestige and literary clout, Barbara Waddington MacAdoo seemed to be just one more lonely, miserable and hungry woman to whom all the trappings of great-lady novelist were nothing at all.

In her eyes no less than in her behaviour Peter was beginning to perceive what amounted almost to a child's longing for love: not more praise for her writing but praise for herself as a woman, an occasional word of tenderness that would take away the creeping coldness of middle age and the fear that her woman's life was already over, unbearably soon. Perhaps, Peter thought, she drank just to forget all that pain, and a resolution of her dilemma in a human and loving way.

It was even more unfortunate, and verging on tragic, that he and Barbara were probably parallel cases. This came home to him as he now painfully felt the limits or range of his sympathy widening; and he realized that just as Barbara had never been able to reconcile her life as a creative writer with her life as a woman, so he had suffered comparably as a man. This was precisely what his own solitude was all about. Peter felt now that he and Barbara should really have been able to help each other. Yet why could *she* not realize how much he was turned off and sickened by the way she continually stank of booze and nicotine.

This and other thoughts he had at first tried to conceal from her, and as far as he knew he had succeeded in keeping the most unflattering estimates to himself; it was again by indirect means that Barbara tore off his mask and as a result took her final step in revenge for his indifference.

He was not aware of what set off this explosion until the crisis was right on top of him and things were literally falling about his ears. One evening at dusk he was strolling back from Crawley New Town where he had gone for his weekly day of rest from Barbara, when he saw on entering the courtyard of the Manor, objects flying through the air, and heard howling and yelling issuing from the house. At first he thought it was just Barbara again, heaving out the cats in her classic, shot-putting style; but, hurrying closer, he saw that the objects were *his* objects — pieces of his property being flung out pell-mell through the window of his upstairs room. The last ones to hit the cobblestones were his suitcase and typewriter, both smashed.

Into the house he ran to find out what the hell was going on and to halt the destruction. The way upstairs was barred. There was Barbara on the third lowest step, drooling drunk and raving; she pushed him down to floor level and, taking advantage of surprise, bounced him all the way out through the kitchen door.

In her hands was a fat volume with red binding, which she kept waving at him belligerently, until at last she stood still and began to spit out a few of the darker thoughts which had been festering in her mind.

—You bastard! You sinister little bastard. Conceited, contemptible shit. Liar. OUT. Get that goddam miserable carcass out of my house and off my property, and don't you ever come near *me* again, or by Jesus, I'll . . . I'll rip your guts out. You hear?

By this time Peter realized that Barbara had broken into his room and not only found, but read, his diary — the red one, sacred to his own eyes and to the eyes of posterity. It was true that in this intimate record he had described his hostess as a bison, using also terms like 'elephantine', 'epic androgyne' and so forth, indulging his gift for vivid physical detail.

The next thing Peter knew, Barbara had rushed up and conked him on the temple with his precious Diary, not seeming to care whether, in breaking the rim of his glasses, she might have injured his eyes. She was off again!

—Chicken! Goddam jerked-off little prick. If you got any prick. Who the blazing bloody hell do you think you are? Dostoyevsky? You're a case, boy. Do you need a shrink! But good. Sly-faced, ego-tripping punk.

—But Bar . . .

—Fuck off. I had a gutfull of your silence and your back-biting and sneaky goddam ungrateful ways. Just take that junk of yours and clear out of here.

—I never inten . . .

—Fuck OFF.

—Just let . . .

—And take this crap with you too.

With her thick, powerful hands Barbara ripped his diary down the spine and flung the two pieces into his face. Then she staggered through the door of the house and slammed it with ferocious finality. Peter could do nothing but gather up the remains of his gear and hump it into Crawley to wait for the London bus in the morning.

He kept wondering, while making this return journey, what Barbara might have put in *her* journal about him; but his only regret was that he would not be at Laurel Manor to harvest any of the vegetables and fruit which he had saved from Barbara's malice and so lovingly tended in her garden.

[1987]

Carmelita McGrath

Jack the Trapper

Carmelita McGrath (1960-   ), a poet, fiction writer, researcher and editor, was born in Branch, St. Mary's Bay and now lives in St. John's. She has won the first prize for both poetry and fiction in the Newfoundland and Labrador Arts and Letters competition. Her published works include *Poems on Land and on Water* (1992), and a book of fiction *Walking to Shenak* (1994). She also edited *No Place for Fools: The Political Memoirs of Don Jamieson* (1989-90), and co-edited *Their Lives and Times: Women in Newfoundland and Labrador, A Collage* (1995).

Oona is the best hunter and trapper on the coast. For thirty years she has travelled the lines, following depressions and slopes, moving inland. Sometimes she takes one of her men with her, sometimes one of the older children, but it is her preference to leave them all behind, the children with Marta and the men to each other. When she comes back, nothing has changed but the stories. Now that Marta only goes to school — out of boredom — on Mondays and Fridays, Oona feels better about leaving the children anyways. When she goes into the woods, there is a leaving behind of all things; compactly, what she needs fits into what she and her machine can carry. Sometimes out there she runs into somebody else and offers them tea. Sometimes in return they offer her whisky. Not for work, she thinks, carrying whisky alone out there on the traplines.

These days there's a sad sight that she encounters out there from time to time, the man Carl, Carl F. Carter, that poor little specimen of a biologist who follows the land in a queer skittish zigzag like a rabbit — rabbit man. One day she asks him about his nervousness, has he always had it, but he only answers that he is just nervous around her, and then rabbits off sideways, up in the direction of Three-Corner Bay where Jack the Trapper disappeared years ago.

Carl is one of the ones who brings whisky with him these days; perhaps he thinks that the men of the community expect it of another man. In case he meets anyone, he'll want to be hospitable. Perhaps he thinks that he'll be one of the men, and then it won't matter that his wife has left him and is spending her time with a man whose reputation with women is bettered only by his reputation at darts. Oona shakes her head after Carl's retreating back, sorry that the man knows too little to do the sensible thing and go home because dark is drawing in and he might encounter Jack himself sitting in the lee and having a boil-up.

Carl moves inland, knowing it is too late to be doing this and not at all confident that he knows the trail. But that woman irks him, her sure confidence, her voice like the cold wind keening up to crescendo as she tells him about the mad trapper and waits, teacup in hand, for him to suddenly change his mind about going farther and decide to call it a day. Call it quits with his tail between his legs. Run away.

"Know what I think?" Marian had said, during one of their conversations in the long warm evenings before her flight. "Know what I think? I think that there are a lot of people here who're running away from things."

"Like what things, Marian? Who and what things?" Marian is aware of how important it is to him to be a scientist. Her irksome vagueness is something he wants to smooth out, and as soon as possible.

"Well, you know, like how a lot of the New World was

settled. Pirates, thieves, criminals, broken hearts. That's who our ancestors were. There's no point in denying it. Who do you know who really wants to delve into their histories? Go really far back? It's because of all the skeletons."

"So?"

"Well, people need to do the same thing now sometimes, you know, can't cope or won't cope or loss of love or the pace of the city just gets to them. So they run away."

"And they come here?"

"Sure. Haven't you noticed, Carl, how many of the outsiders here would be outsiders anywhere?"

"No."

"Oh, come on! Just among the teachers and government workers and the like, I've met three people from recent break-ups and at least four alcoholics since I got here. Except I can't tell who are alcoholics anymore — everyone drinks so much. Oh yes, and a guy who thinks that gays should be sent to live alone on an island, if not shot. What do you say to that?"

"Normal, Marian, perfectly normal, there are people like that everywhere. And much worse. It's just that we don't usually get to know them. A slice of life, this is," he finishes with a grin.

"Sometimes I think it's rubbing off on me. Sometimes I wonder if I'm not running away from something too. You know I was talking to Annie Peckham the other day and she was loaded or stoned or something, about eleven o'clock on a school night, and she was out of it — definitely *on* something. We were eating redberry pie up at her place. I kind of told her casually that I had trouble sleeping. The wind, and the silence. And she just took it as normal. Told me she hadn't slept for a month, until she got some pills from the nursing station. 'You should go down and get checked out,' she said, 'they'll give you something.' And I just nodded my head and smiled. And then she looked at me, meaningfully, and said, 'It's all free you know. All the drugs are free.' And I just smiled and thought, yes, maybe.

A year ago, I would have thought it pretty strange. I would have thought she needed help."

"A year ago we were in Ontario," Carl says, his voice the verbal equivalent of a baleful stare. Carl is from Vancouver and he thinks Ontario is the stuffiest place on earth.

He turns to her, sees a genuine concern on her face. "You didn't get the sleeping pills, did you?" and watches her shake her head. "I love you," he says and goes to enfold her, red hair, eyes like green sparks, the smell of her sandalwood soap. It took him all his life to find her and he doesn't want her to move away now, apart from him, continental drift, although in some ways in their thinking they are, and have already been for a while, worlds apart.

"Let's make love," he murmurs into her hair. She hates the way he announces things always, never daring to surprise her.

Oona has an order to fill, thanks to the many requests for jackets from Etta, the best parka maker in town. Etta always uses Oona's furs when she can get them. They have been friends for a quarter of a century, and once they had shared the same lover. Only when he had died, drowned hunting seabirds, had each known about the other, and it had created a bond between them, a bond of memory and empathy that time only strengthened.

Fur for the hoods, for some, those who made orders from the city, fur even for the cuffs and all the way down the front. Oona is careful not to snicker in front of anyone who she thinks might have ordered one of these. Only she thinks that fox on jacket cuffs is pretty impractical, must only be for people who do not work. How else to avoid grease and blood and oil on them? Oona does not cluck her tongue because this is cash, and she could just as well convince them that they needed fox rears to sit on to pad their delicate kidneys. Money in the pocket, she thinks, and the more the better because she has just found out that Marta is pregnant and the father of her child has disappeared with the boats, gone with a full load of shrimp. Marta will be no good for plant work this summer. Or for fishing or even the smoke house. Oona rolls a cigarette and smiles at the idea of being a grandmother. In good time, she thinks, I'm forty-two. Marta is sixteen. Not like me, Oona thinks, who started so late.

Carl has always been thin but there is something about the woman Oona that makes him feel like a dwarf whenever he meets her. Now, encountering her on the trail, large as life and on snowshoes, he watches as she uses the encounter to stop and roll a cigarette, light up, surveying her surroundings all the time, and finally, "How's it goin'?"

"Fine, fine," Carl says, pissed off at himself for repeating the word, but not knowing how to respond to this question, as general as the horizon, that he had first encountered in the outports of Newfoundland and, now, here.

"Well," Oona smiles, pointing her cigarette for emphasis. "You're the only man I run into out here who comes and goes without taking anything with him. That's good," she grins, "you're not my competition."

"I make notes," he says feebly, "on migrations." There is a temptation in him to use lengthy words she will not understand, the kind of words that put off further questions, although it seems to him that her command of two languages is excellent, and the effect would probably be lost. She is not easily disconcerted. He does not wish to hate her, but standing in front of her he feels that he is taking an exam and is failing. At night sometimes he has dreams about the oral defence of his dissertation, and in these dreams it is Oona who questions him. Perhaps it is just that he is so small and Oona is so big; perhaps, after all, it is as simple as that.

At night, after an astonishing dream in which Carl stands before an assembly of hunters and trappers and defends his dissertation, and Oona is the chief inquisitor, Carl wakes with his throat constricted and Marian does not notice his agitation but continues, at first, to stare at the ceiling and it appears that she has been doing this for quite some time, lost somewhere.

"I've got to get out of here," she breathes. "If only for a while. Carl?"

"Yes?"

"It's different for me. You have your work. You have a sense of purpose, you spend your days doing something you want. I hate substitute teaching. I hate even worse those days when there's nothing to do except go to someone's house and watch the damn soap operas. I don't mean go away forever. Only for a while."

"I wish you didn't do that . . . " Carl says as she reaches for a cigarette. "You never used to."

"Call it a crutch, if you like. I need it. I need more of them, to tell the truth." There is a bitterness in her voice, gone the tenderness that drew him to her like an unfurled ribbon. In the beginning, she had reminded him of what his mother used to say about a cousin of hers who had died young, existing now only in the frame of a photograph, an angel with floating hair and liquid eyes. "She was too fine for this world . . ." The expression had come to mind when he'd seen Marian on campus, and she seemed to him so rare and fleeting that he had wanted to be the bond that held her to the mortal world. If he looked hard, underneath the tired eyes, behind the cloud of cigarette smoke that gave her voice a rasping quality, perhaps he could still find it. Perhaps if he helped her to leave he could keep her as she was. And when his work was done . . .

"Marian," he says finally, giving her the very tenderness that could make her stay, not lecturing for once but only giving her the best of himself. "If you want to go for a while, I'll give you the money for it. Go for a vacation. You can come back when you want. Or I'll meet you this summer back home."

Marian has not anticipated this gift of freedom. She leans into his shoulder, but he will not love her now. For Carl there is love and there is separation, no blending of the two, no other place. Having freed her, he has tangibly let her go. It takes her six days to leave the house. But the weather comes down and she cannot leave town. She looks for a place to stay and wait.

"You're not careful, you'll end up like old Jack the Trapper," Oona tells Carl in the shade of a tuck with cups of tea against a sudden upsurge of wind like needles.

"What happened to him?" Carl asks, not really interested.

"Don't know really," she says. "He lost his fight. He lost his spirit."

Carl walks home on snow that crunches in its brittle freeze as if the ground underneath has somehow gone hollow, as if the earth is really elsewhere, as if one had landed somewhere where the trusted consistency and solidity of the earth had no relevance. This crunch, this echo of disbelief, could drive you crazy if you thought, even for a moment: this alone exists — a hollow earth, a shell of ice.

Ride over it and another thing happens; the hollowness is displaced by the comfort of noise and, no matter how hard you ride, how heavy the burden you carry, it will not give away. Instead, the constant pressure of machine-driven skis makes deep depressions, corrugates, a thousand deep ridges. In the afternoons, the sun gathers a hard gold in these depressions; deeps and highs are defined containers of gold, as if there is after all both depth and richness in the landscape. To ride over it is to choose speed and sound, the noise of mechanization, over the insecurity of your own footsteps.

Carl hears the echo, a grinding sound that reverberates through the body, sees the pools of trapped sunlight. January. He had expected misery to yield a landscape white and flat, faceless, an easy one to leave; instead it has delivered up this clarity.

Along the airstrip, markers made from snow stand like cones along the sides, marking the way for the planes to land, the planes somehow made playful by that instruction to veer in between the cones, so many constructions of a child's whimsy showing the way to avoid accident. From each cone of snow an evergreen branch protrudes, like Noah's green branch, Marian had said, a token of the security of the land. No red triangles blowing in the wind, no arrows or red-amber-green dictates of the busy airports of the outside, no lights. Only the evergreen branches in the uptilted mouths of the doves of snow.

Coming in in the afternoon light, the surrounding mountains fill up with light just like the ruts worn in the snow. The valleys of colour in the midst of the black rock had reminded Carl, on that first visit, of liquor or stained glass. There is the pale gold, the colour of champagne seen through a chilled glass. An iced blue that only the eyes of ice dwellers know well enough to describe, a translucent grey that is like the edges of fur when the light comes through it at the end of a hood.

Flying up the coast on someone else's charter, he had seen colours that he had not seen before, and he had tried to write and tell her about it because there was in him an instantaneous desire to invite her to come and live here with him, so that he could live long enough among the colours to find names for them. He had that feeling that the uninitiated sometimes get, that if he could live long enough among such colours, amid such landscape, his life would be immeasurably enriched, as if he had experienced something deeply spiritual, knowledge that the rest of the world had no access to, secrets that would give him an edge, what kind he did not know, but an access definitely. For Carl, coming here had been as much about the sense of a privileged view of things as it had been about the private habits of migratory animals.

Then when he had tried to write Marian about it, to persuade her that it was worth the trip just to see the colours in the hills, tried to describe the infinite range from white to blue as he had seen it, like being inside an iceberg, his language had failed him. He didn't know the words. He had only been able to tell her about how the ice ended and the dark blue sea with its unknown inhabitants had begun. He had ended up writing the feeble words of a typical proposal, and he had feared failure. Instead she had accepted without question. She had called it a leap of faith.

"He was a white man from England who tried to be an Inuk," Oona tells him another time. "Was running away from something, for sure, the old people said. Came here when I was a little girl. Lived wild, he did. Alone. And always in a hurry. Look," she says, stretching her hand out to enclose the whole of the white open world, the off-white of sky and bay all blended together into a world with no horizon, "where is there to hurry here?"

Oona is drinking today, uncharacteristically, knowing that drink creates a deceptive warmth which convinces you to lie down and sleep. Only today it's warmer, a low front turning everything the same indistinguishable hue, making the air touching her cheeks a pleasant minus fourteen. No danger drinking unless the weather comes down bad. Her husband has come back. Last night he showed up just like that with presents for Marta and her baby, a sentimental man, crying into his beer late at night so that Oona was ashamed of him in front of her children. He had thrown her men out of the house, as if he had any rights. Oona had had to leave. If I leave, she'd thought, he'll leave. He's only in town anyways for a drunk with his old buddies and then he'll be gone. Oona had fought him once, tooth and nail, fought him with her entire body, and she had grown tired of it. She has no desire in her body anymore to fight with men. She is too busy. She has what she needs.

"My husband came back last night," she says, "to pick a fight. He does that every now and again — gets sick of bawlin' out his new wife and kids. Came back because we're going to be grandparents. Tears in his eyes, and everything."

Carl doesn't know what to say. He tries to imagine Oona having dimensions other than the ones he has given her. It is strange. And he does not want to know all about her, as burdened by stories as he is. Oona smiles through the steam of the boiling kettle and waits for his response, but Carl is digging deep inside his knapsack, coming up eventually with a tin of ham, a loaf of bread and a tub of margarine. He places them in front of her, a tea offering.

"So," he says at last, "tell me what happened to old Jack."

"John Furness was his name. There was talk," Oona says, "that he killed his wife. Back in England, that was. Anyway his wife disappeared some time before he came over here. He used to be a minister. Sometimes when he got loaded he would stand in the snow and take his clothes off and pray to God to forgive him, although no one knew what he wanted God to forgive him for. You can imagine a lot of people listened pretty close; they wanted to find out, see, if he really killed his wife. But he never said. Mostly stuff from the Bible. Some of the men used to say that really his wife left him for another man and he went crazy. Anyway, he fell in love with a young girl here and she wouldn't have nothing to do with him because he was so old, and he couldn't stand it. That was when he began to spend all his time alone. All the time alone. Gone for weeks at a time. Lived on what he caught. Then he would come to town, sell his furs, get drunk, and preach another sermon from a snowbank. In the morning then, he'd be gone."

"One time he left and didn't come back at all. We wondered, like you would, what happened. But he was a strange man. Then there were stories, stories that people had seen him moving over the snow at a great speed, down on all fours like the animals he was hunting. And then my David, the young fellow who drowned, he came back one day and said he'd seen him. Jack the Trapper was on his knees and frozen to the ground. David said he'd never forget the look on his face, the queerest look he'd ever seen on the face of a man. Fear, like, but something different. And no marks on the body. David came back in a hurry to get men to go for the body. And when they got there

there was no body. Only marks in the snow like something got dragged. But no blood or fur or signs. Just the marks. Nobody could account for them marks. And, well then, no one believed what David said. That broke him up a lot inside, you know. Like he was crazy or something, seeing things. But the next fall David was drowned himself out hunting for birds. No one ever for sure found out what happened to Jack, you see, because he was gone, that was all, and nobody ever came from England or anywhere to ask about him. Maybe he's still out there somewhere. Perhaps my David saw a wolf and his nerves were playing on him and he thought it was Jack. Anyway, he's a good one for frightening the kids with when you don't want them straying too far."

"Well, I don't know. You tried to frighten me with him. And I'm no kid."

"No," Oona says, sizing him up, "no, I s'pose not."

On a windy day, the kind that bends you in half and makes outdoor work impossible, Carl goes to see Marian where she's babysitting for the afternoon and tells her about John Furness. He wants to amuse her, for her eyes are ringed with dark, flabby circles and her breath is bad as if she's been eating and smoking and drinking all the wrong things. He brings her a fish. He wants to make her laugh but senses only tragedy in her face. At last when it is time for him to go and she has not laughed, he asks her if she has her ticket in case the plane comes soon. She'd slept in and missed the last one, the first in a few days, and he couldn't account at all for her lethargy, the way she moved as if suspended in a slow dream, the way she seemed to have lost control of herself.

"I don't have all the money," she says wearily. "I spent some of it."

There is no need to ask her out of what necessity the money has been spent. Moreover, it seems callous. Tonight he does not lecture her, but she senses that he wants to, that his finger is dying to point. That he has in him enough prepared speeches to last a lifetime. But he's tucked the offensive finger in his pocket, and now he takes it out, folded with the rest of the hand around a wad of money. He presses the money from his hand to hers, and for a minute she remembers handholding in a park on a Sunday afternoon, as if the picture comes from the memory of another incarnation of herself, a snapshot from a more innocent time, perhaps the turn of the century.

"Please go soon," he says urgently. "Please leave as soon as you can."

[1994]

Sources

Avalon, John. "Grimace of Spring." *Protocol* 1 (1945): 4-9.

Bond, Rev. Geo. J. "Uncle Joe Burton's Strange Xmas Box." *Christmas Bells* 10 (1901): 8-9.

Bown, Addison. "A Picture of the Past: A Romance of Newfoundland in the Days of French Occupation." *The Newfoundland Quarterly* 27.3 (1927): 13-19.

Chafe, Frederick. "The Broken Mirror." *Atlantic Guardian* 4.6 (1948): 14-23.

Coady, William E. "Monday Mourning." *Arts and Letters Competition Winning Entries*. St. John's: Department of Education, 1972. 39-48.

Dawe, Tom. "The Apple Tree." *Arts and Letters Competition Winning Entries*. St. John's: Department of Education, 1976. 87-91.

Dinn, Elizabeth. "The Scarlet Jacket and the Middy Blouse." *Atlantic Guardian* 10.2 (1953): 17-24.

Duley, Margaret. "Mother Boggan." *The Fortnightly* 147 (1940): 401-410.

Duncan, Norman. "The Fruits of Toil." *Selected Stories of Norman Duncan*. Ed. John Coldwell Adams. Ottawa: University of Ottawa Press, 1988. 79-90.

English, Anastasia. "A Harmless Deception." *Christmas Bells* 13 (1904): 2-4.

Harrington, Michael. "Lukey's Boat." *Atlantic Guardian* 8.12 (1951): 33-35.

Harrison, S.B. "Near the Walls of Fort Louis." *The Newfoundland Quarterly* 8.3 (1908): 23-24.

Heather, H.M. "Troubled Waters." *Atlantic Guardian* 9.9 (1952): 29-33.

Horwood, Harold. "Iniquities of the Fathers." *A Land, A People: Short Stories by Canadian Writers*. Ed. Michael Nowlan. St. John's: Breakwater Books, 1986. 101-109.

Janes, Percy. "Encounter in England." *A Collection of Short Stories by Percy Janes*. St. John's: Harry Cuff Publications Ltd., 1987. 66-80.

Kelly, Ernest. "Murder Mission." *Newfoundland Story* 5.1 (1951): 35-38.

Kennedy, F.M. "Smallboatmen." *Atlantic Guardian* 9.7 (1952): 29-37.

McGrath, Carmelita. "Jack the Trapper." *Walking to Shenak*. St. John's: Killick Press, 1994. 85-95.

O'Neill, Paul. "The Mulberry Bush." *Twelve Newfoundland Short Stories*. Eds. Percy Janes and Harry Cuff. St. John's: Harry Cuff Publications, 1982. 48-59.

Porter, Helen. "The Summer Visitors." *The Livyere* 2.1 (1982): 40-42.

Russell, Ted. "Algebra Slippers." *Tales From Pigeon Inlet*. Ed. Elizabeth Russell Miller. St. John's: Breakwater Books Limited, 1977. 32-34.

Smith, Janet. "Dark Hill." *Newfoundland Story* 4.2 (1950): 3-8.

Stacey, Jean. "Just Today." *Arts and Letters Competition Winning Entries*. St. John's: Department of Education, 1974. 15-20.

Tolboom, Wanda Neill. "The Legend of Ben's Rock." *Atlantic Guardian* 9.8 (1952): 11-15.

All reasonable efforts have been made to acquire reprint permission for the short fiction included in this anthology. Where an address was available, attempts were made to reach the author. Where we have been unsuccessful in making contact, we have chosen to reprint the article in the belief that the author would like to have the work shared with the reading public in such a collection. Biographical information was unavailable for some of the authors, and we would be grateful for any information about them which could be included in future editions.